This is a work of fiction. Similarities to real people, places, or events are entirely coincidental.

HEARTS ANONYMOUS

First edition. May 22, 2016.

Copyright © 2016 Jonathan Dunne.

ISBN: 979-8215427156

Written by Jonathan Dunne.

Hearts Anonymous
By
Jonathan Dunne

Acknowledgments:

In alphabetical order, thanks to the following who helped in the writing of this book:

Alicia USA

Alyson, USA

Anays, USA

Gosia, Germany

Heather, USA

Jennifer, Canada

Kim, Australia

Lee Ann, USA,

Lina, Greece

Pam, Canada

Maritza, USA

Megan, USA

Nina, Finland

Raven, USA

Rebecca, Canada

Romina, Romania

Sharon, Canada

Tina, Denmark

Victoria, USA

Preface:

'What inspired you to write the story?' is a question I am asked once in a while.

I mostly find this question impossible to answer. I can never figure out that inspirational moment. Lots of little things come together to write a story and I never feel: *Oh, what inspiration! Eureka!* There is *never* a Eureka moment for me. There is however a *work* moment, lots and lots of them, and I work every day to fit the pieces of the puzzle together, and if that means cutting off pieces of the jigsaw piece to make it fit, then give me the scissors. However, there have been specific moments, situations, things I see from behind the steering-wheel, stories my wife tells me, that provide little snippets of future novels, obviously doctored and played around with until the piece fits.

Oddly enough, many of my novels started as misreading, mishearing, and misunderstanding.

The following is a little something of what would eventually become the 'inspiration' for *Hearts Anonymous*...

My 4-year-old daughter, Chloe, ran across a street one morning when we were going to collect the post. She was almost knocked down by an unsuspecting young, faceless driver. On the way back home, I thanked fate that that car hadn't left its destination a second later. What could've started out as a harmless five-minute walk could've turned into a lifetime-nightmare. But it didn't, and as I write this, I take a deep breath of relief (it's not fun re-reading this for the editing process).

This is what had planted the idea-seed for this book: the *what if* syndrome. *What if* and how would I cope with 'if'? Life and Death is all about timing...timing...time... Turn back time... I found myself *seeing* myself in another life, wondering if it is possible to turn back the clock and leave the silly post, mainly bills, for tomorrow. But then again, who knows what tomorrow will bring and maybe it's better not knowing...which is, without giving too much away, what this little novel is about.

I acquired a grandfather clock, dated 1782, for my 40th birthday last year. Its sombre *tick-tock* can be heard right now in my living-room. To think that people heard the same sound and hourly chime 234 years ago is astonishing, and I feel that the clock has been around so long that it has come alive, in a way. If I look, real up-close, into the clock's face, I expect to turn around and find myself in a world without electricity, candle-lit rooms, period costumes, corsets, wigs, and muddy streets with horses. If you check back through my personal blog, you will see a photo of the very clock which has been a big inspiration for me and which has come alive in *Hearts Anonymous*.

Also, around about the same time my daughter ran across the street, my younger sister, Sarah, forwarded me some photos of abandoned amusement parks, and that really brought on a tsunami of creative juices. In hindsight, this might have been one of those 'moments' that got the gears and wheels whirring...

Something else has been an inspiration for me, but that's a secret going to my grave (with me).

A magician shouldn't give away all his tricks, now should he?

Jonathan Dunne, 11th April, 2016.
Toledo, Spain.

Chapter 1

Jack and Jeanie

It is a leaden, gloomy morning, 1st of January, 2015. From a mile up in the air, peering downwards, all that is seen is a giant, multi-coloured Tetris game in the middle of the green countryside.

Floating down into the scene, the Tetris game becomes a multi-coloured sea of old cars in an immense scrapyard, one neatly fitted against the next in a perfect square-mile of dead vehicles.

Pan down another hundred meters on one rusty, olive-green roof. Voices are coming from inside the oxidised carcass.

'Jack and Jeanie up a tree K-I-S-S-I-N-G. First comes love, then comes marriage, then comes Jeanie with the baby's carriage...'

'Aw, c'mon, Jeanie. There's nobody around. If you're embarrassed that the cars will see us, then let me assure that they *are* dead, despite appearances. This *is* a car cemetery.'

'Darling, it's *not* going to happen. I wouldn't even think about it in the back of a cosy hummer, never mind a rust-bucket, dead Beetle.' Jeanie grimaces. 'Even the word *Beetle* is a turn-off.'

'But it's New Year's Day.'

'Not even on Christmas morning, Jack. If you want this kitty to purr, then we need a place of our own with stuff like heat, for example...' Jeanie flicks the heater in the engineless Beetle. 'Heat? No heat.'

Jack huffs his disapproval at Jeanie's unwillingness to live a little and pulls himself through the driver's window, then hauls himself onto the warped roof of the Volkswagen Beetle. 'What's more *private* than this, Jeanie?!' He stretches to the skies, dances a jig on the caved roof, then observes the sea of car rooves around him. He listens to the silence as another flurry of snow begins to fall around them. 'This isn't a traffic jam in Valhalla. It's a scrapyard closed for the weekend and when the cat's away, Jack and Jeanie *will* play...'

'That's probably the point I'm making, Jack. It's a *scrapyard*. How romantic. It's decadent, I'll give you that much.'

'Jeeze, whatever happened to young love?' sighs Jack as he clambers back into the draughty Beetle. He fiddles with some dials and puts the Beetle into gear. He hums the sound of the engine and checks his rear-view mirror before pulling away from a non-existing kerb. He does all of this with a serious expression, so sincere that Jeanie can't keep the giggles away. He keeps on the imaginary road ahead and hums to himself, checking side-mirrors.

'Y'know, uh,' flicking a glance at Jeanie, then back on the road to nowhere, which is kind of where Jack feels this relationship is going sometimes, 'I've been thinking...'

'Oops. I told you not to do that when you're driving, Jackie.'

'No, seriously, I *have* been thinking.' Jack checks more mirrors, adjusts broken switches, then indicates left and turns right. 'And *stop* calling me Jackie...Jeanie.'

Jeanie has seen this behaviour once or twice before: humour – it's Jack's way of dealing with an impending issue. Behind all the bravado, he's a timid soul. 'Penny for your thoughts...'

Jack shakes his head. 'Naw, forget it.'

'No, c'mon, tell me. Here's a penny.' She hands him a coin she finds at the bottom of her coat pocket. 'It's a cent, but who cares...'

'Well, I've forgotten anyway, so...'

'I know you better than anyone, Jack,' smiles Jeanie. 'You just bottled out of whatever mad idea you were about to tell me. I can only say no.'

'Exactly – you *only* say no.'

'No, I mean, I can only say no, which means that I could possibly say yes...'

Jack can't hide the frustration. 'I know what you mean, Jeanie.'

'It's freezing; my fingers are numb. Let's head back to the warmth of your place or my place. I know we're not alone there, but I've had enough of *Herbie Rides Again* for one day.'

Jack and Jeanie had chosen this Beetle in particular because they both pride themselves on sharing a nerdy liking for films on nobody else's list, like *Herbie*.

Jack feels like cracking a smutty joke, something along the lines of: *Again? But there hasn't even been a first time yet!* Jeanie probably won't appreciate that. Dirty jokes are one way of *not* getting up close and personal with Jeanie.

To hell with it, thinks Jack, changing tactics. 'No, now I remember.'

'I thought that would jog your memory. Anything to delay going back to the house...'

'I was thinking that maybe we could, um,' Jack gulps, 'move in together?'

Jeanie hadn't seen that one coming. 'What do you mean? In Old Castle? I still live with my parents in case you haven't noticed, Jack. Those two strangers – that man and woman sitting on my sofa – are actually my parents. Oh, you mean your place? Yes, let's evict your parents. Let's place them neatly in a cardboard box and leave it by the rubbish bins. C'mon, Jack, be realistic.'

Jack sneers. 'Sarcasm is the lowest form of wit.'

'Sometimes I think sarcasm is the only way you will listen. We *don't* have money, Jack.'

'Why am I getting a déjà vu?'

'Because, Jackie, darling, this same topic comes around every few weeks.'

Jack checks his mirrors, indicates to the non-existent kerb and switches off the already off engine. There is a strange silence in the Beetle, almost as if it really had just been running.

Jack turns to Jeanie and blows warm carbon dioxide on her gloved hands. 'I'm your first boyfriend – despite rumours.'

Jeanie giggles and leans over to softly fists Jack's chin with her gloved hand.

'We have been together since forever. We're practically a happily-married couple.'

Jeanie studies Jack before looking out the window at the snow falling on the cars.

'...so let's notch it up and take this to the next level. I know you're trying to be difficult. I *know* that *you* know that I'm not talking about our life here in Old Castle. I *know* you, um, know that, this is getting confusing. I'm talking about our university digs in Limerick City.'

'That's a lot of knows, Jack...'

'What do you think? Let's move in together, Jeanie. We can study side by side.'

'Look at me, Jack.'

'Hmm?' Jack does everything *but* look at her. She knows him too well. He wills his eyes to hers but cannot help the smirk.

With raised eyebrows, Jeanie asks, 'You want us to move in together so we can *study*? Am I understanding this correctly, Jack?'

'Yes...Maybe...'

'Uh-huh. Sure. Why spoil this beautiful thing that we have? Jack, this time is special.'

'Sitting in a freezing crock of a car in a scrapyard, closed to the public, is *special*?'

'Yes. When we're old and grey...'

'Hey, careful, I've already got a few grey hairs.' It's true: Jack has begun to turn grey early in life. 'Though I think it lends me a certain nobility.' Despondently, Jack stares blankly out the window at the falling snow. In another world, very close to this one, Jack can see himself as that grey old man, but Jeanie isn't by his side, and it hurts. 'Why can't you just live for now, Jeanie? I'm sharing my digs with a bunch of lovable morons, you know that. And *your* flatmate drives you nuts.'

'Her name is Ruthy.'

'You've got nothing in common with her. You're grounded, and she's airy-fairy.' What Jack really wants to say is that he's got nothing in common with Jeanie's room-mate and B.F.F.

'Yes, Ruthy does have her head in the clouds, but opposites attract. We share a liking for tequila on Thursday nights at Joe Soap's.'

'Who *doesn't* share a liking for tequila on Thursday nights at Joe Soap's, Jeanie?' Jack sighs with desperation. 'What's the big deal about renting our own place? We'll still be flatmates, only I'll *literally* be your mate and you'll be mine. And we can be cosy and have privacy and spend our time, well, studying and mating.'

'We're not spawning frogs, Jack.' Jeanie takes his hand in hers. 'I'm not ready. It *will* happen, but I prefer to get this last year out of the way, and then we can sing the mating call or whatever it is that you frogs do. *Nothing* is going to get in the way of me finally finishing my law degree. *And* you.'

Jack's clutching at straws. 'But let's divide our time between work and pleasure, just like we do now. There's no difference.'

'Don't take it personally. Degrees mean jobs...jobs mean money...and money means *cosy* and *private*: keywords from my keynote speech today. Besides, I don't think Ma 'n Pa will be too enthusiastic about those living arrangements.' Jeanie mentions every excuse why they shouldn't move in but keeps the biggest reason to herself, which is that she's afraid: afraid that things won't work out when they really get to know each other's annoying little habits and idiosyncrasies. She wants to keep this fairy-tale alive by *not* moving in together.

The despondency in her soul-mate's face says it all.

'The more you wait for something, the more you appreciate it when you get it.'

'No, Jeanie. The *more* you wait for something, the shorter your life is becoming. Carpe diem, that's my motto.' Jack feels that he's losing the argument, and a flutter of panic tingles inside him. 'We're going to be stuck in Old Castle for the rest of our sorry lives.'

'Not true, Jack. We're going to get our degrees and be *shit*-hot lawyers in the city, earning a *shit*-load of money.'

'This scrapyard is as good as it's going to get, Jeanie. We've been coming here since we were kids, and we'll still be coming here when we're old and grey – and we've established that I'm *already* grey, now just the old part is left.'

'Don't be ridiculous, Jack.'

A stroke of brilliance suddenly comes to Jack in a heavenly bolt of lightning. He *knows* Jeanie's weakness. Why hadn't he thought about this earlier? Probably because this conversation has never gotten as far as it has today. Normally, Jeanie would shoot him down outright and that would be the end of it. But today, Jack hears a sliver of hope in Jeanie's tone.

'Y'know what we need?'

'I can think of one or two things, Jack.'

'We need hard cash, so we can rent our own place. We can be *independent*.' And this is Jack's secret weapon: *independent*. 'Our parents aren't going to agree with us moving in together, and the funds will dry up. But if we have our own cash? *Independent*, Jeanie.'

Independence is, and always has been, Jeanie's weakness.

Jack spots Jeanie blinking more than necessary: a sure sign that she's thinking over this proposition without wanting to admit it. Jack *knows* that she's dependent on her folks, as is Jack, but Jeanie is as independent as a tom-cat and has been struggling with that for the last few months. All Jack has to do is mention the magic word and that sends Jeanie reeling.

'And where are we going to earn money, darling?'

In a crescendo of cymbals and angelic chorus, Jack sings *Halleluiah* in his head...

'It'll have to be during the weekend, and it'll have to be here in Old Castle because I get more studying done at home than anywhere else. If I stay in the flat during the weekend, I'll only end up drinking my pocket-money down at Joe Soap's.' Jeanie's very sure of herself because, where and how are they going to get part-time jobs in a place like Old Castle? It's practically impossible to get a full-time job, though things are changing under the new town mayor, Arthur Lawless.

Jack strikes again. 'Pocket-money! Listen to yourself, Jeanie. You sound like a bob-a-job girl. It's time to stop sponging off our old ones and get a part-time job.'

Jeanie's eyes flit around the Beetle's mossy interior, blinking and thinking (the moss only adding to her desperation). 'Okay, let's make a pact. If you can find us two part-time jobs in a place like Old Castle, then I'll *think* about moving in with you, Jack. But I draw the line at being a frog.'

Jack slams on the non-existent horn. 'You've got a deal, babe!' Jack doesn't know how or where he's going to find two part-time jobs in a place like Old Castle. True, the place has picked up since Arthur Lawless became mayor, but still, it is a country-town with limits. Yet he's got his foot in the Jeanie-door.

Jack and Jeanie leave their headquarters and walk hand-in-hand in the falling snow, through the myriad of crock cars. They slip through the same hole in the fence that they'd been coming in and out of since they can remember. They walk up the wooded hill and at the top, they share a longing kiss, then go their separate ways along the brow of the slope. Jack takes a short-cut back to his place through the woods to get job-searching online ASAP, while Jeanie takes the long route home and goes for her sacred, daily jog, wondering if she has just turned the last page of her fairy-tale.

It's all about the future now.

Chapter 2

Scrapyard of Memories

Later on, Jack is surfing the net at his semi-detached house in the suburbs of Old Castle. He is racking his brain for a way to find him and Jeanie work so they can be young, independent, responsible people and move in together under their own steam. Not that these adjectives stick with Jack; all Jack can think about is Open Season in the single bedroom. C'mon, nobody's fooling anybody here. He knows and Jeanie knows, but this part-time job would validate things; a part-time number would bring everything together nicely.

He is checking local news online when, by providence, he comes across a headline:

Country's Largest Amusement Park to open in the town of Old Castle, County Limerick

No sooner has he read the line than he thinks that his guardian angel is looking down on him. A plan is already forming in his brain, and the world is a flowering and beautiful place...

In the photograph accompanying the extensive article, there is a non-descript businessman shaking hands with Arthur Lawless, Old Castle's newly-elected mayor (as the previous mayor had elected himself for alcoholism). At knee-height, holding the mayor's other hand, is a chimpanzee going by the handle of Bonnie. She's grimacing for the camera, like a child who doesn't know why she's got to smile at a square object in her daddy's hand. Anybody else might not understand the necessity of having a chimpanzee at a business meeting but being an Old Castle native, Jack understands the significance of the monkey – the monkey-god. It's a long story and has been extensively covered in a book written about Arthur Lawless and his circus-that-never-was. Everybody in town has read *The Nobody Show* and feels the book does justice to Arthur's doomed efforts that brought him to the brink of madness. But Arthur Lawless *has* lifted Old Castle out of the mire and put it on the map.

With wide eyes, Jack clicks on the *'Read On...'* option.

The proposed and much-debated building of a giant amusement park in Old Castle has been given the green light. The company, Chloma, which will be responsible for the construction, has told us that they are delighted with the decision and will begin construction immediately.

When this reporter asked about the decision to build this amusement park in a relatively secluded area of the country, the company spokesman said that the cult following that has risen from Old Castle resident and current mayor Arthur Lawless' failed attempts at building a circus, gave Chloma inspiration. "We couldn't think of a more perfect site."

When asked why Chloma wanted to tempt fate considering the failed circus, the Chloma representative informed us that they "want to succeed and finish off what Arthur Lawless started. It's not a circus, but it's the same world of entertainment – good, old-school fun. Old Castle has already been put on the map by a series of curious tales that seem to congregate in the town. Books have been written about its characters, and I think Old Castle itself has become a character. We figured that the country's largest amusement park would fit right in. We already have the financial backing and the local politicians plus the Town Hall have given us the go-ahead. Chloma feels that Arthur Lawless deserves to win and we feel that our new amusement park is going to attract people from all over the country and internationally, as well. This will bring revenue into the town and jobs for local people, full-time positions and part-time positions."

Jack reads that last line three times in succession. He stops reading here because the rest is superfluous. His eyes flit over the last part about the jobs once more and pick out the pulsing words: *...part-time positions...*

Jack leaps from the living-room table, startling his folks sitting on the sofa, and makes a bee-line for the phone in the hallway. He punches in Jeanie's number and waits.

Jeanie picks up on the first ring. 'Are you thinking what I'm thinking?'

Jack hears the excitement in her voice. 'Have you seen it, too?!'

'Just saw it on the six o'clock news! I was just picking up the phone to ring you!'

They say in unison: *'The amusement park?'*

Answering back simultaneously, 'Yes!'

'Jeanie, this is a sign! This is providence, girl! How about we meet at the scrap-yard tomorrow morning, and we can plan our next move – literally. What a start to the new year!' Jack can barely contain himself.

'I know!!' Jeanie giggles. 'I've got butterflies, Jack.' She pauses. 'Do you mind if I bring Ruthy, darling?'

Just hearing that name sinks Jack. *'Ruthy?* Why does she have to come?'

'We haven't had the chance to meet over the Christmas holidays.'

Jack lip-synchs a few F-words to himself. 'Okay, but this is *our* plan, Jeanie. Not hers. And why are you so desperate to see her when you speak to her for hours on end on the phone? What's the difference? *And* you share a flat with her... We hardly ever spend time together.'

'We were together this morning.'

'Only because Ruthy was out of town.'

Jeanie sighs down the line. 'I would go into it, but I don't think your little brain could handle it, Jack. See you tomorrow. By the way, don't be so jealous. Jealousy is one noun I don't do.' She hangs up before Jack has time to retract his biting words.

The following morning, 2nd of January, Jack is waiting for his girlfriend and her dreaded B.F.F by the hole in the scrapyard fence. But he isn't worried about Ruthy for now. He is *stunned* into silence. Jack holds onto the wired fence, unable to believe what he is seeing. He watches from the side-lines as his childhood is dragged and torn away by heavy machinery and carted off on the backs of trucks. The scrapyard is being emptied. It looks to Jack as if the clean-up had begun some time during the night. Most of the cars are gone. All that is left are earthy patches in the grass that haven't seen the sun for years.

Jeanie and Ruthy arrive just in time to see the young couple's beloved old Beetle being hauled away, rolled roof over wheels, then lifted onto an enormous truck with a claw, along with another twenty other wrecks destined for some unmarked car necropolis.

The girls are speechless, especially Jeanie, who hides her agape mouth in her gloved hands.

Jeanie observes, 'Never thought I'd say this, but I already miss that old Beetle.' Then Jeanie notices some well-dressed people milling around. She reads the company name on the backs of their vests: Chloma. 'So, this is it.'

'This is what?' Ruthy asks absentmindedly while spiking the tips of her punk-style Mohawk in her fingers.

'What?' Jack is as much in the dark as Ruthy is. He gives Ruthy a vague 'Hello' as she arrives. 'I see you've dyed your hair again? What does blue represent?' he asks snidely.

She gestures to their diminishing scrapyard of memories. 'It's a blue day, wouldn't you say?'

Jack nods vaguely agreeing with Ruthy. 'Good call. How did you know?'

'Just woke up this morning with a gut feeling...'

'I think this is where the amusement park is going to be.'

'Huh?'

'Jack, look at the company name on the backs of their vests: Chloma. It's the same company that was on the news last night.'

Then Jack realizes that he'd seen the same name in the article. 'You're right! So, this is where it's being built.' Jack looks at Jeanie, intent on speaking his mind but is too embarrassed in front of Ruthy to say what's really on his mind: *Adios* to their old life and *Hola* to their new life.

Jack and Jeanie have known Ruthy for a few years. Ruthy had joined them one long-forgotten summer evening a couple of years back. It had been the last day of university before the summer holidays break-up, and everybody was enjoying themselves in the People's Park in Limerick City. Ruthy had just appeared with a six-pack of cider. She sat on the grass by them, offered them each a bottle of cider, and the rest is history. She has stuck with them since, like a stray dog. Ruthy is a mystery; an enigma, as far as Jack's concerned. Jack knows practically nothing about her, nor does he want to know anything about her. All he knows is that she spends far too much time with Jeanie when Jeanie could be spending more time with him...

Except that, very rarely, when the sun shines on her in the same way the sun's rays light up the inside of New Grange on a winter solstice, Jack finds Ruthy mesmerising.

There was a time when Jack would've said the first thing that came to his mind, often opening his mouth without *ever* thinking. But he had grown up a lot recently and grown a conscience with it. That magic thing called love had blossomed between him and Jeanie and everything became awkward after that.

What Jack had wanted to say was that this is a sign: the removal of the scrapyard is the end of their childhood, and the building of this new amusement park symbolizes adulthood and the chance to earn the money they need to move in together.

All of this flits through Jack's mind and fizzles out again when one suit comes towards them with a Chloma vest.

'What's going on?' Jack asks, forgetting any introductions. 'Is this where the new amusement park is going to be built?'

The clean-shaven man looks at Jack and the two girls. He smiles at the girls, but draws a blank at Jack. Jack and Jeanie recognize the suit as the same man in the online newspaper article and the six o'clock news.

He nods, 'And you get rid of this eye-sore in the deal.' He thumbs over his shoulder.

'This *eye-sore* is our childhood,' Jeanie answers back readily.

Ruthy nods. 'We've had hours of fun in these old cars.'

The businessman glances at Jack and sniggers. 'I bet you have.'

'Not *that* kind of fun.' Jeanie's not sure if she likes the guy all that much and has temporarily forgotten about the possibility of part-time work.

Jack agrees with Jeanie, but not for want of trying. He throws her eye-daggers, warning her not to get too cocky with the businessman, because he could be their future employer.

'Well,' answers the businessman, 'now you'll get a chance to sit in cars that actually move – *bumper* cars. And don't forget that the highest rollercoaster in the country will soon be towering above all of this.'

Jack intervenes. 'Um, would there be a possibility of working here part-time? Weekends, for example. You mentioned it in the newspaper...'

'Yes,' he answers readily. 'We will be looking for people to man the attractions and various miscellaneous duties. Take down this number.'

Jack smiles at Jeanie exclusively, then saves the given number in his phone's contact list.

Jeanie thanks the man. 'Don't forget us!' she calls.

'How could I forget you?' says the businessman with an easy smile.

Jack's ready to knock his block off, but the thought of himself and his girlfriend in a double-bed in their own apartment, singing the mating call, quickly overcomes any aggression towards the flirty businessman. "You should be proud..." Jeanie would say and *has* said in the past. "*You're* with me, not him." True, but it still hurts when somebody's flirting with your girlfriend right in front of you. He used to get jealous a lot more in the early days, but he still gets a little green-eyed because of the time Jeanie spends with Ruthy.

The businessman adds, 'This thing is going to go up real fast. We've got a mega-team that will erect this in two months. This is what they do. Ring that number at the end of February and tell whoever answers that you spoke to Jim.'

'Count me in too, Jim!' calls Ruthy. 'We're a package deal.'

The businessman doesn't even turn but just waves back at them, as he joins another group of non-descript Chloma suits.

Jack's fuming. This is *their* gig, not Ruthy's. He's about to speak his mind, and possibly put his foot in it, when he sees that Ruthy has come over all strange and quiet. Bizarrely, she begins to cry.

'What is it?' asks Jeanie, shrugging her shoulders at Jack.

Ruthy tells them, 'I have lots of great memories here.'

'We'll always have the memories,' Jeanie answers and puts her arm around Ruthy. 'Anyway, how long has it been since we actually spent time here?'

With a hint of sarcasm, Ruthy answers: 'Not since you and Jack started going out. I just want to be with you guys. It seems that we are growing further and further apart, and this seems to be the final blow. I hate seeing this disappear because it means we'll disappear – *us*, I mean. I only want to work here because it means we'll be together. I know you and Jack are an item, but that doesn't mean you have to alienate me...'

Even Jack feels guilty hearing these words. 'Nobody's trying to alienate you.' In the back of his mind, he's beginning to regret taking that bottle of cider in the People's Park all that time ago. It's kind of like making the mistake of feeding that mangy stray dog once and now it refuses to leave.

Jeanie, on the other hand, smiles and gives Ruthy a hug as the tears come to her eyes. 'I hadn't planned on crying this morning. Of course you can work with us. But we don't even know if we have jobs yet, so let's not get ahead of ourselves.'

Jeanie looks over Ruthy's shoulder at Jack and throws her eyes to the heavens in a *What am I s'posed to say?* look.

Jack's desperate to tell Jeanie that Ruthy is *not* going to wreck their dream. When, in reality, she's just looking for a job as they are. But it means that he has to share Jeanie's time with her *all* over again.

'Really? Thanks guys! How cool it will be!' Ruthy's excited. 'We've spent all our free time in this place, and now we'll be *working* here. It just seems right.'

'I agree,' says Jack, surprising Jeanie. She flashes an approving smile at Jack and hugs Ruthy even tighter.

Jack genuinely feels sorry for Ruthy. But if truth be known, he knows he has to tread lightly, because it would be only too easy for *him* to become the wedge between the girls, and that isn't an option; he *would* lose. So, not being entirely honest, he accepts Ruthy for his and Jeanie's benefit.

Chapter 3

Written in the Stars

The town of Old Castle becomes a hive of activity over the next few weeks.

Jack and Jeanie have gone back to their law studies at Limerick University. Ruthy, meanwhile, is studying Children's Literature, specialising in medieval children's fairy-tales and folklore. However, on several occasions, Jeanie has mentioned to Jack that she's *never* seen Ruthy open a book. If she's not in the flat, playing gooseberry when Jack comes around, then she's gone for days on end, helping an uncle on his rabbit-farm up in the country somewhere.

Meanwhile, the car cemetery of their collective childhood is now but a fond memory; the cemetery is firmly in the grave. In that place of childhood memories is an amusement park which has taken on the proportions of an extra village, right next to Old Castle. The whole town feels the industrious buzz of hope, many reminded of the days when Arthur Lawless tried to set up the Greatest Show on Earth – Old Castle's slice of Earth, at least. The odds had proven too great for the man, and he almost lost his mind in the process, confiding in a 'borrowed long-term' chimpanzee who quickly became his advisor. Bonnie, the monkey, still plays an active role in decision-making, but these days Lawless has trained the beautiful monkey to give clear and concise answers like any salt-of-the-Earth politician, so he has trained the monkey to give her answers in three straightforward gestures: hear no evil (Bonnie covers her ears and grimaces); see no evil (Bonnie covers her eyes and grimaces); and thirdly, speak no evil (Bonnie covers her grimace). In other words, the monkey has become a politician. Nevertheless, the inhabitants of Old Castle prefer to put their faith in an attractive female chimpanzee, rather than the previous mayor, Moss 'The Mayor', who was – *is* – more monkey than Bonnie will ever be, plus the good people of Old Castle prefer to hear positive news from a monkey-god rather than find an answer at the bottom of a whiskey tumbler down at The Hound.

The big attraction of the amusement park, the rollercoaster, is already drawing crowds from Old Castle and nearby towns as it is being built. Not only locals, but camera crews are also present, documenting the construction of the amusement park and holding interviews with the suits from Chloma. People pull up in their cars on top of the hill to watch the attraction wind and snake its way skywards. Just when people think that it cannot possibly get any higher, the builders add *another* five meters of height. It's so monstrous now that it has reached the top of the little wooded valley in which the amusement park sits.

The top of the rollercoaster is in line with the brow of the hill. Right in the middle of the rollercoaster is a quick succession of three loop-the-loops, which peak at the top of the hill, spiralling along in a dizzying series of hard G-force loops.

Another attraction getting a lot of attention is the giant zombie lying on his back with a ghost train ride running through his thirty-meter Plexiglas gut. Looking downwards from the top of the hill, he looks a little creepy, forever staring upwards with dead eyes.

It is Saturday, 28th of February. Jack, Jeanie, and Ruthy are among the onlookers that have gathered along the top of the hill to watch as the amusement park grows and grows in every way. Jack and Jeanie have been coming here every Saturday morning to see the progress. Ruthy had gone to her uncle's place for a couple of weekends to help out on the rabbit colony. As the park expands, it gradually becomes more difficult to imagine that their scrapyard ever existed. Jack and Jeanie have been making moving-in plans over the phone, as if they already had the jobs and the interview was only procedure. They are keeping their plans a secret from Ruthy for now. That had been Jeanie's idea; she wants to tell her best friend 'when the time is right'.

Jack's response was: 'As if we need permission from her.'

'Will we ring?' he asks Jeanie, not making eye-contact with Ruthy.

Jeanie looks down on the proceedings below. She takes a deep breath. 'Now is as good a time as any, I suppose. He did say to wait until the end of February...'

Without hesitation, Jack dials the number which they were given at the beginning of the year by the Chloma suit named Jim. He waits for an answer and explains who they are, why they are ringing, and the contact name they were given.

The chirpy woman on the other end of the line directs Jack and the two girls to an on-site pre-fab cabin, which they can see from their vantage-point.

Panic lights up Jack's face...

In unison, the girls mime: '*What?*'

'Right now?' exclaims Jack on the phone. 'But, um, we're not really dressed for the occasion,' he jokes. 'We didn't think we would be having the interview *right* now.'

The woman on the other end of the line chimes in: 'This is an amusement park, Jack; suit and tie strictly outside the gates.'

From that, Jack garners that their attire is good to go. He thanks her and makes a beeline for the pre-fab building.

'Like this? *Now?!*' Jeanie looks at Ruthy. 'But Ruthy hasn't even combed her Mohawk!'

A crazy fit of giggles erupts between them as they run down the hill at top speed, laughing off their nervous butterflies all the way to the bottom.

A few minutes later, they're knocking on the door of the pre-fab and are beckoned in by the same friendly voice Jack had listened to on the phone: 'Door's open...'

The pre-fab is colder inside than outside. A lean, ruddy-faced woman wearing a parka-coat and what appear to be several cardigans beneath it, plus a violet woolly hat, is sitting behind a fold-up table. She's wearing an impressive pair of boots and multiple pairs of woollen socks inside.

She introduces herself as Katherine. She tells them, 'Natalie will see you now.'

'All of us?' asks Jeanie.

'Yes, Jim mentioned that you come as a package deal.' She smiles which gives unending optimism to the three hopeful candidates.

Fifteen minutes later, the three emerge from the freezing pre-fab, aglow and smiling.

'We did it!' Jack rejoices once they close the pre-fab door behind them.

Jack and Jeanie smother each other in a hug, knowing the *real* significance of this hug. Ruthy joins the hug. Jeanie lets go of Jack and returns the hug whereas Jack distances himself a little, already fearing the moment when Jeanie will break the news to her. And if Jack knows Jeanie as well as he thinks he does, then that moment is now...

He walks away up the hill, giving Jeanie space to tell Ruthy their news.

A few steps ahead, he turns back to see Jeanie and Ruthy in deep conversation. They are just standing there with their hands in their pockets, while Ruthy looks at Jeanie and listens to what she has to say.

Deep down, Jack feels sorry for Ruthy and begins to regret keeping this a secret. The fact that he's taking her best friend is also playing on his conscience. He has dreamt of this day for a long time; when he would finally win Jeanie over Ruthy, but now he doesn't feel too great and a little petty with it, if he's to be honest with himself. Ruthy, Jack often thinks, seems to be a lost soul, only drifting with the tide.

Then the girls stop their conversation and follow on up the hill towards Jack.

Jack doesn't see any sign on Ruthy's face that Jeanie has just broken the news. 'Did you tell her?' He already regrets saying it...

'Tell me what, Jack? We were just talking about which amusements we'd like to man.' Ruthy smiles at Jack, but the smile fades when she sees Jeanie's seething expression of anger.

Jeanie throws a look at Jack that says all of: *Great, thanks, moron...*

'What's he talking about, Jeanie?' Ruthy starts anxiously spiking the tips of her Mohawk; trying to appear nonchalant.

Jeanie cannot meet her best friend's gaze, so speaks to Ruthy's nail-varnished graffiti Dr. Marten boots. 'Well, I had planned to tell you in my own time, but Jack was never known for his sense of timing.'

'What are you *getting* at, Jeanie?'

'Um, well, y'know, how err...'

Jack kicks in. 'I want to move in with Jeanie; we want to move in together. There – it's out in the open.'

'Real subtle, Jack. *Jesus.*' Jeanie still can't meet her best friend's eyes.

'Is that all? Jesus Christ,' she eyes Jeanie, 'I thought you were *pregnant* or something!' Ruthy attempts a laugh.

'So you don't mind?' asks Jeanie.

'No, why would I? It means cheaper digs.'

Jeanie frowns at Jack and back at Ruthy. 'Huh? What do you mean?'

Ruthy giggles in that Ruthy way. 'I know math isn't your strong point, Jeanie, but four hundred divided by two and four hundred divided by three isn't the same. Instead of two hundred a month, I now have to pay...' Ruthy looks into the sky and begins wriggling her forefinger in the air as she mentally divides...

Jeanie's smile drops when she realizes that Ruthy is dividing four hundred by three...

'Uh-oh,' is all Jack can muster and Jeanie nods her head in silent agreement. Jack takes this as his cue to walk away again, discreetly at first, then picking up pace until he is out of earshot and well into the woods. He cannot bear to watch.

'Ruthy,' begins Jeanie, 'I think you're getting the wrong end of the stick. What Jack means, and, um, what *I* mean, is that we want to move in *together*.' She holds up two fingers to drive her message home and apologetically adds 'two together' in a little voice.

Ruthy's finger stops mapping the sky with numbers. Instead, she just stares at the clouds for a moment, unblinking. 'Yeah, I know,' she answers defensively and walks off in Jack's direction. Jeanie follows.

They catch up with Jack, but Jack plays dumb; the situation is already uncomfortable enough.

'I'm only pulling your leg. I *knew* that's what you meant, Jeanie.'

Ruthy gets the Academy Award for Worst Actress. Jack and Jeanie can clearly see that Ruthy's hurting. She hadn't suspected this bomb-shell and she's trying her best to play along.

'Of course you want to move in together. If I could choose to be a fruit, I'd probably be a strawberry...or a cherry.'

Jeanie frowns. 'Which means?'

'Which means that I'm no gooseberry,' Ruthy clarifies.

Jeanie utters a strained laugh.

Ruthy goes on. 'I think everybody should move in together as a trial period before marriage.'

Jeanie laughs along with Ruthy. The more Ruthy laughs the closer Jeanie is to tears...

'I wouldn't go that far just yet,' says Jeanie, wiping bitter-sweet tears from her eyes.

An odd expression flashes across Ruthy's face. 'Yeah, you're probably right. Anyway, the last thing I want to be is a gooseberry and if that means having to find my own digs and paying *full whack*, then so be it. I can handle it. I'm a big girl with deep pockets.'

Everybody reads the biting sarcasm between the lines.

'Look, I was going to tell you, Ruthy, in my own time, but Jack's got a big mouth.' She throws him more eye-daggers.

'Jeanie, I'm not a kid. I just knew getting rid of the scrapyard was the start of the end for us.' She smiles a little creepily. 'It was an omen, Jeanie.'

Jack pipes up. 'Ruthy, it's just the next step.'

'Yeah, only I'm not on the same step, *Jack*.' Ruthy does that eerie smile again. 'But at the end of the day, we are all on our own path and we cannot change that. It has been written in the stars since before we were born. It's called fate.'

Jack decides to add some wisdom. 'Shit happens, Ruthy.'

'Shit doesn't just *happen*, Jack. You two are so predictable that I'm living in a constant déjà vu.'

Ruthy seems happy with her own conclusion and walks off, leaving Jack and Jeanie frowning to themselves at this peculiar juncture.

Why does Jack get the feeling that there's more to this than they think?

Jeanie, too, isn't sure of the reason for this strange outburst.

Seeing the mild content on her face, Jeanie decides to maximise on this brief ray of light and jokes, 'Ruthy *always* blames interstellar mystical forces on what happens in our daily lives.'

'There's more than meets the eye, that's all,' says Ruthy without looking back. 'Look, speaking of the stars, we've got some celebrating to do! We've got weekend work!'

'Okay, good! That's the spirit!' Jeanie takes a deep breath, only too happy to change the prickly subject.

With a glint in his eye, Jack asks Jeanie, 'Do you want to be the first to try out the rollercoaster?' Jack's imagination is getting the better of him. 'We can be the first couple *ever*. We can sit up front and take her on her maiden voyage. Ahoy there!'

Jeanie grins, 'That would be so cool!'

'And kind of romantic,' Ruthy calls back. 'After all, we *all* know about the Titanic's maiden voyage...'

Jack and Jeanie don't know how to react to Ruthy's odd comment, both embarrassed that she'd heard them.

'C'mon,' Jack deciding to disregard Ruthy's weirdness, 'how 'bout it, Jeanie? We can sit in the front seat.'

'It would be an honour to be the first to ride the rollercoaster, Jack.'

Jack feels a twinge of pity for Ruthy. 'There might be room for three...' In a way, he's just saying it for Jeanie's benefit.

But Ruthy is quick to answer, 'No, no. Go ahead. Gooseberries don't make the height requirements,' she jokes.

Jack smiles a thank-you to Ruthy. He is happy she has declined his offer because he has something very important to say to Jeanie, but he really wants Ruthy (the drifter) to know it first. He may be jealous of the time they spend together, but Ruthy has been one of the scrapyard gang since forever and the closest friend Jeanie has ever had.

That chilly, dark Saturday evening, Jack, Jeanie, and Ruthy climb to the top of the hill that overlooks their new place of work. It looks spectacular, fully-lit for the first time in bright multi-coloured lights. From up here, it looks like a space-ship.

Opening night will be more than just the amusement park's inauguration, Jack thinks and smiles to himself in the comfort of night.

Chapter 4

Grand Opening Night

By the time March 1ˢᵗ comes around, Old Castle is a bustling metropolis. People have come from miles around to attend the opening night of the country's largest amusement park. Families have already begun to queue up at the gates since early this Sunday morning to be the first ones on the rides. Television crews have also come to witness the event.

The atmosphere is electric.

At 4 p.m., Jack, Jeanie and Ruthy are led to their prospective attractions and are quickly shown the ropes by a group of rough and ready individuals who obviously do this for a living (a touch of the circus and bohemian about them). They have two hours to acquaint themselves with their attractions before the gates swing wide to the public at the official opening time at 6pm. Jack and Jeanie complain to deaf ears that there is little time to learn everything. Nevertheless, during the pre-opening two hours, Jack makes numerous escapes to Jeanie's bumper car attraction and whispers sweet-nothings in her ear while making one last final test-run on the bumper cars, laughing their heads off every time they crash into each other. Jeanie's excited but tells Jack to get back to work at the Giant Zombie; they have their futures to think about now.

Ruthy seemingly takes everything in her stride; she looks every bit the true carny with her punk rocker outfit and Mohawk. She had been given the rifle range, jokingly asking her immediate carny boss if she was working in the appropriate section seeing as she was 'mentally unstable'.

At 5.30 p.m., Mayor Arthur Lawless arrives to officially cut the ribbon. He makes a boring little speech before briefly alluding to his time as a circus master.

Holding the mayor's hand is the happy-go-lucky chimpanzee, Bonnie, appropriately dressed in a black tuxedo, complete with maroon dickie-bow and matching handkerchief set into her breast pocket. Completing the monkey's look is the mayor's crazy-days maroon top hat – a constant humbling reminder.

Standing on the other side of the mayor is his dazzling wife, Raquel, but all eyes are on the monkey.

People can relate to the monkey because it's of general opinion that the parliament is mainly comprised of monkeys making decisions and monkey-making decisions. Who knows, maybe Bonnie will be the next president.

After the mayor makes his brief speech, Jim, the Chloma representative, hands the scissors to the mayor, who hands them to the chimpanzee. She is guided in the cutting of the red ribbon to a delightful, *'Awww!'* followed by a rapturous applause. She cuts the ribbon with finesse. Bonnie grimaces a smile for the cameras as the impatient queue of excited thrill-seekers is let in, and a flood of people swarm the amusement park...

Jack had begged with Chloma management earlier in the day to let Jeanie and himself take the helm of the rollercoaster. After much deliberation, Jack finally got his way.

Before they climb in, Jack reaches across to Ruthy and says something in her ear.

'I can't hear you!' she responds.

The cheers and screams of exhilaration coming from the thrill-junkies are deafening.

Jack shouts into Ruthy's ear this time. 'I said...'

When Ruthy hears what Jack says, her face lights up and her eyes grow out on stalks.

Jack flashes something in Ruthy's face.

She screams with happiness and throws her arms around Jack and swears happy swear-words to the heavens...mainly F-words.

But if Jack had been more observant, he would've seen Ruthy pause in the blink of an eyelid as his message sank in; he would've witnessed a fleeting darkness wash over her, especially when her chin was on his shoulder as they briefly embraced. In the back of his mind, he *does* clock the stall, but subconsciously puts it down to probable envy – the moving-in and moving-on syndrome. It wouldn't be the first time he had seen that sudden sullenness in Ruthy.

Arthur Lawless and Bonnie welcome punters on-board the coaster. He smiles for the flashing cameras while Bonnie does that rictus-grin which has everybody in stitches. There's a mad scramble for the rollercoaster. VIPs, Jack and Jeanie, skip the queue and jump into the front seat and strap themselves in. They exchange a kiss. Then they notice Ruthy standing on the side-line by the coaster's docking area.

Jeanie calls, 'Sure you won't come for a ride?'

Ruthy smiles blankly and answers back: 'I'll let you be the guinea-pigs! I'm more of a rabbit person.'

Jack and Jeanie laugh back at Ruthy but sober up when the rollercoaster jolts into life and rolls out along the track. They hold hands as the snout of the coaster begins to climb.

Jeanie looks back over her shoulder and downwards to the crowd. She picks out Ruthy and waves, but Ruthy isn't smiling any more. Not only that, Jeanie witnesses Ruthy turn away and walk off into the crowd. Looks like she's still hurting about them moving in together...

Their car suddenly banks ninety degrees to the left, causing Jeanie to twist around and grab Jack as the rollercoaster rides low on its left side. The coaster then picks up speed as it climbs and drops vertically before hitting the lowest part of the ride and climbs eighty-five degrees towards the twilit sky. Jeanie doesn't have time to ponder her best friend's worries as they climb up and level off a hundred feet above the ground, then plummet into another ninety stomach-turning degrees, before being thrown into a dizzying flurry of loop-the-loops.

As they hit the first one, Jack reaches deep into his jeans pocket and takes out a ring. He had previously removed it from its box to avoid any G-force mishaps.

They go up and around the first loop and pull out of it and are then thrown right into the next one...and then head-first into the last loop...

As they pull out of the last loop, everybody hears a metallic bang from somewhere beneath the coaster...but the vibration gets lost in the speed.

The coaster casts along another ten meters and launches into a straight vertical climb, high over the amusement park, the woods, and Old Castle.

By now, Jeanie is beginning to regret getting on the ride and isn't sure whether to scream or laugh as she reaches for the stars.

This is the moment Jack's been waiting for. 'Jeanie...'

Jeanie can't take her eyes away from the deep drop inches from her side.

Jack shouts to be heard: *Jeanie...*'

She is too scared to speak or look at him. She just wants off; this is the first and last time. Jesus, what had she been thinking when she agreed to get on this?!

Jack pops the question just as the coaster peaks at the highest point of the ride. *'Will you marry me, Jeanie?'* he calls out to Jeanie and the Milky Way.

Jeanie can barely drag her eyes away from the rails in front of their car. But when she sees the ring, she forgets that she's on the highest rollercoaster in the country. Straight away, she spots the cluster of six pink rubies and double-diamonds that are formed like the petals of a flower. She reaches across, fighting the G-forces, and kisses Jack on the cheek (her eyes not leaving the rails in front of them). *'Yes, Jackie darling! I will marry you!!'*

Jack roars in triumph then tries to slip the engagement ring onto Jeanie's marriage finger, just as the coaster drops again and hits the triple loop-the-loop for the *last* time.

They whizz through the first loop. Jeanie snaps back her left hand from Jack and holds on for dear life. They bullet into the second loop with no time to recover from the first loop. Meanwhile, Jack's obsessed with getting that damn ring on her finger...*almost* before it's too late. They are thrown into the last loop. As the rollercoaster exits from the final loop, there is a loud crash in the same place where they had heard it the last time around. A deafening crack erupts below their car...

Jeanie screams in a thrill of horror...

In life, one always hopes that the last sound one makes is *not* a scream. This passes Jeanie's conscience as the rollercoaster leaves the tracks and sails out into the night, high over the woods. Life becomes surreal as their coaster is suddenly flying through the air, leaving the track far behind them. It is almost peaceful...

Jack is thinking that this *isn't* in the instruction manual. Deep down, he's hoping that this is still a part of the ride; some kind of special zero-gravity effect as his stomach lurches...

There is silence for a second, a strange and brief moment as the complete train leaves the rails and catapults right over the Dead Giant Zombie attraction, passing over the Giant's dark unblinking stare, *hundreds* of people, and rolling TV cameras.

On the ground, one child has time to yell: 'Wow, mommy, look! I want to go on that!!'

There's nothing below Jack and Jeanie, only the woods of their childhood. They crash into the trees. Jack feels the branches tear and slice his face, but his thoughts are on Jeanie. He reacts a moment too late. He goes to shield her but as he raises his arm, Jeanie gets pulled out of her seat like a rag-doll as she gets caught up in the branches of a pine tree.

Jack is left empty-handed. He braces himself for impact, ducking down onto the seat where Jeanie had just been sitting. He already knows that his car is going to impact first. As the rollercoaster comes crashing down through the trees, Jack wishes he too had been dragged out with Jeanie...

The crash of twisted metal fills Jack's senses. He feels a light go out somewhere inside him.

Chapter 5

Matters of the Heart

Whose fingernails are these? These are not my fingernails, yet, they look *very much like my fingers.*

'Jack...'

Yes, look, that crescent moon scar by the knuckle of your left forefinger. Unless it's a wild coincidence, but didn't you used to have a scar just like that one? When you sliced your finger trying to open a tin of beans when you were just a kid? You don't even like beans...

'Jack...?'

Maybe they are *my nails, but shorter and tidier than they ever have been. But I don't recognize the cuff of this pyjamas I'm wearing either; it's not mine as these are not my fingernails. The material is too light and plain, just like the walls of this room. These are the hands of a different person, yet they* feel *like mine...*

'Jack, can you hear me?'

'Yes, he's showing signs of coming around. Look at his eyes fluttering...his eyeballs are racing behind those lids. He's probably surfacing from his long sleep and his brain is trying to update itself...'

You've got quirky dog wallpaper in your bedroom at home. These walls aren't the walls of your rented flat next to the university either because they are puke green – not easy to forget. You're an old man, in old-man pyjamas, surrounded by old-man walls. Where am I? Wait!

'Jack...'

I know *where I am! These are the walls of my – our new apartment. Jeanie!! The one we said we would rent when we save enough money by working the weekends at the amusement park...unamusement park...*

'Jack, can you hear me?'

'Jeanie?'

Pause. 'No, Jack. This is your mom.'

'Mom?'

Jack feels a hand lay softly on his shoulder. Suddenly, he flinches in his bed and ducks from the tree-tops coming at him. *'Mom?! Look out! The rollercoaster...'*

'Jack, *Jack*, you're safe. You're okay. You're alive. You're *alive*, Jack!'

Jack hears his mother crying for the first time, but he's not sure if he's hearing anything really because he's probably dead...

'Jeanie, I need to see Jeanie.' Jack tries sitting up in bed as he recognizes his mother for the first time in what seems a life-time. Has she started to lose her hair? She seems to have shed more kilos than what is healthy and the bruised blue bags under her eyes, along with that withered look of yellowed parchment that makes her almost unrecognizable.

What has happened?

Jack looks around him and discovers that he is in a hospital ward – *private* ward – surrounded by expensive, beeping machines. Standing on the other side of glass to his right, which turns out to be one complete wall of the room, Jack spots his father wiping his eyes. He, too, has become the shadow of a ghost with a head of grey hair and an unhealthy paleness about him.

His father blows him a kiss.

Something else doesn't add up; what's with the tinsel and Christmas decorations on the wall of the room?

'Where's Jeanie?' A sudden shearing pain in Jack's chest sends him falling back to his pillow in a limp daze. Stars burst before his eyes and splinter before fizzling out to reveal his mother's face...

A nurse enters the room and checks Jack's vital signs. 'Jack, my name is Heather. I've been looking after you for the last nine or ten months...I've lost count.'

'Excuse me?' Jack croaks, really freaking out now. He has *never* seen this woman in his life. He reacts by pulling the blanket further up on his chest in defence.

Heather smiles. 'There's nothing I haven't seen three times a day, *every* day, since 1st March. Don't worry, Jack.'

Hearing "don't worry" makes Jack *worry*. 'First of March?' Jack repeats in his dry croak, not quite understanding.

'Yes, that was the night of the accident.'

Jack pauses as he feels the sickening lightness in his stomach, recalling the moment the rollercoaster left the rails, and that empty feeling of being at the absolute mercy of the accident Gods. *'Where's Jeanie?'*

Jack's mother looks back over her shoulder at her husband and turns to face her son with a haunted expression. 'Jack...'

Jack's memory is on over-drive. 'I couldn't catch her. I wanted to shield her, put my arm around her, but she...' Like suddenly waking up from a dream where one is about to lose their life, Jack's mind seems to blank out as soon as that dreadful moment comes when his girlfriend – blink-and-you're-gone-fiancée – is yanked out of the coaster like a Cabbage Patch doll. It is there, in the dark recesses of his mind, but it's fighting not to reveal this particular memory to Jack.

The nurse gives Jack a swift, smooth injection and tells him that it's a 'painkiller', which is a little too general for Jack. She then goes to leave the room but makes some clandestine sign to Jack's mother, in plain view of him. Jack witnesses his mother pause, then nods reluctantly at the nurse who has stalled at the door to wait for his mother's response, before easing the door closed behind her.

'Jack, Jeanie's gone.'

'Gone where?' He already *knows* where, but he refuses to understand. The pain in his rib-cage consumes him, and he squirms in agony.

'Jack, Jeanie didn't make it in the accident.'

Panic rises in Jack's chest. His heart begins to hammer wildly. He wants to run and scream, but he's connected up to this machine which he now understands to be his heart-monitor. The beeps suddenly pick up in tempo until it's beeping so frantic that it's practically a deadline.

Nurses and doctors storm the room and curtly tell Jack's mother to leave.

Jack's parents watch through the wall of glass as the medical team swoop in around their son. Jack's mother cries again. Crying has become a daily activity for them both; the weeping sobs sneak up on them in the least likely of places, from their own en-suite bathroom to the frozen food section of *Tesco* supermarket. Jack's fight for life has sapped them of their life, aging nine years in as many months. This isn't the first time Jack's mother has told him that Jeanie didn't make it. If counting, this would be her *fourth* attempt at telling her son that Jeanie had died in the rollercoaster accident. This attempt is also a resounding failure, leaving Jack's weakened heart shy of an attack for the fourth time in a row.

These encounters with his mother have manifested as a series of lucid dreams for Jack, but then he sinks back into an amnesiac fairy-land, drug-induced, warm and scluggy reverie. Scluggy was a word he invented when he was three years old. Jack's folks had secretly marvelled when he had repeated that word over and over again the first time he had come around at the beginning of November, three weeks ago. How the mind can store and file information and spit it out more than two decades later, like an Alzheimer's patient taking a stroll down memory-lane...

'Happy Christmas, Jack.'

Jack hears these words and manages to open his eyelids a fraction. He sees his mother and father sitting on either side of his bed.

His mother exults, 'He's awake!'

Then his father says: 'He always loved Christmas. Jack?'

'Huh?' It takes all of Jack's energy to get one reedy syllable out.

His mother speaks softly, 'We brought you some presents. It's Christmas day, Jack.'

Jack's eyes focus in on the world. The blurry faces become his parents. In the back of his mind he remembers his mother telling him that Jeanie had died in the accident. 'Jeanie?'

Jack's mother glances across at his father and vaguely gestures a shake of her head, as if not believing something.

'He doesn't remember,' says his father. 'Tell him.'

'*You* tell him,' back-answers his mother.

Jack's father solemnly shakes his head.

'Jack,' his mother starts, 'Jeanie was killed in the amusement park accident. Do you remember anything?'

Jack nods. 'I thought it had only been a bad dream. I should've stayed asleep.'

His folks frown, refusing to read between the lines. Or maybe their son simply meant that the nightmares happen while awake so best to stay asleep, for now. But forgive them for thinking the worst, as in, a really long sleep – just like the one Jeanie is in right now.

Jack's mother asks, 'Do you remember the accident, Jack?'

A flashing strobe-light memory explodes in front of Jack's eyes. He recoils as tree branches cut and tear at his face while he sails downwards through the tree-tops of the pine wood surrounding the amusement park. He raises his hands to his cheeks and feels the deep gashes that have long since healed over, leaving eternal memory-scars. Jack recalls flying through the air just as the screams erupt. Then, Jeanie is snatched out of their car in what looks like the sudden jack-knife of an opening parachute in his mind's eye.

On instinct, Jack reaches out and grabs at sterile hospital air...

'Shush, it's okay. You were so lucky, Jack, so, *so* lucky.' His father's chin jitters and he fights to get the rest of the words out. 'It's a miracle that you're alive. Now, I don't know what you mean, exactly, about "staying asleep", but you have to know the reason you're *alive*.' He repeats: 'It's a *miracle*.'

Jack is still groggy, *scluggy* even, and he struggles to keep his thinking-process in check. 'What do you mean?'

His parents exchange dark glances.

'What?'

Jack's father can't hack it anymore. He claps his hand to his mouth and leaves the room like the nervous-wreck he has become.

'Jeanie saved your life.'

This line wakes Jack, *shakes* him. 'She couldn't have. She couldn't have because I failed to save hers. I tried to guard her, but she got caught up in the branches...' Jack begins to cry. Listening to his own words confirms his worst living nightmare. For a tiny moment, he had hoped that he might be still raving, under the influence of medication, but his mother's grave reaction is heart-breaking.

'Jack,' his mother continues, but treading lightly, 'Jeanie literally *did* save your life.'

'That's not possible. I saw her dragged out of the car. You told me yourself that she died in the accident.'

She stalls. 'Yes and no...'

Jack's caught for words. 'I'm not in the mood for mind-games, mom.'

'Jack, Jeanie was an organ-donor.'

Organ donor???!

This line sends off alarm-bells inside Jack. His head begins to swim. There's something creepy coming...

'Your heart stopped. The shock of the accident gave you a massive heart-attack. You've had a heart murmur since you were born. We knew about it, but the cardiologist told us that it would never be an issue. The doctors said that it was a weak link, but you'd lead a normal life. It's quite common apparently.' She says this trying to make light of the situation. 'After the accident, you were kept on a life-support machine – clinically, um,' she stops and composes herself, '...dead...for an hour before you underwent a heart transplant here at the hospital. You suffered brain trauma, and they've kept you sleep-induced to help you recuperate.'

Jack's breathing becomes erratic as the full implication of his mother's words begin to take shape in his blurred mind. *No, please don't tell me that...*

'Jeanie broke her neck when she hit one of those trees, but her heart kept working. You have Jeanie's heart. She saved your life. If she hadn't been so fit and into sport, her heart wouldn't have been big enough. And the luckiest thing is that you share the same blood type.'

Jack considers this same blood-type thing for a moment, never knowing it before now. If only he was discovering this under better circumstances.

A whimper escapes Jack before uncontrollable pining, *heaving* weeps come from him as his mother confirms his deepest, darkest suspicion. His mother holds him tight. But as Jack bawls, the mind-blowing fact that he will always have Jeanie's heart fills him with a strange melancholic happiness and wonder *beyond* words. To think that his fiancée lives on inside him – *literally* – is just about too much for him to understand in his half-drugged state.

'She had a big heart, Jack.'

'Yes, she did.'

Chapter 6

Money can't buy Love

Christmas week of 2015 passes by quickly. Jack spends more and more lucid hours sitting up in his bed. The machines have been taken out of his room. The bed-sores that had begun to surface a fortnight earlier are worse than ever now. Heather, the nurse, tends to his sores every day, cleaning and dressing them. Soon, Jack will be able to walk around and spend less and less time confined to his bed.

Friends and family pour in to visit Jack, even people he doesn't know in Old Castle. The whole town calls in, except Ruthy – Jeanie's best friend and Jack's best friend/arch-enemy. Ruthy is the only string tapering Jack back to his previous life, and he never thought he would think that. But he *does* notice her absence. In a way, she is the one person he really wants to see; all the others live on a different planet, or so it seems nowadays, including his family. Maybe she had visited while he had been asleep, though the grape-vine and inner-circle (family) observers claim Ruthy has not visited once since he had been hospitalized on that fateful Sunday evening. Nine months and counting…

But the odd thing is that, deep down in the sour water-well of his subconscious, Jack could've sworn that he had seen Ruthy many times in a recurring dream, sitting by his bedside during his darkest hours following the accident.

On New Year's Eve, the hospital grants Jack's parents 'special circumstances outside visiting hours' to stay with their son until midnight to ring in New Year. Jack's sister, Molly, who works as a reporter in Dublin, has come to spend New Year's Eve with her brother. Several times, Jack catches her on the brink of crying, looking in awe at Jack as if he's some kind of miracle-child with an angry scar running the length of his chest. Whereas in actual fact, it is *Jeanie* who is the miracle child. After all, it is *Jeanie* who has performed the miracle. Not five minutes have passed in all these monotonous, bed-ridden hours when Jack hasn't stopped thinking about his dead Jeanie – his Jeanie in-a-bottle. He's comfortable to broach the subject of Jeanie in his head, but dare not speak her name aloud because that makes her absence reality, if that makes any sense. He cannot even utter Jeanie's name without feeling a physical pain of loss, yet he shouts and yells her name inside his head, hoping that she will hear him on the other side.

A few minutes before midnight, Jack's family vow to each other that 2016 will be a year of healing and recovery, convincing each other, as if Jack isn't in the room.

Jack tries to hold a smile and is *screaming* inside.

His elated folks have one final message before the clock strikes twelve bells...

'Jack,' his mother says, 'we've got some really great news that is going to help with all this healing and recovery.'

Jack can't possibly imagine what great news can come of all this agony and anguish. He looks at his father and sister who are beaming back at him through misty eyes. They obviously know something he isn't privy to. 'What? What is it?'

His mother looks at his father. In a voice, barely under control, she says: 'Will you tell him or will I?'

'*I* will,' answers Molly. 'If that's okay?'

They nod and smile.

'Jack, you took the job at the amusement park to get extra pocket-money...'

For a second, Jack's heart – Jeanie's heart – skips a beat: they *know!* His family knows why they had wanted weekend work. As far as he recalls, Jack hasn't told anybody – not unless he muttered something in his nine-month forced hibernation; his second gestation. His heart beats a little faster. This strange feeling hasn't left Jack, knowing that he's got Jeanie inside him – her *heart*, of all things. What a gift! What a beautiful, *beautiful* thing. That warm, fuzzy, *scluggy* feeling hasn't left him since his mother told him.

But what Jack's sister says next makes him forget *everything*.

'You're the richest man in Old Castle, Jack.'

Jack attempts a smile for his family but cannot muster one up. 'I don't understand.'

His father chuckles, 'You got your weekend money.'

'That and more,' adds Jack's mother with a Cheshire Cat grin. 'Whatever it was you were saving up for...you got it...with interest.'

So they don't know...

Jack's lost. He feels a cold sweat coming on. 'Will someone just tell me?'

'Jack, when you signed that contract for weekend work, you were also given an accident insurance policy. Do you remember signing that?'

Jack shakes his head. 'I just remember paperwork.'

'Told ya,' Molly chimes to her parents. 'Thanks to that paperwork,' says Molly, 'you've now got enough money in your account to never work another day in your life. The amusement park paid up big-time for your injuries.'

'Be wise and invest it,' his father finishes. 'The amusement park forked out *big* insurance money, Jack. Big bucks.'

While Jack had been sleeping a deep comatose sleep in a private hospital ward (with a great view of the city at night if he had been awake to see it), he had become a rich sleeping celebrity.

All of this is too much to take on board for Jack. He is speechless.

Molly adds, 'We don't know why you and...' she pauses, realizing nobody has mentioned the pink elephant in the room, 'Jeanie wanted extra cash. But now, in a roundabout way, you've got more money from the amusement park than you could've *ever* wished for. Why did you want weekend work anyway?' Molly giggles. 'I *know*; I'm a nosey-parker, but you *are* my little bro.' But the grin dissolves from Molly's face, along with her parents' smiles, when they see tears come to Jack's eyes.

'Jeanie and I were going to be married.'

His parents and sister share the same expression of utter shock. There is silence in the room.

'We took weekend work to raise enough cash to rent an apartment of our own in the city...until we finish university.' Jack recalls when he had mentioned moving in to *study* together and how Jeanie had told him that study was the last thing on his mind...something about chirping frogs. 'I asked Jeanie to marry me while we were up on the rollercoaster...the last loop-the-loop.'

'And what did she say?'

Everybody, including Jack, stares at Molly as if she enjoys dark humour, but they can see the honesty in her face and that she hadn't really thought before opening her mouth.

'She said yes.'

Jack's mother bites her lip and wills the tears away, but they squeeze their way out anyway. She holds her son's hand tightly.

Molly grows red and begins to well up, while Jack's father just stares off into space.

'I didn't get time to put the engagement ring on her finger...' Jack wonders where that diamond and ruby ring is now. Darkly, Jack adds: 'I'd swap all that money just to hold her hand again...to have enough time to shield her from the trees. The money won't bring Jeanie back.'

The others look at each other briefly and lower their heads, almost in shame, presuming that money could buy them out of this one. But that hadn't been their goal; the last thing they want is to upset Jack.

'Jack,' his father says, 'you don't see it now, but money does help and *will* help some time in the future.'

Midnight comes and goes with twelve bitter-sweet bell chimes.

Jack's mother says, 'Jack, we've one more surprise...'

Jack responds flatly: 'I can do without any more surprises.'

'No, you will like this news,' Molly assures him. 'Go on, mom, tell him.'

'You're coming home tomorrow.' Jack's mother looks at her watch. 'Well, technically, today.'

'You're coming home on New Year's Day,' observes Jack's father, 'so let's wipe the slate clean and make this year the best one yet.'

If only it were that simple, thinks Jack. 'What about the other people on the rollercoaster?'

'Some were in the I.C.U for a few weeks,' Molly answers, 'while others were lucky enough to escape with scrapes and bruises. The front car – your car – took the brunt of it.'

The following morning, the mayor of Old Castle, Arthur Lawless, comes to visit with his aide, Bonnie, the chimpanzee, along with a pleasant Limerick County newspaper reporter who introduces herself as Gabrielle.

Jack poses for a photo with the mayor while Bonnie sits on the bed next to Jack, staring at him while helping herself to a bag of grapes some sympathiser had left.

Mayor Lawless wishes Jack a 'Happy New Year' and to 'keep your dreams alive' which is open to interpretation, considering the mayor's past dreams.

The mayor then leaves to entertain the children's ward with Bonnie being the star attraction.

After the doctors finally make their rounds, Jack is told he is free to leave the hospital. Many of the nurses and doctors who have cared for Jack during the previous nine months have come to see him off.

Jack says his goodbyes, he walks out the front door and is surprised to see, not his family waiting to collect him, but Ruthy.

Chapter 7

Return Visit

The fog is thick on this New Year's Day, mid-day Friday, 2016.

Ruthy is standing there in the foggy car-park by her idling old Fiat belching blue smoke. She looks good. She had dyed her Mohawk fresh-leaf green. Jack's sure it symbolizes something, but he's not sure yet because green is for envy, and he cannot come up with *anything* she could possibly be envious of now.

Jack scans the hospital car-park for his family, but it is only Ruthy who has come.

They had obviously planned this between them.

Secretly, he's happy that they hadn't told him because he would've been nervous; anxious about having to face Ruthy, and consequently, facing the painful truth of what has happened. Up until now, Jack has been cocooned in the sterile, artificial hospital microcosm.

He takes a deep gulp of fresh air (as fresh as the city and Ruthy's Fiat can offer). For the first time in his life, Jack appreciates the air that he has always taken for granted.

An intoxicating cocktail of fog, fresh air, and Ruthy's perfume hit Jack all at once and he's suddenly back on that killer coaster. He freezes, seeing nothing in front of him now but the tree-tops coming towards him at two-hundred miles per hour...And then he's back in the hospital car-park just as fast. Flashback gone.

'Jack...'

Jack doesn't hear Ruthy call his name because Jeanie's heart is hammering in his chest and ears. She must be excited to be out of the hospital too, or maybe she's excited to see her B.F.F, Jack ponders, feeling for a tiny moment what Frankenstein's monster must've felt like.

Maybe it is better when one doesn't know whose heart or lungs they have working in them; perhaps nobody should have told him that he's got his deceased lover's heart in his rib-cage.

Jack tries to over-ride his morbid thoughts and come back to here and now.

'Yoo-hoo!'

This time, Jack hears Ruthy...

'Hop in.'

He pauses for a moment before ambling over to the Fiat. He hands her his over-night bag which had turned out to be his over-year bag; his mother hadn't been thinking clearly when the doctors told her that her son would need an impromptu heart transplant.

Ruthy pops Jack's bag in the Fiat's boot while Jack sits in the passenger seat, his knees jamming up against the glove compartment.

Ruthy sits in and drives off, all flair and flame.

No words pass between them as they turn left out of the hospital car-park and head west towards Old Castle.

After fifteen uncomfortable minutes pass, Jack cracks and decides to break the ice with a safe compliment. 'I like your hair.'

'I needed some colour in my life,' Ruthy answers readily without taking her blank stare off the N21 motorway ahead. 'Blue wasn't doing it for me anymore. The blues, y'know.' She looks at him and makes eye-contact for a fraction longer than necessary.

'So, why green?'

'Fresh beginnings.'

Jack nods. He understands now. 'So what's been happening in Old Castle during the last forever?'

Ruthy smiles. 'Um? Well, I haven't been around much.'

Jack doesn't feel confident enough to ask Ruthy why she hadn't visited him. Not yet.

'Well,' says Ruthy, 'I s'pose they told you about the elephant?'

'*The what?*'

'The stolen elephant and the zoo-keeper?'

'I would've remembered that topic.'

As they drive along the N21, Ruthy tells Jack the story of Mick Munroe, the zoo-keeper with Alzheimer's, who had stolen his best friend, an elephant, after being fired from Dublin Zoo. They ended up in Old Castle after travelling an epic, cross-country night-time journey so that they wouldn't be seen – 'it's difficult to hide an elephant.'

Jack thinks about it. 'Yes, it is.'

'They became urban legends.'

'Are you serious?'

'They even solved a few crimes on their journey.'

Jack feels the smile on his lips and face. He hasn't genuinely smiled for almost a year, and the muscles are out of practice. 'This just gets better.'

'Apparently, Mick was tired of sticking Post-Its to the fridge, so he stole an elephant instead to remember something of his life...as one does.'

'Cool.'

'*Very* cool,' Ruthy agrees. 'He even took part in the St. Patrick's Day parade in Old Castle – that's when the police caught him...'

'*Police?!*'

'Yeah, the police wanted to catch him because he was solving more crimes than they were. Only they didn't catch him, because he got away. Rumour has it that Mick and the elephant are hiding out in some house in Old Castle as we speak, but nobody knows where. They're the stuff of legend, Jack. Word on the grapevine is that Sinbad...'

'Sinbad?'

'Yeah, the elephant...They say he died. Though some still swear that they see the giant, hulking shadow of an elephant and that of a man, wandering the secluded roads around Old Castle.'

Jack looks at Ruthy with a grin. 'You just made all that up? I know you're studying literature. Maybe you need to take a break from it.'

She looks at him and giggles, 'No, it's true.'

Not another word passes between them. Ruthy stares forward into the thick fog while Jack feels they're driving too fast, until he sees that she's only doing sixty kilometres-per-hour on the motorway. The accident on the rollercoaster has imprinted itself on him, and he clinches every sphincter in his body on every bend, white knuckles clutching either side of his seat without even knowing it. However, having the windscreen wipers on full blast *isn't* clearing the fog. Jack decides to say nothing to Ruthy and keeps his observation to himself; he can do with a laugh.

On the outskirts of Old Castle, Ruthy suddenly veers off the motorway and takes a different route to the normal one.

Jack frowns. 'I don't live this way.'

'I know.'

Ruthy doesn't offer more insight, so Jack has just got to ask the burning question: 'So, where are we going?'

'Enjoy the ride.'

Where had Jack heard that before?

'You'll know when we get there.'

Jack's stomach pitches when he catches sight of the tops of the three loop-the-loops rising high over the woods surrounding Old Castle. His heart begins to thump and he's not sure if it is his or Jeanie's heart anymore; they have become one somewhere along the way. Again, Jack finds it a comfort in knowing that his fiancée is locked inside his treasure-chest forever. A warm feeling of fullness would probably be how Jack would best describe it: that scluggy vibe. 'Turn back...'

'We have to face our fears, Jack.'

Panic rises inside Jack. He reaches for the door handle, but the doors are locked. 'Let me out, Ruthy...'

Before he knows it, the Fiat is pulling into the main thoroughfare of the ill-fated amusement park now known as 'Titanic' if the streams of graffiti are anything to go by.

The sight that greets Jack through his window leaves him breathless and without sufficient vocabulary.

The amusement park has become a derelict ghost town. The rides stand eerily still in the heavy fog.

Jack remembers reading about the *Marie Celeste* at school and now he cannot help thinking that what he sees before him is very similar. Everything is as it was left on that fateful night in March, last year. The electricity supply had been cut. The bumper cars rest where they had stopped almost a year previous, but now on a bed of green moss. The end of the Slippery Dip slide is disappearing into the woods which has begun to claim the park; the same woods that had claimed his Jeanie (but not her heart). The ghost train is sitting at the mouth of the giant zombie and is living up to its name by having nobody but ghosts riding it.

But Jack is afraid to look at the rollercoaster ride; something physically stops him from turning his head in that direction.

Ruthy opens his door. Tentatively, he gets out and she takes his hand in hers, which Jack finds a tad disturbing yet comforting.

Ruthy leads him to their worst nightmare – the rollercoaster. Jack looks upwards at the snaking, swirling tracks, the tops of the loops disappearing up into the cloud of fog. But he clearly sees where the rails had snapped, left jagged and twisted in the air. Jack notices the graffiti on the wall surrounding the rollercoaster's docking area: a stencilled six-foot wide broken heart. One broken half is black and the other broken half, blood red. Painted across the black half of the broken heart reads: *Hearts* in careless canary-yellow, and across the other red half is *Anonymous* in dripping white spray paint.

How ironic, thinks Jack. This heart sums up him and Jeanie in every way.

But it is the cemetery flowers that bring it all home to Jack. Plastic bouquet upon wreath have been tied to the steel grid-work legs of the rollercoaster. All dedicated to his Jeanie.

Jack turns away and contemplates how nature has gone to work on the doomed amusement park. 'It's completely overgrown,' is all he manages to say. 'In such a short time...'

'Well, it has been almost a full year.'

Jack thinks about this. 'I'm missing ten months of my life. How can I get those back?'

'Maybe you can...'

'I *can't*, Ruthy. They're gone in the wind, just like Jeanie.'

Ruthy leads him to the bumpers and sits into one of the cars. She beckons Jack to join her, but Jack is in a time-warp. 'Jack, I need to talk to you about something. Sit next to me.'

Jack feels a little uncomfortable about sitting so close to Ruthy. Jeanie isn't around anymore and maybe it's the fact that she isn't around that is the problem.

I...am...here, he hears Jeanie's heart thump in his ears.

Jack isn't sure why he feels guilty, but he sits in next to Ruthy and takes hold of the little steering-wheel. He cannot help but think of that day at the scrapyard when he suggested that he and Jeanie move in together.

'Jack, you're probably thinking why I haven't visited you all this time.'

'Santa Claus could have visited me and I wouldn't have known, Ruthy.' Jack lies.

She smiles a little. 'Well, I never visited. Not even when you finally came around – when they brought you out of the coma.'

Jack senses that there's more coming.

'This is my guilt trip, Jack.'

'What does that mean?'

'It means that guilt has been eating at my insides for the last nine months and I've organised this trip to tell you why I haven't visited you in the hospital...'

'Yeah?'

'I wanted to visit, you have to know that, but I couldn't bring myself to look at you in that ICU bed with machines beeping all around you.'

'It's not your fault, Ruthy.'

'Yes it is, Jack. I should've never let you or Jeanie get on that ride.'

Jack looks at Ruthy, not really understanding what she's getting at.

'I don't know if you remember waving to me as the ride began to climb. Do you remember waving back at me, Jack? Jeanie was waving too.'

From the deep recesses of Jack's mind, he recalls that moment. His face becomes darker as he recalls that particular moment, clearly seeing Ruthy's worried face in the queue. 'I remember.'

Ruthy takes a deep breath and continues. 'Jack, I kind of knew about the accident before it happened, as clear as you're sitting here now. I saw the accident right before it happened, just like in the script. I screamed to stop the ride, but nobody heard me. By the time the guy did hear me, it was too late, and he wasn't paying any attention to me anyway. You almost died and I could've saved Jeanie...' Ruthy hides her face in her hands and cries.

Jack decides not to take Ruthy too seriously because she has a tendency towards the dramatic and the mystical, so he plays along with her in a figurative way: *if only...* 'And so could I.'

Ruthy gazes at Jack questioningly, sniffling and wiping the tears from her puffy red eyes.

'I tried to block her from the branches, but everything happened in a split second. I was too late. I didn't get my arm around her in time...'

Jack finally lets go of almost a year's worth of anger and regret in a sobbing wail. Ruthy stretches her arm around him, and the two of them cry for Jeanie in the rusted and lifeless bumper car.

After what seems like an hour, Jack finally takes his face from Ruthy's shoulder, embarrassed that he's let his guard down. He is ashamed and doesn't want to catch Ruthy's eyes as he straightens up, but they do make eye-contact. For a brief moment, Jack feels himself drawn to mystic Ruthy, her sharp features, full red lips, dark eyes, and statement leaf-green punk hair-do. But Jack also sees Jeanie in Ruthy's face; it's difficult not to. She was Jeanie's best friend and they shared moments Jack will *never* know. This is the closest he has been to Jeanie since the accident. Or is it this desperate longing that forces Jack to see his dead fiancée in her B.F.F's face? Ruthy is his planet, and he feels her gravity draw him in...

They're about to share a kiss when Jack pulls back and mutters the age-old cliché: 'This isn't right.' He pauses. 'I saw Jeanie in you, Ruthy, just now. I saw her matrix in your face.'

She smiles gently and places her hand on his chest, moving her fingers till she feels the beat of Jack and Jeanie's shared heart. 'You are the closest I will ever get to her, Jack. I guess we will always have Jeanie with us.'

Jack's not comfortable with the situation and squirms a little until she gets the message and removes her warm palm. But he *does* agree with her. 'I feel the same, the *very* same. I look at you and I almost feel and hear Jeanie. It's as if we are a substitute for Jeanie...for each other, I mean. Does that make any sense?'

More tears trickle from Ruthy's eyes. She nods agreement.

'But you know what?' Jack smiles in an attempt to clear up the situation. 'She *is* in me. It's such a relief to get the topic out in the open; my family had been skirting around the issue. Understandable, I suppose.'

Ruthy's moist eyes widen. 'Yeah, weird, right? It's a little macabre, but it's true, Jack; she *is* with us. Not only in memory, so maybe we should be rejoicing?' She pauses. 'I know it's a bad thing to say, but sometimes I think it would've been better if Jeanie had been buried with her heart. It kind of leaves things undone...unfinished. Don't you think so?'

Jack hadn't thought about this ghoulish idea. 'But where would that leave me?'

That dark image of Jeanie lying in a pine box with an empty chest doesn't sit well with him.

Ruthy can't bear to bring herself to look at Jack. 'Do you forgive me? I could've stopped it, but I didn't.'

'Don't be silly. Do *you* forgive *me*?' Jack answers back.

Ruthy smiles, wipes her tears away, and nods.

Jack does the same and puts his arm around Ruthy, realizing that Jeanie's heart lies between them both. Jack guesses that he will have to get used to having odd moments like this one; almost a feeling of looking over his shoulder. The more he thinks about his new heart, the more he can feel Jeanie's spirit thumping inside him. He thinks about what Ruthy had said about leaving things unfinished...

'Do you think she's really gone?'

Jack's question shocks Ruthy. 'What do you mean?'

'Do you believe in the after-life?'

'I've seen a lot of shit, Jack, so I'm keeping an open mind. You mean, do I think Jeanie's ghost is hovering around this derelict amusement park?' She stops to think before looking him in the eyes. 'I can't rule it out.'

Jack, normally, wouldn't entertain such nonsense, but the topic has struck a chord with him. 'What if her spirit isn't at rest?' Gulp. 'What if she's looking for her heart?' A crazy giggle comes from Jack at the thought of this. He feels guilty for laughing but if he didn't laugh, he would either run screaming to get away from his heart or lie down in a darkened room and hide himself from the world forever.

Ruthy's profound expression is enough to tell Jack that Ruthy hasn't contemplated this particular scenario. She looks about her warily and pauses before she answers. 'If she's anywhere, she will be in the woods. She won't be in the cemetery, that's for sure. That wasn't her style.'

The fact that Ruthy doesn't tell Jack that his idea is utter nonsense *is* a little disconcerting, to say the least.

Jack looks around him at the encroaching woods. It's only a matter of time before Mother Nature takes over and hides the place and its tragedy forever, as it should be.

Jack's heart continues its thump-thump...thump-thump in his chest, a forever gently knocking reminder.

Chapter 8

Deathday and Birthday

It's time that you put this thing to bed, Jackie...

Jack is sitting at the top of the twenty-five-meter high Slippery Dip slide, looking out across the invading woods, looking as if he's about to launch himself downwards on a free ride. The place should've been shut down, as in closed off to the public, but the amusement park owners are involved in an insurance dispute and the amusement park, A.K.A the Titanic, has been left abandoned like the Marie Celeste instead. It's only a matter of time before there's another accident here...

Jack likes to come here to think, or rather, to remember, and has been coming here since Ruthy made a surprise visit to this place the same day he got out of the hospital.

He scans the woods from his vantage-point in the vague hope that he might spot the spectral vision of Jeanie, hovering amongst the trees that killed her, glowing luminescent like a nuclear victim. Desperate yet scared to see her, Jack is sorry that he ever pondered that creepy topic with Ruthy that day sitting in the bumper car. Anyone else would've dismissed the crazy idea point-blank, but Ruthy bought into the idea, even seemed to revel in the thoughts of her ex-B.F.F's ghost guarding the doomed amusement park. And now, he cannot get that unnerving vision out of his addled brain. Sitting here alone in this eerie place, Jack feels the shiver of goose-flesh as he deliberates on that macabre notion that Jeanie *might* rise from the cold, worm-infested grave and come whistling for her heart.

At this juncture of deathly thoughts, Jack whistles long, soulful, bum-note toots and scares the living shit out of himself despite having a clear view of the whole park and woods from up here. If truth be known, he's been a nervous wreck ever since the rollercoaster wreck.

But more than Jeanie coming back from the dead, Jack is thinking about Ruthy's comment that Jeanie's death is unfinished…as long as her heart is beating in Jack's chest. As long as Jack is *alive*, Jeanie *won't* be dead.

It's a catch-22, Jackie…

Right now, in this dark period, it seems more likely that Jack will die before Jeanie will.

That same Friday, January 1st (every day seems to melt into one nowadays), Ruthy and Jack had almost shared a kiss in the defunct bumper car. And that too has been playing out on a loop in his mind's eye.

Jesus, what had he been *thinking?*

Jack curses himself. 'You *fucking* idiot!'

He'd been thinking of his fiancée when he had moved in to kiss Ruthy. It's called desperation and the unwillingness of the brain to let go. After all, Jeanie, as his almost-wife, had been so close yet so far. She had said 'Yes' to his marriage proposal five seconds before she was non-living matter and mulch, almost like a sick, cruel, demented April Fool's Day joke.

Today is Sunday, the 14th of February. It is Jack's birthday and he doesn't have his valentine. A month and a half has passed since that brief close encounter with Ruthy. He hasn't seen or heard from her since then. Ruthy has a tendency to do this; just disappear. She's probably gone to save some rabbits.

Unknown to himself, Jack smiles at this thought, imagining crazy Ruthy running around some paddock after semi-wild rabbits. Only Ruthy…

His eyes trace the bumps and dips of the steep slide downwards to the bottom below which disappears into the undergrowth. If he were to launch himself from here now he would end up feet first in the same vegetation that has already swallowed up the bottom of the slide and drastically changed Jeanie's immediate and long-term future. Jack stares at the bushes and trees at the bottom of the slide in a haze of confusion. Eleven months have passed, and not one *day* has passed; time doesn't heal all wounds. Jack's wound has been growing like an ozone-hole in his chest and that desperate, longing, pining, almost gagging loss has grown, grown, *grooown*, like a tumour inside him, remembering his bride to-be. Knowing that Jeanie's heart had saved him in her death has been an eerie comfort, but of late, it has been tormenting Jack. And it all started with Ruthy's passing comment that Jeanie isn't fully dead. Her beating heart has become a constant reminder of his guilt. Jack will *never* escape this remorse of having not been able to save her; every thump-thump of her donated heart will be a thump-thump in his head, building little by little to the great headache his own life has become. All that blood-money in the bank won't save him *or* Jeanie now...

Then something enters Jack's head which he hasn't ever thought about...his old heart. Where is it now? Probably vapour in the ether, somewhere high above the hospital incinerator. It's a morbid subject, but doesn't it deserve a better send-off than that?

But, worse than that, is his own guilt for living while Jeanie had to be taken.

Jack has been coming here every day for the last six weeks. This place has a strange hold over Jack. Something calls to him every day from this place. Maybe it's his guilty conscience, perhaps Jeanie's ghost whispers to him subliminally, but not loud enough to understand that she's calling him, so he comes on instinct. Or maybe it's just that Jack can't let go...

Yes you can, Jack. Just ease your fingers from the iron bars and let yourself go...let yourself drop, Jackie. You'll land right into my lap. I'll have my heart back and you'll have me back. Happy ever after. The End...

'I'm coming, Jeanie...'

Jack has induced himself into some kind of trance, or has the empty amusement park done it? Perhaps it is Jeanie's voice in his head and chest? He cannot tell the difference any more. *Who the fuck cares?*

Instead of pushing himself down the slide, Jack gets to his feet and clambers up onto the edge of the structure, grabbing onto the scaffolding. He stands on the ledge and looks out across the horizon, then down at the hard unforgiving concrete twenty-five meters below. If he jumps from here, he'll probably land on his new Mini (it was the only thing he had invested in because he needs a car, and it wasn't without a twinge of guilt as he signed the contract at the nearest Mini show-room). He's already been hospitalized for months and he doesn't fancy that again, so takes a few steps to the right of the Mini where he *knows* he will do the job right.

Jack finds his balance and stands with his arms held out like a tight-rope walker who is about to fall onto a net of concrete. He keeps his eye on that horizon, then down a little at the tree-tops of the woods that had claimed his beautiful Jeanie. He reckons that if the woods is the last thing he sees (as it was Jeanie's), then he had a fighting chance of meeting her on the other side...in the woods probably.

Just as Jack moves to step off the barrier, a *crow* suddenly appears from nowhere and squawks anger in Jack's face, frightening the living (almost dead) bejesus out of him. The frantic bird hovers and flaps wildly, so close that Jack feels the air buffeting on his sweat-clammed face. He grows dizzy, unable to focus in on the bird, then gazes boggle-eyed at the concrete below.

He loses his step and plummets...just managing to turn in mid-air and grab onto the scaffolding.

Swinging in the wind, Jack realizes, to his detriment, that it'd been his own conscience speaking to him, not Jeanie. Or had it?

It would be so easy to just let go now. The adrenaline going off in his body is almost too much to bear; he freezes, afraid to move and equally terrified of letting go. His whole body trembles and if he's not careful, the shake in his hands will jiggle him free of the scaffolding.

And then the moment of truth hits him, no, it *thump-thump-thumps* him. It's Jeanie's heart going off in his ears and temples!

It's Jeanie's heart that he will be killing!!!

Jeanie's voice screams in his head: *I gave you this gift of life, Jackie! How dare you throw away this priceless Jeanie souvenir! You think that I want my death to be in vain? Take yourself and my heart to the nearest ICU heart-patient who will appreciate a second-hand heart!!!*

Jack almost passes out as this nightmarish realization dawns on him...

With all his effort, he manages to pull himself upwards, straining every muscle and sinew in his upper body to stay alive. He manages to find a hold and hauls himself over the top of the barrier and flops in over the ledge of the Slippery Dip like a landed fish.

He lays there, sobbing in self-pity, too exhausted to stand, pale, and light-headed to the point of being sick.

Jack had just tried to commit suicide.

How fucking dare you take my life for a second time! I own you, Jackie. You're all mine, you fucking puppet!

The seething anger inside Jack is maddening. Of course Jeanie would say this! Why wouldn't she?!

He gets to his feet with a fury ready to split him down the middle and break Jeanie's cursed heart. He roars at the sky, *'Why me?!'*

And then he remembers the crow that had, intentionally or unintentionally, saved his life by giving him a good old fright. He looks about him; the bird is gone, but his wrath isn't.

He gazes at the trees and bushes below, smothering the landing area of the slide. He backs up to the tall wall of the slide and runs full belt and launches himself head first down the slide in a bid to outrun himself and his heart. Jack pummels down the Slippery Dip, gaining air each time he leaves a bump and slams hard into the oncoming dip. He rockets downwards, slamming his chest onto each rise and lifts into the air, then lands halfway into the next dip before hitting the last rise. On the other side of the rise, Jack clears six feet of ground before crashing into the briars, bushes, and branches. He is jack-knifed in a headlock of thorns and stinging nettles.

But it hasn't killed him nor has he outrun himself... nor has he outrun Jeanie's parting gift.

He scrambles on his belly commando-style along the last five meters of the slide which angles slightly upwards to slow its would-be occupants. He drags himself through the thorns, happily cutting his face and ears. He was clinically dead for Christ's sake. What's a few thorn pricks?

Arriving at the end of the slide, Jack lets himself fall off the side onto the leafy floor of the woods that hadn't been there a year ago. He then crawls on his sorry hands and knees back towards the main thoroughfare of the amusement park.

Suddenly, Jack spots something amongst the decaying leaves and moss. It glints and winks up at him as if it knows him. He frowns and digs a little more. His heart is already beating faster.

Jack picks up a ring.

Not just any lost old ring. Jack recognizes this ring and tears come streaming down his bloodied face. He *knows* this ring; Jeanie *briefly* knew this ring.

He studies its eye-catching jam-tart pattern: 'Six pink rubies divided by double-diamond clusters on an eighteen carat white gold shank.' Jack reams it off as the seller had done the day he had bought it on Henry Street in Limerick City.

The ring looks just like a tiny precious flower, growing here in the dank, decaying ground. Jack had saved up for a year to buy this ring; a year-long secret he had kept and a big gamble with it. This was their engagement ring. The last time he had had this engagement ring in his hand was upside-down on the second last loop-the-loop of the killer coaster. He had a fleeting glance of it *almost* on Jeanie's wedding finger just before his life was turned upside-down in so many ways. The irony was that she could only get it onto the first knuckle of her wedding finger before the coaster's G-forces pulled her the other way. She tried to slip it onto her finger, but her life was taken first.

Maybe I had never been yours to begin with...

That disturbing voice, sounding like Jeanie, but not her, creeps over his shoulder and whispers in his ear.

Jack crawls out of the undergrowth and gets to his feet. He stares into the gemstones of the engagement ring that never knew an engagement. The ring is hypnotic.

What are the gods trying to tell him?? Not only does he have his dead girl's heart, but now he's got her ring too!

Jack asks himself, 'What's next?' as he crosses slowly to his Mini, all bloodied and torn. He sits in and starts the engine but is in no hurry anywhere. Peering upwards, he locates the position where he had just been hanging from, blowing in the wind, and traces his fictitious flailing body falling to the concrete. He stares at the spot on the ground, virtually seeing his broken body splayed right there in front of him. He flinches as he hears pretend-Jeanie's voice screaming in his ears:

How dare you, Jackie! How fucking dare you do this to my memory! Talk about kicking a girl when she's down!! Prick!!!

He turns up the radiator to full and sits there, also raising the volume on the stereo to drown out Jeanie's wild accusations. Again, he asks whoever will listen: 'What's next?'

After what seems a life-time, Jack makes a decision: 'Maybe I should wait and see what happens next?' Unable to shake the feeling that all of this is happening for a reason. As the first drops of rain begin to land on his windshield, Jack puts the car into gear and races out of the haunted amusement park, as if the Sleeping Zombie were about to break his shackles as Gulliver had done before him and reach out for the speeding Lilliputian Mini. Jack tries to wash what has just happened from his mind, not daring to look at the amusement park receding in his rear-view mirror, for fear of being reminded of what he has just attempted.

As he exits the main gates, he catches a glimpse of the 'Hearts Anonymous' broken heart graffiti....

As Jack drives home with a new sense of purpose, born-again but guilt-ridden, a crow appears from nowhere in front of him and smashes into his windscreen.

Jack slams on the brakes and the Mini skids a full five meters, sliding along on the wet road, before coming to a jolting halt and facing the opposite direction – back towards the amusement park, funnily enough.

Jack sees the bird in the middle of the road in his rear-view mirror. It's still alive; he can see it flapping helplessly back there, pulling itself around in circles like a one-armed man rowing a boat.

He jumps out, races back, and picks up the broken bird. He looks at it and cannot help wondering if this is the same crow which had startled him out of his suicide.

And save your life, Jackie, as I have done...Never thought I'd be compared to a crow, Jackie...

'Hang in there...' he whispers to the crow and lays the bird on the floor behind the driver's seat. He takes off his ripped duffel coat and builds up a wall around the dazed bird, before throwing the Mini into gear, and speeds off towards the centre of Old Castle where he knows a veterinary clinic.

Heavy traffic around the town square slows Jack up considerably, and by the time he pulls into the vet's front yard, his worst fears are realized: the crow had died somewhere along the journey.

A shattering wave of guilt and sadness washes down over Jack. It's ridiculous to even contemplate, but he can't deny his conscience which is telling him that he had killed the crow because of his ridiculous anger-speed. He failed the crow as he had failed Jeanie. Yet, the crow had saved his life, (if this is the same crow, but what are the chances of that, and it doesn't matter now anyway), and he had finished its life.

As far as Jack is concerned, this *is* the same crow.

Jack's too distraught to figure out this cryptic clue for now. But he does know where his next stop is: the taxidermist.

This crow means too much to him now to simply fling it over the next hedge. He is going to keep this bird, stuffed, where he can look over him, and likewise, the bird can look over his shoulder as he or she had done at the amusement park. Maybe it will bring him good luck – though that might be a tad optimistic seeing as he killed the bird. As the saying goes: the lucky rabbit's foot brought him/her about as much good luck as it did the rabbit.

He doesn't have Jeanie's body, but does have her heart. He doesn't have the crow's heart, but does have its body. Murphy's Law.

It's crazy to even contemplate, but Jack is really beginning to think that there are greater forces at work now. A puzzle that needs to be solved. Who could he speak to? Who would know anything about a parallel universe and what's already written in the stars?

Ruthy.

Chapter 9

An Unfortunate Meeting at Joe Soap's

That evening, Jack decides to take the initiative and rings Ruthy.

'Hello?'

'Ruthy...'

'Jack, how are you? It's been a while. I'm up to my tits in studying. Final exams coming up...'

Trying to hide his numb-state melancholy, Jack jokes: 'I'm not sure I need to know how far up your studying reaches, Ruthy.'

They share a laugh.

Ruthy explains, 'Sorry, I'm just stressed with everything. Anyway, what's on your mind?'

'I've been thinking a lot lately.'

'The good or bad kind?'

Jack decides to skip the succinct fact of how a crow had saved him from suicide earlier. He also leaves out about finding Jeanie's engagement ring. 'It's a long story. What are the chances of meeting this weekend? Are you with the rabbits or in Limerick?'

Jack senses an awkward pause down the line. 'Unless you're busy, that is.'

'Um, no, no. What's it about anyway? Just give me the gist.'

Jack throws it out for the fun of it. 'Parallel universes.'

'Hmm, maybe I can find time for a coffee *if* you come to me. You know where I am, right.'

How could Jack forget? He practically lived there... 'Uh-huh. When's a good time?'

'I'm going to pull an all-nighter, study 'n shit, so how about, let me see, in an hour's time? I'll top up on caffeine and that'll take me up to midnight.'

'Sounds good.'

Jack pulls up on Henry Street in Limerick City, just after 7 P.M. He walks a block to Ruthy's block in Mount Kennett Place and presses the bell.

Ruthy's voice comes out of the speaker. 'Jack?'

'Speaking.'

She buzzes him in. He skips the dodgy-looking lift and takes to the stairs instead. The last time he had climbed these stairs was to visit Jeanie; it seems just like yesterday. It is a strange time-warp indeed.

When he gets to the top of the stairs, she is waiting for him in the hallway at her front door. She's changed her hair colour again, opting for a turquoise Mohawk.

'Wait, I'll get my jacket.' She turns, but does a double-take and gawks at the cuts and bruises on his face. 'Jesus, Mary, and Joseph, what happened to *you?!*'

'Long story.'

She ducks inside, shouting, 'Oh, by the way, happy birthday, Jack!'

Jack thanks her and waits. He'd almost forgotten that it was his birthday; it was *almost* his deathday...

When Ruthy appears again Jack almost falls backwards down the stairs. It's the jacket that Ruthy is wearing.

Ruthy sees him stare at the jacket and looks down at herself. 'I didn't think you'd recognize it,' she tells him apologetically. 'I never had the, um, heart to speak to her folks about the clothes that she'd left behind. I was going to donate her stuff to charity, y'know, that Oxfam shop on William Street, but I didn't have the heart...sorry, another unfortunate pun when I probably never mentioned heart in my life...sorry, I just did it again...'

Jack assures her that he's cool with it (when he's not really).

'I heard about this woman who makes pillows and teddy-bears out of clothes, but I thought that would be a little strange...yet oddly comforting.'

Jack smiles and nods. 'I know the feeling.'

'The thoughts of somebody else wearing her stuff really put me off the idea. And burning them or throwing them into one of the street bins isn't an option.' She pauses. 'Does it bother you that I'm wearing Jeanie's stuff, Jack?'

For a tiny moment, it actually *does* bother Jack; a slight hint of resentment came on first seeing Jeanie's army parka. But the more he thinks about it, the more he likes the idea. 'Jeanie is *everywhere...*' he answers cryptically. 'Who better to wear her clothes than her best friend?'

Ruthy beams. 'That's the spirit, Jackie.'

Jack freezes momentarily, hearing Jeanie's pet-name for him, but lets it slide. He adds, 'It's kind of why I'm here actually.'

They walk down the stairs.

'I don't get it.'

'Let's get our coffees first, and I'll tell you all about it.'

'O-kay, McCain.'

It is a freezing evening, and the rain-drops are biting icicles. Ruthy leads Jack onto Mallow Street and down Fox's Bow alleyway. They pass a busy restaurant named The Oyster Shell owned by Michelin-star Chef Connors. After that, they stroll by an equally busy tattoo parlour. They stop outside a little bistro named Joe Soap's, an old favourite haunt, especially Tequila Night on Thursdays.

They duck inside, led by their red noses.

The bistro is warm and lively, mainly students and arty folk of all ages, the majority not having an artful bone in their bodies.

Ruthy orders two lattes from the Spanish waitress, and she sits into a cosy corner by Jack.

'So, what's all this about, Jack? I didn't even know you had my number. I think it's the first time you've ever *called* me.'

'Jeanie gave it to me once; "for a rainy day" was her reason. I guess she was right.'

The Spanish waitress leaves their enormous mugs of milky coffee on the low table in front of them and whistles off into the crowd again, all business.

Jack sighs. 'I don't know where to begin.'

'You haven't been sleeping well. I can see the bags under your eyes...behind the scars and cuts. Jesus, Jack. What've you been up to?'

'I can't get Jeanie off my mind.'

Ruthy nods, waiting for more disclosure.

'Better said: I can't get Jeanie out of my chest.'

After nothing else comes from Jack, Ruthy prompts him. 'Which means...?'

'At the beginning, it was a nice warm fuzzy-wuzzy feeling knowing that I had her heart.'

'She used to say that – fuzzy-wuzzy.'

Jack smiles. 'But now it has become a guilty obsession. Every thump of her heart is chipping away at my soul, Ruthy.'

'You're a poet, but you didn't know it...' jokes Ruthy but gets serious when she sees that Jack isn't amused.

'It's a constant reminder that I owe her everything, and I'm on a *major* guilt-trip...a trip that has no end, I think. Every move I make I hear Jeanie's voice, approving or disapproving, only it isn't her voice. The voice is so real and seems to have a mind of its own. I *know* it's all in my head, but I can't help it. It's getting stronger by the day. At the rate I'm going, I won't be able to distinguish between her thoughts and mine.'

Ruthy's eyes are turning red with building tears. 'Right after we hung up on the phone this evening, I promised myself I wouldn't cry,

Jack. Why can't we just get on with our lives?' She blinks and a single pair of tears break and roll down each cheek into her coffee.

'I want to, Ruthy. I want nothing more in this world than to get over Jeanie's death. But that's it right there: firstly, this world is acting weird lately, and secondly, I'll never get over Jeanie's death, because she's living inside me. She's a part of me now; literally, metaphorically, and every other way.'

'Jack, you've got to get that shit out of your brain.' Ruthy dries her eyes with the heel of her hand, then takes a gulp of coffee. 'Thinking like that is going to wreck your head. That's *your* heart in there...' she pokes his chest, '*your* heart. It's your heart because it's *your* body that's making it beat, not the opposite way around.'

Jack rolls this over in his mind. 'Ruthy, I'm getting these odd signs lately.'

'This is the parallel universe thing you mentioned?'

Jack nods. 'I was sort of joking.'

'Jack, there's a lot of shit in this world that we don't see, but it exists. Some of us do see it, but the majority can't, or rather, don't *want* to see it or *read* the signs. You know when you say to yourself: what a coincidence! You think it is coincidence? There are other forces at work, my friend.' Ruthy runs her Mohawk between her palms, smoothing her spiky turquoise hair upwards from her scalp. 'Sometimes we get so many coincidences that we cannot call it coincidence anymore.'

'I had a weird day today, Ruthy.'

'Go on.'

Jack swallows some coffee. 'I'm going to tell you everything because I want you to get the whole picture.'

So Jack tells Ruthy how a crow had startled him out of his attempted suicide and how he had gone down the slide instead, in the vague hopes of having his neck broken by the same woods that killed Jeanie. Then killing a (the same) crow which had saved him, which is now being stuffed as he speaks. Then the cherry on the cake: the engagement ring.

During Jack's story, Ruthy's expression turns from curiosity...to mild terror...to absolute horror...to mind-boggled.

'Jesus, Jack. I didn't realize things were *so* bad. I should've stayed with you longer, besides getting bogged down in my studies and...everything else. You see, Jack, finishing my degree is the only excuse I have to not think about Jeanie. It's the only thing which keeps her face on the other side of the door. That's why I haven't been around much in Old Castle, because I expect to see her face around every corner. You're right, Jeanie *is* everywhere.'

Over time, Jack had forgotten where Ruthy actually comes from. He was unable to call to mind that Ruthy had *never* lived in Old Castle, but she had been there so often at the weekends that Jack had, more or less taken it for granted that she lived there. She's from the city, apparently, and he has always known her to be living with Jeanie in the apartment.

Jack produces the long-lost ring and hands it to Ruthy. Sad delight comes over her face. She studies the ring in a reminiscent way, like looking at the face of an old friend.

She hands it quickly back to Jack and hides her cries behind the enormous coffee mugs. 'I found it while scrummaging around in the woods on my hands and knees.' Jacks says in serious earnest, 'Ruthy, I can't go on without her. I can't go on knowing that her heart is keeping me alive when she's dead. That's the sick irony. You can't imagine how that feels.'

'Jack, I'm not copping out on you, but I think you need professional help.'

'Ruthy, I came to you because you believe in something else. You don't rationalize and deduce everything with science, which is what some shrink is going to do.' He pauses. 'Now, this is going to sound crazy, but I think these things are happening for a reason – and not only today. I think I killed that crow that saved me for a reason. I think I found Jeanie's engagement ring for a reason. I believe there's a reason why I'm sitting here talking to you instead of being pizza scraped off the concrete of the amusement park.'

'Do you believe Jeanie died for a reason?'

Jack cannot answer that question, nor does he really want to, because that would mean having to analyse.

'This is going to sound really out there, but I think I've been given a second opportunity by someone – some*thing* – somewhere.' Jack gulps before speaking again. 'Jeanie, I've been having strange dreams.'

'I'm Ruthy...'

Jack realizes what he's just said. He reddens up to the gills and covers his face in his hands for a moment. 'Sorry.'

'That's okay. What dreams aren't strange? I've got a list as long as my arm. I've kept a dream diary for the last three years. Every dream is different, even if you think it's a recurring dream. There are tiny differences.'

'Well, this is where it gets weird: my dreams – my dream – is always the same.'

Ruthy sits up. 'That is odd. What happens in the dream?'

'I go back in time.'

Jack waits for a response from Ruthy, but doesn't get one. In fact, she just stares blankly at – *through* – him. 'It's like a badly cut black and white silent film. We are there, so happy, sitting in the rollercoaster and waiting for it to move off...then we are screaming in silence before we hit the trees...then I'm right back there again, sitting in the coaster, but this time I've got my arm around Jeanie and the other hand in my pocket, clutching the engagement ring. I know that, this time, I will be able to save her because of the arm symbolism. But then it goes back to the first version again: we crash, then I'm back there with her and waiting to move off with my arm around her again...'

Ruthy thinks about this. 'Jack, there's nothing so odd about your dream. Books were written on how to read dreams, but it's all bullshit. They're abstract and each person will find their own meaning.'

'But it's the same dream over and over again.'

'No it isn't. I'm sure if you hold the dream up to the light, you will find little differences in each one. Dreams are like snow-flakes, Jack. Your brain is playing out what it thinks should've happened.'

'But what happens if your brain plays out this fantasy so much that you don't know fantasy from reality anymore? What happens if you believe your dream so much that you *make* it happen?'

Ruthy's lost. 'What are you getting at?'

'What if we *could* go back in time?'

An odd reaction flickers across Ruthy's face. 'Yeah, um, Jack. That's *doesn't* happen – in Hollywood, maybe. You're delusional.'

'But you said yourself that you saw the accident that night before it happened. You *saw* into the future.'

Ruthy stays silent for a long time. For a second it seems as if she's about to say something, but the moment passes. 'It's easier to see into the future than go back in time, Jack. People get premonitions all the time. You just have to be sensitive to it.' She checks the time. 'Who wants to go back in time anyway?'

'*Me...*' He should've never opened his stupid mouth about this.

Ruthy adds, 'Y'know what your problem is?'

Jack shrugs. 'Please, be my guest.'

'You're *living* in the past.' She gives him a tragic look. 'Get with the future...' She considers him. 'Are you okay?'

'Apart from the attempted suicide, everything is just dandy.'

'You look strange tonight, Jack. I'm worried.'

Jack finds himself unable to drop the subject. 'But in my dream, Jeanie and I go back in time.'

'Yeah, in your *dreams*. Have you not ever heard that expression? It's sarcasm; it means that it'll *never* happen. Never.'

'My dream keeps taking me to the same point, like as if, trying to give me another chance...or trying to tell me something.'

'Dream logic,' Ruthy confirms. 'Believe me, Jack. I'm a spiritual person, and I'll be the first to believe when somebody comes from the future. But for now, I'm afraid I have to be content with my instinct and my occasional third eye into the near future. And my third eye now sees me going back to a night's study and finishing my analysis on symbolism in the Grimm Brothers fairy-tales.' Ruthy weighs up her next words before speaking them. 'Jack, you have to snap out of this. Jeanie's *gone*. It hurts me to say this, but she's gone. I had to let go too.'

So she's already gotten over her? 'I can't let her go.'

'You have to!' Ruthy's snappy return draws a few stares.

'She's not gone,' Jack raises his voice. 'She's here!' fisting his chest.

'Look at her heart as a goodbye present.' Already Ruthy regrets saying it.

'How can you be so, so *heartless*?'

Jack gets up and leaves, turning back at the door of the café to yell, 'Pardon the pun!' without a hint of a smile.

He slams the door of Joe Soap's behind him. As he passes by the window, he briefly glances at Ruthy sitting on her own in the café, trying to avoid staring eyes. Already, Jack feels bad. She had only uttered those biting words to wake him up and get on with his life. But he can't go back now, out of embarrassment more than anything else.

He retraces his steps back along Fox's Bow alleyway, power-walks down William Street, crosses O'Connell Street, onto Henry Street. He gets into his Mini, then drives west to Old Castle, driven faster by blind anger and self-pity.

Once in the darkness of the County Limerick countryside, Jack suddenly switches off his headlights while travelling at seventy miles per hour along the N21. The intravenous thrill is adrenaline-fuelled. He's never felt so scared in all his life as right in this moment, but it feels so *fucking* liberating.

He loses his bottle a second later as a dreadful shock assaults him, imagining another car with a maniac driver at the wheel, just like him, crossing over into *his* side of the motorway with *his* headlights also switched off...

Scrambling for the lever, Jack swerves back into his lane. He switches on his full beams as a car appears from over the brow of the hill, flashing its lights at him and hammering on its horn as it passes to his right.

If Jack hadn't diverted when he did, that car and his car would now be a smoking concertina.

Jack skids to a stop on the hard shoulder. He takes the Mini out of gear and switches on his hazard lights. As he does this, a delirious laugh bubbles up from within him – the thought of putting on his hazard lights after what he has just done is just *too* funny. A cold sweat beads on his forehead and the giggle vanishes as fast as it had come. Shakily, he opens the window and sticks his head out to clear his addled brain.

He drives off with his head out the window, breathing in deeply as the rushing wind clears his madness away.

He ducks back inside and flicks through his music library, opting for some Marilyn Manson. Quickly, he decides that his frame of mind isn't in the right place for Manson, so chooses Vivaldi's *Four Seasons* instead.

Something else is becoming clear now as he drives home: Jack has a death-wish.

Maybe Jeanie's heart is turning stale on him and is trying to finish what was started on the rollercoaster almost a year ago.

Jack would've told Ruthy this, but Ruthy doesn't want to know anymore.

Clocking up his near-death experiences, Jack arrives at the conclusion that he has used up four of his lives (three today alone): the rollercoaster, attempted suicide saved by a passing crow, driving at night with no lights and suddenly bottling out as a car comes over the brow of the hill. In a video-game, Jack would be more than likely dead, but a cat has nine lives. Jack doesn't fancy tempting fate five more times.

When Jack arrives back at his place in Old Castle, he sees that he's got a text from Ruthy...

J, I've found something! My hands are shaking right now with excitement. Pls ring me when you get home, R x

Chapter 10

The Unending Fairytale

Back in his bedroom, Jack reads the message a second time. He is perplexed and wonders what it could possibly mean. However, Jack is more concerned with the cryptic X-for-kiss at the end of the note. Why is it there? Why, oh, why? Jack knows that the best thing to do is call her, but they had left on bad terms at Joe Soap's. He pauses before he dials her number, gawping at his phone for advice. Jack has learned that it's sometimes better not to think, but to act. Then again, sometimes he acts without thinking which lands him in hot water.

Ruthy answers on the first ring. 'Jack, you're not going to *believe* this!'

'Ruthy, I never thought I would say this, but *I'm* the believer – you're the *dis*believer, remember?'

His near-death experience, Jack realizes, has prompted him to think in a different way. Pre-accident, Jack didn't believe in anything that couldn't be explained by science, but now, he finds himself pondering the afterlife and everything in between. But he refuses to become one of those people in those documentaries who speak about going down the tunnel of light and personally speaking to God before being sent back to Mortalandia.

'Well, Jack, what if I tell you that I might be a believer, after all?'

'I'm listening...'

'Y'know when you were saying that you were getting messages that seem to be saying something? The ring...the crow...etc...'

'Uh-huh...' *I just drove along the N21 with my headlights off in the pitch dark and imagined another car, also with its lights off, stray into my lane with another suicidal, just like me, behind the wheel...* 'What about it?' *I've got a death-wish...*

'Well, as you know, I'm studying a degree in children's literature and in that there is a section on Folklore and Fairytale.'

'Fairy-tales?' asks Jack with incredulity. He looks at his phone as if half expecting to see it sniggering back at him. She's not taking him seriously. He is on the brink of hanging up.

'Don't hang up!'

He hears her distant voice as he's about to thumb the red button.

'Not *all* fairy-tales are about fairies, Jack. I could crack a joke about that, but I'm not in the mood and it's too late. I don't know if you know, but many fairy-tales are metaphors and allegories and many have their roots in actual medieval happenings.'

Jack decides to play along for now. 'No, I didn't know.'

'Uh-huh, well, fairy-tales contain hidden meanings and secrets also. Tonight, I came across a German fairy-tale called *The Clockmaker's Daughter* written by an anonymous author. It's also known as *The Unending Fairy-tale.*'

By now, Jack's beginning to wonder where all of this is going to end. 'Does that mean I'll be here all night?'

'Ha, ha.' Ruthy answers readily, '*Not* exactly. I'm trying to help you.'

'Okay, okay. It's just that when you said, "the Unending..."'

'Now,' Ruthy cut him off, 'in this tale, to cut a long story short, there is a clockmaker who lives with his only daughter on a blustery, snow-capped mountain in the heart of the Black Forest of Germany. The year is 1777.'

'As in Black Forest gateaux?'

'On the side of this mountain is a dark Gothic castle. The castle has been handed down from generation to generation. An eccentric by the name of Count Friedrich Olenberg lives in his descendant's castle with his only daughter, who, I might add, is a known beauty in the Black Forest.'

'Is that a euphemism for a pros–'

'*No*, Jack, it's not. A woman can be a known beauty and not charge for her services. *Jesus, men!*' she huffs. 'Anyway, where was I? Oh and by the way, the clockmaker has worked every day of his life to keep his family warm and free from hunger by creating exquisite clocks.'

Jack's losing interest, not seeing the relationship between his present dilemma and a two-hundred-and-something year-old fairy-tale set in the Black Forest of Germany. 'He had a lot of time on his hands...' quips Jack.

'A *lot*, Jack.' She hears the sarcasm but plays along for now by giving her own little play-on-words. 'Big time. Where was I? Okay, yes, so the clockmaker has a *terrible* argument with his daughter because he doesn't approve of the boy she wants to marry.'

'What father does?'

'Yes, but what father goes to the trouble of *killing* his future son-in-law because he is his competitor's son. There are two high-end clockmakers in the Black Forest – Olenberg is one, and the other is the daughter's lover's father – her future father-in-law. Olenberg cannot live with this idea, so decides to nip it in the bud.'

'This is better than *Top 10 Serial Killers*. Have you seen that?'

'No. So the Count, yeah, feeling a tad miffed about this situation, decides to hire the services of a...'

'Hit-man?'

'Close. A travelling shaman.'

'Of course he does...'

'Uh-huh, he hires this travelling shaman to cast a curse on his daughter's lover.' She sighs. 'I'm starting to think that it might've been easier just to read the tale to you over the phone...'

Jack's finding it difficult to take any of this seriously. 'Have you seen the prices they're charging for a simple curse lately?'

'Okey-dokey, Jack. So now, this is where it gets interesting.'

'Oh, I'm riveted. Go on...'

'Well, in killing his daughter's lover, the clockmaker becomes guilt-ridden and filled with black grief beyond measure...'

'Black?'

'*Beyond black*,' she repeats for Jack's amusement, 'because he sees that his daughter is slowly withering, *dying*, without her loved one. He is sorry that he never allowed his daughter to be with the man she loved; something quite simple.'

Jack says hopefully, 'That's it?'

'No.'

'Oh...'

'Seeing his daughter slowly die, coupled with his infinite sadness and misery, the clockmaker becomes a recluse to the tower of the castle and begins to build something behind closed doors; not even his daughter knows what he's up to. For *five* years, she only sees him briefly at meal-times before locking himself up in the tower once again.'

'Did he have a bathroom in the tower?'

'Yes, Jack. A big one...en-suite...power-shower...spa. Where was I? On the 14th of February, 1782, Olenberg presents his daughter with an extraordinary gift.'

'14th of February? My birthday. What is it?'

'What's what?'

'The *gift*...'

'Oh, sorry. I didn't get you a gift. But I will, I promise. Look at this tale as your gift –'

'No, *Olenberg's* gift? To his daughter? What was it?'

'A time-machine, Jack.'

Pause...

'Look, Ruthy, it's getting late...'

'Olenberg made it his life mission to build the ultimate time-machine. Interesting to note that all clocks were once called time-machines.'

'Oh, sorry. I thought you were going to tell me that he had built a capsule that travels in time.'

'He did – the *ultimate* time-machine. He found the formula to travel in time.'

'I keep reminding myself that this is a fairy-tale. Did she go back in time?'

'No. The daughter refused to go back in time because she spoke to...'

'The travelling shaman?'

'Yes.'

'He doesn't do much travelling for being a travelling shaman.'

'Whatever. The shaman told her that should she go back in time, the clock couldn't be used to alter what has already passed. This upsets the balance of things, and, by doing so, only opens up other side-effects. It is dangerous to play around with what has already happened because it will have consequences. Altering what has happened in the past will always catch up with the time-meddler, sooner or later. She relayed this information to her father, the clockmaker. The clockmaker paid heed to the wise shaman's words. Never second-guess a shaman.'

'I think he made a mistake. Those shamans are high as kites most of the time; if they're not smoking hashish, then they're drinking hallucinogenic cocktails. So, it was a complete waste of time? That's what you're saying? We don't even know if the time-machine ever worked?'

'Which brings me nicely to the end of this tale.'

'The end?'

'The end only because there is no end, Jack. The rest of the tale is lost in time – no pun intended. It's called *The Unending Fairy-Tale* because nobody knows its ending.'

'What do you mean?'

'Well, don't you see?'

Jack's losing his patience now. 'I'm not as bright as you, Ruthy.'

'Jack, this Olenberg guy is said to have really existed, and his great-great-*great*-grandson is alive today, by all accounts.'

'*Now* you tell me?'

'Yes! And shares his great-great...'

'...*great* grandfather's name? Okay, I get it. Friedrich Junior...'

'You can call him what you want, Jack. But, yes, from the research I've done, he carries the same name. But to avoid confusion, I think you're right. Let's call him Friedrich Junior. Up until recently, there have been sightings of this recluse in the village of Bladd that sits at the bottom of the mountain.'

'Are you being serious right now?'

'During the summer, he is said to appear now and again to stock up on provisions, but he hibernates for the winter. *Nobody* sees him. He's like a ghost, Jack.'

'I'm not sure I like where this is going, Ruthy. But if I'm thinking what you're thinking, then it is *you* who needs to see a professional. And this Oldenberg –'

'Olenberg...'

'Whatever. This guy is a character in a medieval fairy-tale, and you're telling me he goes down to the local super-market to stock up on Red Bull and beans to get him through the winter?'

'His descendant, Jack, *descendant*: Friedrich Junior. It is said that this Olenberg character – only he isn't a character because he *actually* exists and is carrying on the clock-making tradition and makes top-class Cuckoo Clocks, but apparently he's got a *special* clock which has been handed down through the generations from the original Friedrich Olenberg. The same clock that appears in *The Unending Fairy-Tale*...Jack!'

'Ruthy, please, don't make this any more difficult than...'

'Why don't we go and find this time-machine and –'

Jack explodes. '*You're* beginning to sound unending, Ruthy, and the only cuckoo here is you! I bared my heart – *our* heart – and soul to you tonight at Joe Soap's, and you return this trust by taking the piss out of me?!'

'Ja-'

Jack hangs up on Ruthy for the second time tonight, ending his birthday on a sour note.

Chapter 11

Count Friedrich Olenberg

A week passes. All that Jack has done during this time is mount his stuffed crow on the wall of his bedroom. The taxidermist had perched the crow on a branch which Jack had taken from the woods that surrounds the amusement park, thinking it quite apt. The staring crow is the last thing that Jack sees at night and the first thing he sees in the morning.

Stuffing his dead saviour isn't...

How 'bout stuffing me in your bedroom, Jackie? No, let me rephrase that: how 'bout bringing me back to life in your bedroom, Jackie? Hmm? I was your first saviour...

...the only thing Jack does during the week: he constantly thinks back to his regretful conversation with Ruthy. But he hasn't changed his mind about how he treated her. She's taking the piss; she's playing with fire. Silly girl.

On Sunday night, running into Monday morning, 22nd February, Jack is lying in bed, unable to sleep. His stuffed crow's eyes glisten off the porch light outside his front window. There's something bugging him tonight but for the life of him, he can't figure out what it is. Yes, he's got that thing with Ruthy, but that isn't it. There's something else nagging his subconscious.

He's just easing himself into a slumber when it suddenly comes to him: the blood money!

It's the insurance money that is playing with his emotions – those bloody notes running into their thousands in a bank account. Jack doesn't *want* the damn money. He bought the Mini because he needs a car, but anything else seems lavish and unfair to the memory of his dead fiancée. Even finding a place of his own in Limerick City doesn't feel right. He also contemplates going back to University to pick up the pieces and continue from where he had abruptly left off a year ago. He could use the money for his college fees, and that would be an honourable cause. But again, he cannot face that choice.

Going back to reality without Jeanie isn't an option for now. It seems that she is everywhere, *more* than when she was alive, if that's possible.

Jack makes up his mind to sort out that little blood money problem the following day.

And having solved the issue, Jack sleeps a relatively deep sleep.

The following morning, as his parents busy themselves around him getting ready for work and the daily chores, Jack drinks a coffee and studies the frosty lawn through the back window, specifically, the patch of lawn beneath the crab-apple tree, which has begun to bud again.

Once his parents are gone, Jack takes a walk down to the bank in the town square.

To the bank-teller's dismay (her name-tag tells Jack that her name is Jennifer), Jack proceeds to withdraw most of the money. He leaves a few thousand in the account for any emergencies that may crop up and weekly rental money which Jack prefers to give to his parents, seeing as he's living at home. He feels better about it this way.

Once back at home, he finds an old biscuit tin. He rolls the insurance money into tight five-hundred euro note bills, puts the money in a plastic bag, and places the bag inside the biscuit tin.

Jack then goes outside, grabs the shovel from the little greenhouse, and carefully slices off a sod of lawn. He lays the sod carefully aside and digs a deep hole under the crab-apple tree. Into the pit he places the biscuit tin, along with the memory of Jeanie – if *only* life were that simple.

For a tiny moment at least, Jack finds a tincture of closure, filling back that hole in the ground and replacing the sod of lawn. His folks will never know the difference; they will *never* guess that there is a tin box full of five-hundred euro notes just under the sour-apple tree, which Jack feels appropriate, as the experience *is* a bitter-sweet one.

As he back-fills the shallow grave, he recalls the aloof grave-diggers filling in Jeanie's grave, just another job for them, tossing earth as if they were at home pottering around in their own garden. Jack should've slapped one of them, but they were just doing their job...but all of this had been seen through Jack's third eye, because he had been in a coma when Jeanie's heartless corpse had been filed away forever under *U* for Underground.

On Sunday evening, exactly a week to the hour, following his blow-out on the phone with Ruthy, Jack's watching the *History Channel* in his bedroom when something very interesting comes on.

A documentary all about time-travel.

The first fifty minutes are dedicated to the hard science of time-travel and interviews with physicists and job descriptions that sound, to Jack, as if they're from space.

Mild amusement soon turns to boredom once again. Jack looks up at his crow and begins to nod off...When suddenly he is jolted from his sleep with an aggressiveness, as if somebody under his bed has just kicked upwards, lifting him off his mattress.

He starts up in bed and looks around for the cause of his sudden shock. Had he dreamt again of that moment when the ride leaves the tracks to the deafening crescendo of twisting steel and screams, the sickening surge in his insides as Jeanie is snatched from the car?

Jack looks around the room for anything that could've fallen over or made a bang in any way, but everything is as it should be. For a crazy second, he thinks that the crow has moved, but she's there, gazing eternally down at him.

Then he hears the name that had slammed him out of his slumber, as if the man himself, bearing that same name, had frantically shook his shoulders, telling the fool to *wake the fuck up, now, Jack!!!*

'Olenberg...*Olenberg*...*OLENBERG!*'

The same name Ruthy had mentioned in her fairy-tale is coming out of his telly. He wipes the sleep from his eyes and focuses on what he is seeing on his portable telly.

The narrator is speaking of a reclusive old Count living in the mountainous region of the Black Forest of Germany and the last in a long lineage of Old World monarchy.

The camera-crew film Olenberg's gothic residence from far-off, hidden amongst the black fir trees that give this forest its name. Grainy, shaky footage taken through the trees, stalks the old man as he appears at his great door briefly but disappears again. The narrator tells Jack that Count Friedrich Olenberg, descendent of the original Count Friedrich Olenberg, refuses to speak to them and forbids any filming of any description, which explains the poor footage. The narrator goes on telling Jack that these few seconds is the only known footage of the antisocial Count. Jack watches in amazement as the Count appears again briefly in his front cobble-stone yard dated to the rest of the gothic castle from the 1200's. The crooked, old man leans on a walking-stick and is wearing what appears to be an olive-green robe.

Jack spots a large dog walking by the old man...only it isn't a dog. Just as Jack is straining his eyes to see what, exactly, is accompanying Count Olenberg, the narrator informs him that the footage is over twenty years old, and nobody has been able to identify what type of animal appears with the aged Count; it's just a morphing blob on 80's celluloid.

The documentary then goes on to interview local people in the vicinity of Castle Olenberg, in the village of Bladd. The general consensus is that Count Olenberg is a ghost. He is seen very rarely by locals and when they see him he is gone as fast as he appears, sometimes inexplicably so. Like a hibernating mountain animal, the Count comes down from the mountain during the good weather to stock up on tinned goods, apparently. Castle Olenberg remains snow-bound until the first thawing of late March. One old man is interviewed and mentions, in subtitled German, that Count Olenberg was last seen a year ago in the local family-run shop which sells a little of everything or 'knick-knacks' as the subtitles read.

But many locals refuse to speak to the camera. The interviewer combs the streets of Bladd, looking for a local to talk to, but a pattern soon emerges: tourists don't know what he's talking about and locals refuse to talk.

The interviewer sums this up by commenting that, "In fact, the town of Bladd seems to be hiding a secret."

Olenberg is indeed a ghost.

The narrator with the rich, husky voice then tells Jack that the closest the public will come to the modern-day Count is through his elaborately carved Black Forest cuckoo clocks. He only makes a handful a year and each clock sells for lots of money around the world, owing to its aristocratic and artistic origins. An unnamed third-party individual sells his clocks at auctions; seller and buyer never meet. The auction-house refuses to disclose any information relating to its famed client, Count Friedrich Olenberg, though they do confirm that he is their client.

"However," the narrator continues, "legend has it that Count Olenberg is guarding a secret: a special clock which not only tells the time, but *alters* it. Urban legend and word-of-mouth has it that Count Olenberg is said to be in possession of a timepiece which transports its occupants in time. But as was previously mentioned, Count Olenberg moves with the grace of a ghost. Only *time* will tell if rumours are to be believed."

Quite unable to believe what he has just seen, Jack picks up his phone with a shake in his hand, then rings Ruthy as the credits roll. He's almost convinced now that all of this is happening for some obscure reason.

The phone rings a few times before Jack hears the click.

'Oh, so you're talking to me again?' Ruthy doesn't bother with formalities. 'What's up? You do realize it's one in the morning. You're lucky you caught me, um, studying...'

Jack looks up at his stuffed crow. He feels it's a female and is thinking about calling her Clara after a girl from Spain he once dated in another life, very far from the one he's leading now.

Jack can hardly contain his excitement. 'I owe you an apology.'

'Apology accepted – I *always* accept apologies. What apology am I accepting?'

'Olenberg...the time-machine.'

A lengthy pause comes down the line. 'Why the change of heart – sorry, I had it said before –'

'I've just watched a documentary about time-travel on the *History Channel*. The first, like, fifty minutes was heavy shit about astrophysics and the speed of light and *stuff*, but the last fifteen minutes or so, was all about this Count Friedrich Olenberg – *your* Olenberg from *The Unending Fairy-Tale!*'

Jack listens to the open line. Ruthy's response comes a little later than he had expected. It *doesn't* come...

'I can't believe it, Ruthy! You were right. He *is* a distant, *very* distant, relative of the Count. The documentary maintains that he's hiding something up there on that mountain – the secret of time-travel. It's completely nuts, but the fact that this guy even exists and the *History Channel* is paying attention to him is beyond belief. This is the stuff of dreams.'

'That's what I was telling you, but you wouldn't listen. Never dismiss your dreams, Jack.'

Jack doesn't know how to respond. He's not sure he even understands. 'Ruthy, will you come with me to the Black Forest?'

'Ok!'

Jack continues as if he hasn't heard Ruthy's answer. 'I know it's a lot to ask, but I'll treat you to the finest hotels and spas and whatever you want...Don't you *see?* Jeanie has given me this money to find Olenberg's secret!' Jack has already convinced himself that Jeanie organized the insurance money from her celestial accounting-desk. 'Wait, you *will come?*'

'Why not?' Again, Ruthy answers as if Jack has asked her to go for a milky coffee at Joe Soap's. Ruthy doesn't even think about it. She agrees wholeheartedly, as if she *knew* what Jack was going to propose.

A silence looms on the other end of the line. 'But I thought you didn't do fairy-tales?'

'This guy *exists*, Ruthy.'

'Jack, don't you think you're taking this a *little* far? I mean, last week you shot me down at Joe Soap's, left me sitting there like a fool. Now you want to go to the *Black Forest?* And what will you do when you get there?'

'Wait, I thought you just agreed to go with me...'

'Yes, I did. But I want to know that you're thinking clearly first. I just want to make sure that *you're* sure of what you're doing. I'm not talking you into going to the Black Forest...You're doing this off your own back.'

Jack thinks that this is self-evident. 'Of course! I'll track down this Count and see if this time-machine really exists.'

'If it does?'

'I'll go back in time.'

'*Hello?*'

'Ruthy, I haven't been able to find the right reason to spend the insurance money on. But this is it. I'll *buy* myself time.' Jack reflects on the past few crazy weeks. 'I knew all of this had to have logic. Remember I told you that all of these events had to have a reason? Well, that money is to buy *time*.'

Ruthy interrupts, 'I'm not going to take responsibility for this if it doesn't turn out the way you want it to, Jack.'

'Deal.'

Ruthy imagines the desperation in Jack's face down the other end of the line. She bets that he's got that brainwashed look about him; that same look when somebody explains numbers and calculations to her. She knows Jack's every little nuance and gesture. She knows him a lot better than he thinks.

'You do realize that this is fucking crazy, Jack.'

'Haven't you ever wanted to be a fairy-tale princess? Have you ever wanted to *live* in one of those fairy-tales that you study? Look at it as research.'

'Well, yes, but then I've got to deal with big bad wolves, trolls, and *all* kinds of shit. Life isn't a fairy-tale, Jack.'

'It is if you look at it the right way. Listen to me! It's *you* who should be trying to convince *me* of this! Ruthy, let's chase down this Count and see if the rumours are true. Then, when we find out that it's all smoke and mirrors, we can come home knowing that we did the right thing by Jeanie. If I *don't* go, the doubt will always be there. Once I know the truth and time-travel is impossible, duh, then I'll wear my heart on my sleeve – pun intended. But right now, I need to know that that crazy old recluse doesn't have a clock that offers time-travel as an added extra.'

Jack hears Ruthy snicker a little at that last comment.

'We both know that this will be a wild goose chase, Ruthy.'

'Do we?'

'Ruthy, I'm not stupid or delusional. We both know time-travel doesn't exist, and if it does, it's reserved for the mega-rich. Let's go there, discover the inevitable, and come home with our heads held high. Look at this trip as one of therapy and healing. I think we should do it on 1st of March – it will be Jeanie's first anniversary...'

'And the wedding anniversary that never happened...'

Jack answers reluctantly, 'I guess.'

'Okay, I agree. 1ˢᵗ of March works on many levels; it's like coming full circle and that ties in with the last loop-the-loop of the rollercoaster.'

'Great. Ruthy, I'm still on that *fucking* last loop-the-loop and I want off.'

'If that's what it takes for us to get on with our lives, then I'm up for it.' Clearing her throat for comic effect, Ruthy adds: 'Um, you mentioned that this trip is on you...'

'Package deal...promise. Come join me on my delusional flight of fancy. Look at this as extended research for your MA thesis or whatever it is that you study or do.'

'Jack, that's a *very* good idea. You're *right*; I can kill two birds with one stone.'

Jack looks up at Clara, the crow.

'How many other people will have gone to the trouble of tracking down a modern-day fairy-tale character?'

'I like it. So, if you don't mind, I'd like to get back to the symbolism of *Jack and the Beanstalk*. Did you know that the beanstalk symbol supposedly represents...'

'A phallic symbol?'

'Yeah, *no*, smart-ass. It represents...'

Jack, feeling a little closer to his old playful self, hangs up on Ruthy. He knows she is smiling at her phone right now.

He is right. Ruthy *is* smiling at her phone. Ruthy is fucking ecstatic right now, but not necessarily for Jack's stalk, bean or otherwise.

Unable to sleep, Jack slips out, grabs his car-key from the little mirrored wooden key-box on the wall by the front door, and drives down to the abandoned amusement park to gather his thoughts and think about his impending trip to the Black Forest.

This place still has a fierce hold over him, like a drug, and he, its addict.

He sits there in the intermittent moonlight hanging high over his Mini; a thousand thoughts hurrying across his mindscape as the wispy clouds race across the nightscape.

Chapter 12

The Trip

Jack prepares for the trip extensively over the following hours.

After a little online GPS research, he discovers that Castle Olenberg overlooks the Murg valley in the Northern Black Forest, near the historical town of Bladd. Bladd, Jack recalls, was the little town where locals had been interviewed on the documentary he had seen on the *History Channel*. He's surprised that the castle has been so easy to find, but then again, it's difficult to outrun Big Brother Google's eye.

He makes a note of the GPS coordinates for Bladd, but soon finds out that the castle doesn't seem to have coordinates. Once he finds Bladd, he's sure he'll track down the castle. Finding a castle can't be that difficult...

But they need to get there first. So, without further ado, Jack learns that the closest major city he can see on the map is Stuttgart, so he books first-class flight tickets to Stuttgart from his local airport, Shannon. He chuckles his way through the exciting booking process, wondering if he should book return tickets for himself, *considering* that he is going back in time and that concept gives Jack a great kick.

But that leaves the problem of Ruthy. Where will she go if Jack goes back in time? And he's also presuming that this special clock offers international European destinations and not just Germany.

The best thing is to forget about time-travel because it doesn't exist. So, Jack should continue planning an itinerary that will be an average round-trip to Germany's picturesque Black Forest for a week; just your average sight-seeing holiday. Look at it as disconnecting from all of this, Jack.

In hindsight, he recognizes that leaving a few thousand in his bank account was a good idea. Without his credit card, he wouldn't have been able to book anything.

Once in Stuttgart, they will need independent transportation – this isn't the guided tour version. So Jack happily passes his card through Stuttgart airport's car-rental facility. He books the fanciest shiny black sports Z3 BMW he can find. Jack's not going to spare *any* expense because all of this is for his long-lost love; it's the least he can do, considering she gave him her heart. *And* he promised Ruthy first-class service and he will be true to his word. *Nothing* has been so important to Jack since he woke on a hospital bed. He's determined to do it right the first time. It's all about the trip now.

He then reserves two single rooms and the all-inclusive package deal in the finest five-star hotel, Hotel Bladd, situated in Bladd's town-square. He doesn't find the hotel by chance; Ruthy messages him and tells him about the place. He doesn't ask how she had heard about it, suffice to say that the reviews on *Trip Advisor* are stellar. The hotel is known for its "old-world charm" and "five-star service which is impeccable".

Ruthy's got good taste in hotels, at least.

On the 1st March, just a few hours after booking everything, Jack wakes with a new sense of purpose for the first time in exactly one year.

He has slept with Jeanie's engagement ring beneath his pillow and searches for it with his fingers. Switching on the bedside lamp, he gazes sleepily at the shimmering ring, its flower shaped pattern; six pink rubies for petals and a cluster of diamonds where the pollen goes, all held together by a shank of eighteen carat gold. It is a fairy-tale ring. He looks along the inside band to find the inscription in Edwardian scribe which Jeanie probably never got to see: J + J, March 2015.

He climbs out of bed and gets ready.

Just after five a.m., Ruthy's Fiat pulls into Jack's front yard on this lead-grey morning when nothing stirs.

Jack smiles to himself; he wasn't sure if she was going to turn up. Thank God she has, because he's paid a small fortune for this little wild-goose adventure.

Through Jack's living-room window, he first sees Ruthy's Mohawk that seems to glow on this dark morning. She has dyed it *again*: love-heart magenta pink...which symbolizes? What frame of mind is Ruthy in, Jack ponders?

He meets her in the front yard with his five-day luggage.

Ruthy is standing by her car. 'So, we're *actually* going through with this?'

'I guess so.' Jack gets a sense of déjà vu, thinking back to the day she collected him from the hospital. He waves the tickets at her. 'First class...'

'Maybe I *am* the princess in this fairy-tale, after all.'

'Five stars all the way, baby,' jokes Jack, making light of it all, but inside his rib-cage his borrowed heart flutters nervously.

Jack gets into the overly-warm Fiat.

Old Castle is like a ghost town at this hour of the morning. Cats gather around the stone cross in the main square but apart from that, the town is dead. Jack feels like he's just passing through and hasn't actually lived here all his life.

During the hour-long journey, Jack and Ruthy talk about Jeanie, openly and fondly. Ruthy takes her hand from the wheel briefly and pulls down the hip of her jeans to show Jack a new tattoo. It is a cute pink pom-pom type creature with big googly eyes. Around the pom-pom are the words: fuzzy-wuzzy forever.

'I like it.'

Jack has a love-hate relationship with tattoos, but there's no denying that a tasteful tattoo on a good-looking girl raises that girl in Jack's estimation. Jeanie had a tattoo of a koi fish on the nape of her neck. It happily wallowed there forever, under the shade of her long blond hair...not that it brought her much luck.

'It's the nearest I can get to having a piece of Jeanie forever,' smiles Ruthy.

'Well, I've got her heart,' Jack jokes, '*nah-na-na-nah-nah...*' (of the opinion that it's better to embrace his donated organ rather than keep it hidden). It's therapy, though sometimes it can seem darkly comic. But today is the start of something new...

They pull into Shannon Airport's public car-park a little after six am.

'What time is boarding?'

Jack checks his itinerary. 'Eight-thirty. We've got time for a coffee.'

Jack and Ruthy pass through passport control and stop at a little café to have a latte and a Danish pastry. They speak about lots of things; things they'd never spoken about when Jeanie had been around. Stuff they had never known about because Jeanie had always been between them. Even sitting in this airport café, Jack feels that she is sitting between them, filtering their messages.

They are in deep conversation about their lives with Jeanie, almost like a belated funeral wake, when a woman's voice comes over the loud-speaker announcing their flight.

They pick up their things and make a bee-line for the gate. They slide into the fast-lane queue. Jack's stomach flutters when he hears German being spoken somewhere behind him in the line. For the first time, it dawns on him that this is *really* happening.

They board the Airbus A320. An attractive flame-haired air-hostess with striking turquoise eyes shows them to their first-class seats. She tells them that her name is Nina and that she will be looking after them during the flight.

Ruthy whispers to Jack with a smile, 'As if we need looking after,' as they take their seats.

Before they know it, they are above the low blanket of cumulus cloud that constantly sits over Old Castle. They resume their conversation about their lives that had revolved around Jeanie.

'Jeanie was our planet, and we were her moons.'

Jack couldn't have put it better himself. They had always known each other, but through Jeanie. Conversation about Jeanie led to other topics.

Jack is starting to feel that he is only beginning to know Ruthy right now, today, the 1st of March, as they fly at thirty thousand feet over the English Channel. More than that, Jack discovers more about Jeanie as he listens to Ruthy tell various stories about their escapades they'd had together.

This trip has already been worth it.

Nina, the air-hostess, asks them if they would like a drink.

Feeling that they're celebrating something, Jack and Ruthy order wine.

Before they know it, they have begun their descent. The captain tells them that there's a storm over Stuttgart, so they have to circle in the sky to dodge the bubbling dark cloud formations the passengers can see from their windows.

Turbulence suddenly surges the plane before it levels off again.

Ruthy downs the rest of her red wine and grabs onto the back of Jack's hand, and Jack, freaking out completely and right back on the killer coaster, is only *more* than happy to take her hand in his.

As the plane rides the storm, Jack struggles to keep his breathing steady. Ruthy sees Jack practically having a panic attack. She tries to calm him by rubbing the back of his hand and telling him that it's 'just some turbulence.'

Once below the angry cloud, the plane evens up. Jack and Ruthy simultaneously look down at their white-knuckled, inter-locked hands, and share an awkward giggle.

Rain begins to stream along their window.

Jack leans over for a better view and sees that it is absolutely lashing out there. Rain hadn't been in his plan because he was booking a full five-star service and rain didn't feature in it.

'Did you bring wet-weather gear?' he asks Ruthy.

Her expression tells him that she brought about as much wet-weather gear as he did: zero.

Nothing is going to get in the way of Jack's objective. 'Minor detail.'

'I don't want to get my Mohawk wet.'

'A Nohawk.'

Ruthy's snorts and guffaws fill the Airbus.

'By the way, why bright pink?' Jack signalling to her hair colour.

'Love.'

Jack decides that that can be left open to interpretation and doesn't dwell on the subject.

Jack and Ruthy give each other nervous, excited smiles as the A320 glides effortlessly onto German soil, sending up a spray of water outside their window.

Ten minutes later, they descend the steps and walk into Stuttgart's Terminal One building.

They stop off at the first over-priced clothing stall and buy raincoats.

At the car rental in the main Arrivals building, everything runs smoothly and Jack is given the key to the sexy little Z3 BMW he had booked for the week. Following a short walk, they find the car-park and Ruthy's eyes are out on stalks when she sees the car they have rented. 'I've never had the pleasure of travelling in a car with no back seats.'

'Told ya,' Jack affirms. 'You're the princess in this fairy-tale.'

Ahem, if Ruthy is the princess, then who or what am I? Snow White? If only things were as simple as giving me a kiss to wake me up...

They stuff their small suitcases in the BMW's smaller boot. Jack sets up the GPS and enters Bladd's coordinates he had copied from the net. The GPS quickly locates their route. It tells them that their journey will take the best part of three hours.

An hour or so after leaving Stuttgart airport, Jack and Ruthy begin to see the first black fir trees of the Black Forest. As their BMW's GPS guides them through the region, Jack cannot help mentioning, 'I think we're coming full circle – or the full loop, both work.'

'Which means?'

'All of this ended and started in another forest – Old Castle's woods. The more I think about it, the more I'm getting a déjà vu. *Everything* is on a loop, Ruthy.'

Ruthy smiles knowingly at him. 'The Unending Fairy-Tale.'

The rain begins to fall even harder, if that's possible.

Jack and Ruthy thought they'd seen heavy rain in Limerick, but the rain in the Black Forest tells them that all they'd ever seen was a shower back home. The skies have grown dark and the whole thing is quite ominous and foreboding; it is fitting because Jack and Ruthy are about to enter their own unending fairy-tale.

Chapter 13

Hotel Bladd

Two hours and something later, Jack and Ruthy exit the A5 at Rastatt. They have entered Murg Valley. Forested hills and snow-capped mountains surround them on all sides.

One snow-capped peak, in particular, catches Ruthy's attention, and she screams for Jack to have a look at it; they almost end up in a close-encounter with the steel barrier running along the autobahn (Jack had been taking advantage of the high speed limit).

'What?' Jack strains his neck to get a view of what has just driven Ruthy berserk. *'What?!'*

'I think this is the start of our fairy-tale, Jack.'

'Jesus, I thought you'd seen a U.F.O or something!'

'No, just the breath-taking countryside. This is where fairy-tales are born.'

'My princess…' Jack utters the words without thinking and immediately regrets and *doesn't* regret saying it.

Ruthy looks at him momentarily, and they share a flashing hint of a smile before Jack reddens to his ears. He fiddles with the heating of the Z3 (turning it down as it's just become a little too hot for comfort) and squints to see through the pelting rain, which is beginning to turn to sleet. He checks the GPS and according to the screen, they should be arriving in the town of Bladd within the next twenty minutes.

As they drive the last few miles, Jack retraces his steps that have led him up to here; an incredible sequence of events that could seem prophetic if stared at long enough or just pure coincidence.

'All of this is happening for a reason,' Jack opines.

Ruthy nods vehemently. 'It is.' She says it as if she's got no doubt whatsoever, that all of this was meant to be.

'You told me about Friedrich Olenberg over the phone. Don't you think it's an amazing coincidence that I should see this same guy on the *History Channel* just a few days later when I'd *never* heard of him in my life?'

'Even if you hadn't seen that documentary on Friedrich Olenberg, we would have ended up here eventually, some way. It's written in the stars.'

Jack admires her conviction; he loves how she has no doubt about happenings beyond what our senses tell us. 'And here we are, just about to enter the town which was featured on that documentary. If I think back a little further, the statistics increase...Clara saved me from becoming bacon and mushroom pizza on the concrete floor of the amusement park. My life was saved and almost cursed at that amusement park.'

'*Clara?*'

'Yeah, my crow. Remember I told you about it at Joe Soap's?'

'It didn't have a name the last time...'

'Yeah, I thought she deserved a name seeing as she saved my life.' Then Jack goes on to tell Ruthy the redemption part of the story when he had the crow stuffed and which now guards his bedroom back in Old Castle.

'I think you're right about everything being on some kind of loop. The crow is a metaphor for Jeanie.'

'Well, I don't know if I'd go that far...'

'Yes, in resurrecting the bird, you've helped resurrect the memory of Jeanie.'

'Which brings us back to our fairy-tale: we're here to resurrect her.'

'That night in Joe Soap's...'

'I remember that night didn't end so nicely.'

'And I'm sorry, Ruthy. I thought you were taking the piss. I was brittle. I was going through a very dark moment in my life – my borrowed life. I was looking for a reason to live. Try to see it from my point of view.'

There's silence in the Z3. The radio seems to grow louder. The forest around them becomes so dense that the trees meet over the winding road until they are driving through a tree-tunnel.

The BMW's headlights switch on as they enter the darkness.

As the gloom envelopes them, Jack decides to get something out in the air. 'Ruthy, I know we haven't actually spoken about this, but I know we are both thinking it, so why not get it out in the open...'

Ruthy suddenly looks at Jack's dashboard-illuminated face in surprise. As if he's about to say something that will change everything for the better and worse.

'We both know that fairy-tales don't exist. We are doing this for the memory of Jeanie. Like you said, resurrecting her memory and putting her to rest at the same time. But that's all.'

Jack smiles while tears well in Ruthy's eyes. They are both happy in the darkness of the tree-tunnel.

'You're wrong about one thing: fairy-tales *do* exist. Millions of *existing* parents read *existing* fairy-tales every night from *existing* books to kids who, funnily enough...'

'...*exist*, yeah, I know. I mean it's fantasy, not reality.'

They drive back into the light at the exit of the tree-tunnel. Everything that had to be said was said, and they soon leave their little conversation behind in the safety of the tree-tunnel as they enter the charming Old Town of Bladd.

The town looks just like it's out of a fairy-tale with its rickety rooves and medieval beams on colourful house facades. They drive through the snaking one-way system; quaint, narrow, cobblestone streets. If it weren't for people's clothes, iPhones, and transport, Jack could swear that he had travelled back in time a few centuries. The GPS takes them up a steep incline to an imposing old building overlooking the town square. The place is enormous in all its old-world beauty and charm. At the door stands a doorman wearing a top-hat and tails.

'This is our hotel,' says Ruthy, gawking at the building. 'This is the one I told you about.'

Jack nods and smiles. 'You know your hotels.'

'I've never stayed here before.'

This strikes Jack as an odd thing to say but the cold is intense and there's no time to think as the doorman greets them with a smile and opens the main door.

They thank the doorman and step inside to the warmth. They are greeted by an immense hallway of warm colours and ancient wood-panelling of various hues. The whole wow factor is quite a rustic one and it suits the atmosphere *and* the town.

Ruthy grabs Jack's arm on impulse and squeezes it, letting out a whimper of joy. 'I never thought researching an MA thesis would be as fancy as this.'

Jack gives his name to the receptionist behind the counter, clocking her name-tag: Emily.

She smiles and gives them their keys and outlines the services which are included in the price: spa, thermal baths, and 24-hour room-service access, 'plus three square meals a day.'

Emily, the receptionist, finishes with an enthusiastic, though robotic smile. She hands them two plastic room-cards which are the only sign of anything *modern*.

Jack thanks her for the keys and information, and the bell-hop insists on taking their luggage.

Jack murmurs to Ruthy: 'I don't know if I fancy eating three squares a day. For the cost of all of this, you'd think that they might throw in a trapezoid, or even, dare I say, an *isosceles* triangle.'

Ruthy giggles and is helpless as she snorts laughter in the bell-hop's face while they climb two floors in a whirring, old-fashioned lift, reminiscent of a cage.

The courteously blank bell-hop pulls back the cage door and leads them to their bedrooms: 2204 being Ruthy's and Jack's 2205.

In the hallway of the second floor, Jack and Ruthy make plans to meet for lunch in half an hour. Jack goes to his room and Ruthy goes to hers to freshen up.

As Jack pushes the card into its slot, he reflects that everybody he has met in Bladd, so far, has been extremely nice; they don't look like people hiding something as was given the impression on the *History Channel* documentary. Then again, he has only come in contact with people who deal with tourists; artificial and false. He makes up his mind to probe a little further. He won't get a real feel for the place until he meets the locals.

Half an hour later, they meet in the hotel restaurant for lunch as planned. The place looks and feels like a giant log-cabin. There is a homely feel to the place. Dapper waiters and waitresses glide to and from the kitchens to the tables and back again. Logs crackle in a large open fire. The mantelpiece is a slab of decorated amber-coloured wood with leaping stags, wild fowl, and huntsmen.

On the wall above the fireplace is a giant hand-carved Black Forest cuckoo clock. The largest Jack has ever seen. His grandfather had one in his living-room which Jack's uncle had brought from this same region during the seventies, but this clock is almost the size of Jack's new Mini. The timepiece has many characters and intricate patterns, ranging from carved black fir trees and mountain-backdrops to frogs and soaring eagles.

The clock's bone-hands strike two o'clock. There is a gong, followed by two cuckoo calls, and then rotating dancers roll and prance to Beethoven's *Moonlight Sonata* while entranced dining tourists gaze on in amazement.

'Do you like the clock?'

Jack turns around to see a cute waitress with a Latina look. 'Oh, um, yes, it's amazing.'

The waitress takes pride in telling him, 'It's an Olenberg clock,' even though Jack hasn't asked.

Jack nods and thanks her for the voluntary information.

'Let me find you a comfortable table.'

The waitress is gone off again by the time Jack realizes what she has said. He turns to Ruthy with wide eyes and excitedly tells her, 'She just told me that this is an Olenberg clock!'

A table of tourists, to Jack's left, stare at him.

Ruthy whispers, 'Calm down.' She looks at the enormous work-of-art which is the centrepiece of the restaurant. She nods as if she's not surprised. 'Are you beginning to believe me now?'

The waitress whizzes back to them. 'Are you ready to sit down?' She glances momentarily at Ruthy's Mohawk, then at Ruthy in general, with the slightest hint of disdain. 'Let me show you to your table...'

She walks off. Jack and Ruthy follow her through the myriad of restaurant tables. The waitress leads them to a cosy corner and seats them at their table. 'My name is Maritza. Just call me if you need anything.'

Jack takes this as his cue to ask her how old the clock is.

'Probably around,' Maritza theatrically counts on her fingers, 'two hundred and thirty or forty years old. It's an original Olenberg.'

Jack finds this fascinating, to think that this clock was ticking back and forth all that time ago and is still working today with the same *tick-tock* people long since dead were also listening to.

Jack and Ruthy order roast piglet, which is the house specialty, according to Maritza.

It arrives on the table in an instant, faster than any Chinese restaurant, and is a little graphic for Jack, as it arrives fully intact, ears, snout, hooves and even bristles.

Ruthy, on the other hand, looks like a scavenger. 'I'm famished. Did you see how she looked at my hair?'

'I don't see hair when I look at your Mohawk. I see attitude.'

They both snicker.

The exquisite taste soon overcomes the split piglet lying on the serving plate in front of them. Ruthy orders a glass of house wine, and Jack sticks to water.

'C'mon, live a little,' Ruthy eggs him on.

Jack tells the waitress that he's sticking with his choice.

Once the waitress lithely turns on her heels, Jack says to Ruthy: 'This isn't a pleasure trip; this is a guilt trip. I don't feel comfortable enough yet to drink wine.'

'It didn't stop you on the plane?'

'That was different...'

'Lighten up, Jack. The last thing Jeanie would want is to see you depressed. I *get* the guilt trip thing, but can we not have a little fun while we're doing it? Hmm? After all, we both know this is a wild goose chase.' Ruthy finishes her point by tucking into the suckling pig and stuffing her face with roast potatoes. 'Okay, so how do we do this?' Ruthy asks, digging into her handbag for something.

'Firstly, we need to find his castle. It can't be too far from here because he comes down here to stock up on food for the winter. Wherever it is, it must be well off the beaten-track. I couldn't find GPS coordinates for it.'

'I brought you this. It's a present.' Ruthy hands Jack a battered, old edition of *The Clockmaker's Daughter*.

Jack looks at her in surprise.

'It's a first and last edition.'

What does that even mean? Nevertheless, Jack is bowled over with the gift. He never thought he'd be left so gobsmacked with a fairy-tale. 'This is the story you told me over the phone?' He looks at the clock on the wall and now the fairy-tale doesn't seem so fantastical and inaccessible anymore. As a matter of fact, it's beginning to take on a life of its own.

Ruthy nods. 'I thought it would make a good memento and maybe bring us some luck.'

'This must've cost you...'

'Special circumstances...' smiles Ruthy. 'It's even signed.'

'Signed? But I thought you told me it was written anonymously.'

Ruthy opens back the front cover and shows Jack the eloquent inscription: *Anonymous...*

'Duh...' Jack gets a fit of laughing.

Ruthy laughs too.

Jack holds the book and flits through its yellowed, time-stained pages. The illustrations are amateur enough, and the book itself is something that Jack could probably stick together in an hour if he were so inclined.

However, there is something odd about the inscription: and that is that the writing is clearly newer than the book which is obviously very old. And "Anonymous" is written with a gel pen. Jack's no expert, but he's sure gel pens didn't exist two hundred years ago.

He's close to mentioning it but decides against it. He doesn't want to hurt Ruthy's feelings. Obviously somebody had written that inscription to squeeze more money out of the buyer, i.e. Ruthy. Jack's a little surprised at Ruthy's naivety, especially considering that she *studies* literature. He feels a twinge of pity for her.

He decides to broach the subject when the time is right.

Jack flicks back to the first page of *The Clockmaker's Daughter* and begins to read...

The warm, cosy atmosphere of the restaurant, plus the heady effect of the wine, and Jack's soft words seem to hypnotize Ruthy. She listens to Jack's voice and stares at the hypnotic pendulum of the Olenberg clock above the fireplace, ticking back and forth.

The fairy-tale puts her under its spell...

Chapter 14

The Clockmaker's Daughter

"'Once upon a time, there was a clockmaker and his daughter who lived on the side of a windy mountain in a splendid castle in the Black Forest of Germany. The castle was known for many miles around, and it was owned by a Count named Friedrich Olenberg. The same Count also built clocks of the highest standard for the land's nobility and the kings and queens of other countries.

One day, the clockmaker's daughter tells her father that she has fallen in love with his competitor's son.

In a transport of rage, Count Olenberg travels to the deepest and darkest heart of the Black Forest to speak to a shaman living in a house of rock...'"

At this juncture, Jack comments, 'What's a travelling shaman doing living in a house of rock?'

Ruthy tells him that she cannot *always* be right. 'Even the bible isn't trustworthy...'

Not wanting to get into a bible argument, Jack continues:

"'The shaman in the cave concocted a potion. He put this brew over an open fire and waited for the bubbles to tell him the truth. When the potion began to simmer, the shaman was already gravely shaking his head, causing the clockmaker unending worry. Soon, the potion was bubbling over and with each bubble pop, the shaman was convinced even more.

He took the concoction from the fire and set it aside and told the clockmaker that he will only find happiness when this young man no longer exists because his future son-in-law will be the ruination of the Count. His future son-in-law will be an extraordinary clockmaker.

The Count couldn't bring himself to ask the shaman how to kill the young man, so he decided on something else.

For a princely sum offered by the clockmaker, the shaman agreed to cast a curse on his daughter's lover. The shaman wasn't to blame, but the person who paid the shaman is the guilty one. The shaman wasn't fully human and remained above the fray of humanity. The shaman did good and bad for the right price, which, more often than not, wasn't money but possessions.

The shaman agreed to cast a curse on the boy in exchange for an Olenberg clock. Time was immaterial to the shaman, but the shaman and the scavenging magpie liked shiny things.

Count Olenberg agreed to give away one clock to save a thousand others.

That night, the shaman conjured up a tonic and slipped it into the young man's supper which was cooling on the window-ledge; a fitting potion from one clockmaker to another, thinks the devious shaman.'"

'How convenient that his supper happens to be out in the open...on a window-ledge in a *forest*...full of *insects* and *birds* and *squirrels* 'n shit...'

'Just go on with the story, Jack. Nobody's asking you for an analysis.'

Jack clears his throat. "'*The following morning, the young man woke and screamed when he saw himself in the looking-glass. Unless the glass was lying, he had aged forty years overnight. A haggard, jittery old man with white wispy hair stared back at him with sagging jowls and bags under his watery eyes. He tried not to believe that it was him, but he did vaguely recognize himself.*

Unable to face his father, the young man met secretly in the forest with the clockmaker's daughter. She didn't recognize her lover at first, until the man convinced her by telling her secrets only they know...'"

'Naughty...' interjects Jack.

"'*The clockmaker's daughter broke down in sobbing tears, but vowed that she will always love him....'"*

At this point, Jack asks, 'How can a beautiful young maiden go on a date with her grandfather? Gross. Did Viagra exist in medieval Germany? Bet it did – some kind of dock-leaf growing wild.'

'Read on, whenever you're ready.'

"'The stricken man went back to his family mansion and told his father, who is Olenberg's enemy and competitor.

His father was livid with rage and desperate with pity that he would outlive his son which is a perversion of nature. He knew that his son suffered an ageing curse and vowed to find the culprit. The clockmaker promised to find his son's enemy if it took him the rest of his life and hired the services of a shaman known to the family and a counter-curse.'"

Jack breaks from the story once again. 'What's with all the shamans??'

Ruthy's expression warns him to continue.

"'The following day, Count Olenberg's daughter went to visit her cursed lover and was met by his weeping parents at the front door of their forest mansion.

With deepest regret, they informed the clockmaker's daughter that their son had died peacefully in his sleep at the ripe old age of ninety-seven. He had aged another three decades during the night. They went on to tell the heartbroken girl that a shaman known to the family had come to inspect the body and informed them that their son had indeed been the victim of an ageing curse, which is essence of time, a sprinkle of belladonna, a dose of bad weed...'"

Again, Jack breaks from the tale: 'Bad weed? There's nothing like bad weed. He should go back to his supplier and voice his opinion...'

Jack's reading the fairy-tale, more for Ruthy's benefit than his; his mind is solely focused on finding Olenberg's castle.

He reads on, not finding much humour in Ruthy's wine-rosy expression.

"'...and deadly mushrooms...'"

'Yeah, he definitely needs to have a word with his supplier...' utters Jack between lines.

"'...found on the dank, rotting forest floor. It had been the work of an experienced shaman unknown to them or their own shaman._

The clockmaker's daughter returned to her castle. She told her father that her lover had died of old age at twenty-eight.

She was stricken with grief and hid herself in the tower of the castle for days on end.

The days grew into weeks, and the weeks into months.

It broke her father's heart to hear his daughter crying with agony and loss. And very soon, he regretted what he had done.

He made a night-time visit to the shaman and explained that he had made a terrible mistake and should have never gotten in the way of true love. The shaman told the Count that it is too late. The man had died and no potion would bring him back. The curse might have been reversible if he was alive, but nothing or nobody, not even the mountain gods, can bring back a dead man once he crosses over.

Count Olenberg told the shaman that he was afraid that his daughter might do something terrible to herself, unable to live without her lover. The Count offered his castle to the shaman, but the shaman refused, saying that hate, jealousy, and sadness had sunk into the pores of the castle and he wanted nothing to do with it. Castle Olenberg was a place of bad luck.

A terrible argument broke out between the Count and the shaman. In a fit of rage, and silently afraid the shaman would take out a revenge curse, Olenberg unsheathed his sword and killed the shaman with one deadly blow, which sent his head spiralling into a boiling cauldron while the body was left standing for a few moments, almost in surprise.

The Count left, saddened that he couldn't bring the boy's life back, but happy that he had ended the shaman's.

As well as fearing for his daughter's life, he now feared for his own life. He knew that it was only a matter of time before his competitor discovered that it was he who had the shaman curse the boy. After all, their business *was time. His competitor would easily see that it had been Olenberg who had cast a fitting curse-potion.*

But for now, Count Olenberg was happy because the only curse he feared was that of the shaman, but he was no longer alive to cast the curse.

Time itself soon became the clockmaker's greatest enemy. The tick-tock of his clocks drove him to insanity and he dug an enormous hole at the bottom of the tower where he planned to bury his clocks forever. He didn't deserve to have anything that he loved anymore.

He dug all night and went to bed in the morning and slept the entire day.

That very night, Olenberg suffered a horrible nightmare. He was back at the house of rock with the shaman. He beheaded the shaman and the head plopped into a boiling cauldron, just as it had done in reality. But the shaman had already been brewing up a curse for another secret benefactor and the shaman's head was added to the curse in the cauldron. In a perversion of potions, the shaman's severed head raised out of the cauldron, all burnt and melting, half skull and gooey flesh."'

'Did you mention that this fairy-tale is for *kids*? This is one of those cool, twisted gothic fairy-tales...'

'Just finish the story, Jack.'

"'It looked at Olenberg with stark, lidless eyes. The hovering head, shrouded in steam, told him in a raspy voice that he had cursed himself – the deadliest of all curses: guilt. And for that reason, the shaman was happy in death...

Just as the Count started up in bed in a cold sweat, he heard the single scream. The scream belonged to his daughter and it was outside his bedroom window. But how was this possible? His bedroom was on the fourth floor of the castle. There was nothing but a sheer drop outside his window.

He fell out of bed and scrambled to the window and poked his head out. There, on the ground, was his daughter in the dress which her lover had once bought for her.

His only daughter had thrown herself from the tower.

The clockmaker recalled his nightmarish apparition: the worst of all curses – guilt. He had caused all of this.

He fell to the timber boards of his bedroom floor and heaved long, wailing doleful groans of sheer guilt before rushing downstairs, and out into the night in his robes and night-cap. He threw himself to his daughter's side; her porcelain face lit silver-pale in the moonlight.

He laid his head on her chest and wept and wept. But it was only when he could weep no more that he heard a thump...then another...and another. And now, Count Friedrich Olenberg heard the thump-thump of his daughter's heart.

He lifted his head and looked at her still face. It was a freezing night, but he saw to his utter disbelief, her breath fogging at her lips; faint, almost nothing, but she was breathing!

She was breathing because she had landed on the pile of fresh earth which Olenberg had dug to fill in his clock-grave. The soft earth had broken her fall. Or maybe his clocks had saved her life?

The clockmaker picked up his daughter and brought her inside and stayed by her for a week and a day until she woke.

When she came to, Count Olenberg confessed his crimes to his daughter but assured her that he had done it out of undiluted love.

His daughter locked herself in the dungeon of the castle, telling her father that he had taken her and her heart prisoner.

This, in turn, broke her father's heart, and he almost lost his mind.

Some lost hours and days after his seething daughter locked herself in the underbelly of the castle, Olenberg, who himself had aged a decade in just a few days with worry and guilt, suddenly snapped out of his temporary lunacy. He realized that his clocks had always been his salvation. They had provided him a good life for himself and his daughter. If he hadn't been digging that grave for his clocks that night, his daughter wouldn't have landed on that small mountain of fresh earth he had dug.

Clocks were his escape and it is in his clocks that Count Olenberg, clockmaker extraordinaire, would find redemption.

That night, he vowed to the souls of the young man and the shaman that he would invent a clock that would take everything back and make everything right..."

Jack lifts his eyes from the pages and glances at Ruthy. 'This is starting to get interesting...'

"'He promised himself that he would die helping his daughter and others; it's true what the shaman had said – the curse of guilt is far worse than any potion concocted by a shaman. To rid himself of the guilt that slowly ate into the marrow of his bones, Olenberg vowed never to think of himself again, but to think of others. He would sweat blood until he invented a clock which would alter time itself.

After many sleepless nights and hours of torturing himself, studying the stars and the rotation of the planets, Olenberg finally came up with a formula that would alter time. He discovered a tiny black hole in time and harnessed it. He then built an enormous grandfather clock around the black hole, big enough to allow a couple of people to stand inside its case.

A year after his daughter had taken to the dungeon to live, her father came to visit her. He told her that he had a surprise waiting for her in the tower.

His daughter grew angry and hissed at her father that she never wanted to see another clock in her life because time had been lost since her lover died to, ironically, time. The clockmaker told his daughter that this was a special clock.

Reluctantly, she left her prison dungeon and climbed to the top of the tower with her father. There, she saw the most splendid and enormous clock she had ever laid eyes on, standing tall above her on a pedestal. The clock was painted in ebony black and gold leaf with a splendid gold face and baby cherubs singing from the four corners. But this clock was different. Instead of having one face, it had several smaller faces, each face divided into fractions of time and degrees of the planet.

The Count told his daughter that he could send her back in time.

But Olenberg's daughter surprised him by telling him that the past had nothing for her now.

The past must stay in the past, she told him.'"

Again, Jack looks into Ruthy's wide pupils. Her expression waiting on his every word...

"'She climbed into the clock, and the Count locked her in. He turned forward the five hands of the clock which marked date, time, hours, minutes, seconds.

Inside the clock case, Olenberg's daughter began to feel dizzy before the floor seemingly fell out of the clock. She travelled through the black hole, from 1782 to...'"

'Well, where's the rest of it?'

'It ends there,' says Ruthy, quite drunk by now, but floating merrily.

Chapter 15

Dead End Room

Jack looks up at Ruthy. He notices that she's wiping her eyes with the heel of her hand. 'You're not *crying*? I don't read that bad, surely?'

'It's such a beautiful tale, Jack. It is so romantic... I just got caught up in it all over again.'

'Caught up in the *wine*, you mean. Don't think I didn't see you putting it away as I read. That poor waitress is earning her money today. And what do you mean with "all over again?" Have you read it?'

'Sure. I told you about it over the phone, remember? And I had a sneaky read after I bought it.'

'Hmm. I'm not sure romantic would be how I'd describe it: chopping off heads that land in boiling cauldrons, for example, that wouldn't be classed as romantic. Poisoning people is not romantic, if you *really* think about it.'

'*Gothic* romance, Jack. It's a sub-genre. It is a dark love-crime.'

Jack raises his eyebrows. 'I'll take your word for it.'

Jack rifles through the pages. He notices that the primitive illustrations are just the image of the man he saw from a distant camera lens on the *History Channel*, right down to the lime-green robe he appeared to be wearing. 'It doesn't add up.'

'What?'

'The old guy, Count Olenberg Junior, who I saw on that documentary was wearing the exact same clothes this guy in the illustration is wearing.'

'Don't forget that this clockmaker is a direct descendent of the original Friedrich Olenberg. He has been handed down the castle, the clocks, the whole shebang.'

'Yes, I get that, but handing down his *clothes*? Surely a member of the aristocracy can afford his own clothes? It's just odd.'

Ruthy downs her glass of wine and looks about for the nearest waiter or waitress. She speaks like a mystic clairvoyant for laughs. 'All will become clear when we meet the Count.'

Jack answers back, 'And that's another thing: apparently, he doesn't take kindly to strangers turning up on his doorstep.'

'Jack, I thought you might have figured out all of this before getting here.'

'No. My plan stretched as far as booking into this hotel. We need to come up with a plan.'

'Well, I think it's quite straightforward. We need to find his castle, which shouldn't be too difficult because it *is* a castle.'

Jack tells Ruthy that he did some online research, and the location of the castle is vague at best. 'Like there's a map of the Black Forest and then Castle Olenberg kind of like two-thirds of the way up, but that's about it.'

'We'll knock on his door. When he answers, we need to tell him that we are there to satisfy our curiosity and to put the death of Jeanie behind us. When he confirms that he *doesn't* have a time-machine, we can bid him good day and be on our merry way. Speaking of merry way...' Ruthy raises her glass to the nearest waitress.

'Hi, my name is Lina,' she announces with a beaming smile that *almost* reaches her eyes. 'Can I help you?'

'More wine, please.'

Lina disappears and appears seconds later and tops up Ruthy's glass. She offers wine to Jack, but he's adamant on staying clear-minded. Deep down, he feels Jeanie's presence, and he wouldn't want to be seen as enjoying himself; that's not why he's here. Jack is tempted to join Ruthy in her merriment, but he wants to stay focused on his objective. Then, once he has confirmed that time-travel only exists in fairy-tales, he'll kick back and let himself go.

Jack, Jack, Jackie, I'm part of you, darling. In the deep or shallow end of your mind, I hear it all in Dolby surround-sound. There's nothing you can hide from me now...nothing...nothing...

'This wine is good...I'm feeling a little tipsy.'

'Just because you're tipsy doesn't mean that it's good wine,' opines Jack. 'But I, however, am a wine connoisseur,' he jokes. 'I *know* this wine is a good wine because I've seen the price.'

Ruthy sniggers. 'Let's order dessert. Do you mind? Or is it too pricey?'

'Okay, but then we go on a scouting mission.'

'I think you'll have to carry me,' adding, '...if I fit through the door.' Ruthy's gawping at the Black Forest gateaux arriving at the next table.

She hails Lina once again and points to the Black Forest gateaux being placed on the table by them.

'Let's flesh out the locals and see what they know of Olenberg. That's how we're going to get to him.'

'If you say so.'

When the waitress delivers a pair of Black Forest gateaux to their table, Jack seizes the moment. 'That clock...'

'Yes?' says Lina with a graceful smile. 'It's an original Olenberg,' she repeats proudly and almost robotically, as Maritza had done before her. It's as if it was drilled into her and which she spouts out when the right button is pressed; tell-tale sign of dealing with tourists every day.

'Why is it here?'

'The Count donated it to our hotel. It had been in the castle for over two centuries, but the Count decided that it would look nice over our majestic fireplace.'

Thoughts begin racing through Jack's mind. 'Uh-huh. So, it's not one of the new Olenberg clocks?'

'No, no. We've got the real thing right here. If you want to see a similar one, you'll probably need a personal invitation to have tea at

Buckingham Palace. I believe they've also got an Olenberg just like this one – not that they appreciate it.' She says it with a mild hint of scorn.

'But why did Olenberg donate it to *this* hotel in particular?'

Lina's smile falters a fraction. She smoothly excuses herself, telling Jack and Ruthy that she is "required at another table" before wandering off into the middle of the bustling restaurant.

Jack follows her with his eyes...

She *doesn't* stop at any table, but instead, sails through the tables and disappears into the kitchen.

'Odd,' Jack comments. 'She was definitely dodging that question,' he observes.

'Who?'

'Was her name Grace? No, Lina...the waitress.'

Jack and Ruthy dig into their Black Forest gateaux and wolf it down.

After the delicious dessert, they make their way back to their rooms to freshen up.

But on the way out of the restaurant, Jack stops another busy waitress while Ruthy walks on ahead. Jack decides on a more direct approach to see where that gets him. 'Excuse me, could you tell me the way to Castle Olenberg?'

The waitress, name-tagged Romina, just stares at Jack with dramatically-raised eyebrows, as if asking: *are you for real??* She then answers back in German. It's easy to pick up from her gestures and the vague word 'English' that she probably hasn't understood his question.

Jack vaguely apologizes and lets Romina get on with her business.

But as they leave the restaurant, Jack spots something from the lobby that stops him in his tracks. He sidles up next to the restaurant entrance by a queue of guests waiting to be seated, and listens.

Meanwhile, Ruthy is looking at him with a ruddy, perplexed face from the lobby.

Jack re-joins Ruthy. 'So what do you make of that?' he asks her.

'Of what?'

'The waitress...'

'*Which* waitress? The one you were eyeing up? Marisa.'

'No, and I *wasn't* eyeing her up. It's MariTZa.'

Yes, you were...

'You just admitted it.'

'Why would you care anyway? I'm referring to the waitress we just spoke to – Romina, I think her name-tag said. The one who doesn't speak English when I asked her about Castle Olenberg...'

'And?'

Jack peers over his shoulder and points to the left, directly behind the main doors of the restaurant. 'Have a look...'

Ruthy backs up a few steps and loiters around the door for a moment when she clearly hears and sees the same waitress in full fluent English conversation with an American couple, recommending places to see in the local area.

She skips back to Jack. 'She speaks English!'

'*Only* when she likes the topic of conversation,' Jack answers cryptically. 'So why didn't she want to speak about Olenberg?'

Just as they are getting into the cage-lift, Jack spots something a little odd. Maybe he's wrong, but Jack could swear that he's just seen a queue of waiters with food on plates heading down to nowhere. And not just any food; Jack clearly sees steak on every plate being carried by five or six waiters and waitresses – *raw* steak.

'*What the fuck...*' mutters Jack, doing a double take. What are they keeping down there? What confuses him is that the first waiter is carrying a bottle of wine and a single glass. For a second, Jack thinks that they might be discarding leftover food, but this doesn't seem to be the case. The green sign on the wall with the illustration of a stick-man on some steps shows that the stairs downwards lead to an emergency exit.

He jams his hand in the door, levers it back, and slips out.

As it shuts quickly behind Jack, Ruthy calls from the rising lift, 'Where are you going *now?*'

'You go on up,' Jack yells back. 'Help yourself to the mini-bar. Keyword: *mini*. You've already drunk half the cellar.'

'Maybe it's not a bad idea,' answers Ruthy. 'I've got a headache coming on.'

Jack leaps the five steps down to the lobby and takes a right to the left of the restaurant entrance. Stealthily, he tip-toes down the hallway, maintaining enough distance behind the last waitress, who he discovers is Lina – the waitress who had played dumb when Jack had gotten up close and personal about Olenberg and went to hide in the kitchen.

He follows the queue of waiters down a myriad of narrow hallways and down more steps until he feels the freshness which tells him that they are well below street-level now. The concrete floor gives way to rough cobblestones, and the walls are no longer walls of a building, but that of rock. Suddenly, it's chilly.

Somewhere along the way, Jack realizes that the hotel had ended and a cave had begun.

Finally, the row of waiters stops outside a door at a dead-end. The waiter in front, carrying the bottle of wine and a glass, knocks, and they wait before being let inside. Each waiter disappears into the room with a plateful of *raw* steak.

A dead-end room? thinks Jack. *Odd.* He follows up the rear, looming as close as he possibly can but staying in the shadows.

Just before the door shuts, Jack has sufficient time to see the amazing decoration with rich velvet burgundy wallpaper and a shimmering chandelier. The room's hallway (what Jack can see of it) leaves Jack's room looking like a one-star hostel.

If he has paid for Hotel Bladd's full package deal, then how much has this guest paid? And *who* is this guest? More importantly, what kind of guest eats twenty raw steaks with a bottle of good wine? Jack had heard about people occasionally eating raw meat for its natural properties, but this seems to be leaning more towards cannibalism.

As Jack's eyes adjust to the poor light, he sees that there's something not quite right about the dead-end. The wall, which is the end of the tunnel, vaguely reflects the lighting in the hallway. As if it were made of plastic. It reminds Jack of the walls at Disneyland Paris; from a distance they look real, but home in a little closer and a fibre-glass sheen is evident...

The door of the room suddenly clicks open...

Jack flees back down the hallway, running like the clappers, but trying his best to keep light-footed, almost to float if he can.

At the top of the stairs he stops, peers around the corner into the lobby to see if anybody sees him. When the coast is clear, he appears nonchalantly, then mills around as if *nothing* has just happened, looking at everything and nothing while he waits for the waiters and waitresses to return.

After a short wait, they finally appear at the top of the emergency exit stairs. And speaking of emergency exit, Jack doesn't see one.

Chapter 16

Emergency Exit

In the hallway, Jack knocks on the door of room 2204. Ruthy doesn't answer, so he knocks again...and then again.

Jack looks out one of the many windows lining the second floor while he waits for Ruthy to answer. He realizes that dusk has fallen outside. It gets dark in the Black Forest faster and earlier than Old Castle. They've already wasted most of today, Jack thinks a little ashamedly, reading fairy-tales and stuffing themselves. They need to get out on the streets of Bladd, suss it out, and see if they can get directions to Castle Olenberg and be done with this.

Ruthy must be in the shower, thinks Jack, so takes this opportunity to go back to his room and slip a few packets of biscuits and bottles of water from the mini-bar into a small backpack he had brought along for such excursions.

Again, he goes outside and knocks on Ruthy's door.

A voice yells from inside. 'Can't you see it says *do not disturb?!* You are *disturbing*. Now fuck off 'n die, please. Thank you.'

Jack can't believe that this is Ruthy saying these words, but it *is* her voice and it sounds slurred.

He puts his ear to the door. He's sure that he hears Ruthy sobbing. 'Ruthy, it's Jack. What's the matter?'

'Oh, Jack. I...I thought it was the, uh, cleaning service.'

'Ruthy, I almost fucked off 'n died,' jokes Jack, but Ruthy continues crying. 'C'mon, let me in.'

There's silence for a moment before Jack hears her feet pad along the carpet towards the door.

She opens up and Jack's taken aback at the state of her puffy red face. Her Mohawk is all gone to hell. Jack had once seen a half-drowned rat down by the river Arra in Old Castle, and Ruthy bares a vague resemblance to said rat. He quickly deduces that it might not be the best time to compare her to a pathetic, soggy rat.

Ruthy throws herself at Jack, and he has no choice but to put his arms around her to save her from falling down his front. She cries on his shoulder as Jack spots, over her shoulder, the open mini-fridge. The stench of alcohol from Ruthy's breath confirms his suspicions.

'How long have I been *gone?*' he asks. 'Surely I haven't been gone that long.'

'I just had a little tipple – purely medicinal, of course.'

Jack then clocks the pile of empty mini bottles strewn around her bed and bedside locker. 'A little tipple from *twenty* different bottles? Don't tell me you drank all those in the short time I was gone? Y'know when I said *keyword: mini*, I kind of meant it in a *mini* way.'

Ruthy looks distraught and not in any humour. 'Jack I gulped the whole lot down to forget...to *forget*, Jack.'

Jack's confused. 'To forget me? Or just to forget?'

Ruthy's blurry eyes study Jack for a moment.

'Forget what?'

'My past.'

'Have you killed somebody?' quips Jack, as usual not learning that the situation has gone beyond anything that can be salvaged with humour.

Ruthy's response shocks him, and he's beginning to regret ever asking the question.

'Yes, I have.'

'Uh-huh. Do you mind if I ask *who* you killed? Minor detail...'

Ruthy doesn't answer for a moment but just clings onto Jack as if she were hanging off a cliff-face. 'I killed Jeanie, and I killed a part of you...and maybe I'm killing us, too.'

Jack feels that same rush of anger and confusion that grabs him when Jeanie is mentioned. But he shouldn't pay much heed to Ruthy; she's drunk. 'Killing a lot of birds with one stone, Ruthy. Hmm?'

He pries her from his shoulders and looks into her blood-shot, droopy eyes. 'You didn't kill anyone. A faulty rollercoaster killed Jeanie, and as a direct consequence of the accident, my heart stopped beating. Get that into your head and stop this self-pity because it doesn't suit you.'

'Time stopped there.'

'No,' says Jack. '...just my heart and the bit of Jeanie around her heart.' *How strange,* Jack ponders. *How beautifully weird...*

'Don't you see, Jack? Time *did* stop there.'

'I don't know what you're talking about.'

'I've done a terrible thing; I could've stopped it.'

'No you couldn't. How would you stop a rollercoaster travelling at I-don't-know miles per hour?'

Ruthy garbles, 'You don't understand... I realize now that all of this is a mistake...'

'I *understand* more than you think, Ruthy. And none of this is a mistake. All of this is supposed to happen.'

'Yes, you've got that part right.'

Jack doesn't have time for this cryptic self-indulgence. He wants to get out of this stale room. Jack has only a few days to find Olenberg, but how can he leave Ruthy in this state?

He takes her by the hand and leads her to her bed. He lays her down and tucks her up under the blankets, fully-clothed, and sits by her.

She begins to utter slurred, sleepy words that are difficult to grasp.

'Jack, I knew...'

'Shush, get some sleep. You'll feel better when you wake up. That's a lie; you'll have one hell of a hangover after all that vodka and gin.'

'And whiskey... Jack, is it possible to love two people at the same time?'

'Sounds like a line from a film. I think one must prioritize their love.'

Ruthy answers back, 'You should work in administration, Jack. Wife: File 1. Bit on the side: File 2. Crush: File 3. And...' And the rest of Ruthy's sentence is lost to slumber.

The stress of the trip has caught up on Jack, and he lays in the bed next to Ruthy, above the covers, crossing no imaginary lines. Jeanie's not far; she's here right now, forever-thumping, with them.

Jack wakes, disorientated.

To his right, Ruthy is sleeping off her hangover. She seems peaceful enough.

His intention, before he nodded off, was to do some research around town, see if anybody can tell him anything about Olenberg or the whereabouts of his castle. He checks his watch and sees that it's four in the morning. Three more hours sleep will hit the spot. So, Jack creeps from the bed and leaves room 2204.

He looks up and down the hallway. It is very quiet, almost eerie, not a sound. He goes to reach for his room-card when he realizes that he has left it in his room. He'd been so excited about the prospect of tracking down Castle Olenberg that he left it in the room when he had gone to knock on Ruthy's door again.

Having no other choice, he takes himself down to the lobby.

When he gets there, he sees that the night-shift receptionist is on duty. Feeling a little stupid and incredibly tired, he approaches and explains to the man behind the desk that he has left his card in his room.

The receptionist (Tony by his name-tag) gives him that same Stepford smile everybody else has given him at the hotel. Tony happily assures him that it happens every day (and every night) and hands Jack a new card with Bladd's winning smile of the month. Just for the fun of it, Jack decides to see just how long that smile lasts before it cracks.

'Excuse me, we are new to the area and are looking for some interesting places to see. Can you recommend any?'

'Oh yes,' Tony jumps in. 'The Black Forest is teeming with all sorts of interesting sights.' Tony then goes on to tell Jack, in his strong German accent, about the myriad of tourist attractions in the local vicinity and as Jack had suspected, Castle Olenberg *isn't* on his bucket list.

'How about Castle Olenberg?'

Bang!

There goes the smile... Adios, smile!

A tiny flicker of a hairline crack, but it *does* crack. 'I'm afraid Castle Olenberg isn't open to the public – not that I know where it is. I believe Count Olenberg is a very private individual and wants to keep it that way.'

'Uh-huh. So you don't know where it is?'

Tony comes over all vague and shakes his head, gazing through his computer's screen and obviously lying through his shiny white teeth. 'If you are interested in Olenberg clocks, there is one in the restaurant. It is closed now, but you can see it tomorrow morning for breakfast. Breakfast times are from...'

But Jack isn't interested in breakfast times, which is obviously just a detour from the prickly topic of all things Olenberg. Jack cuts him short. 'Why *is* the clock here, as a matter of interest?'

Tony chuckles, a little too hysterically for Jack's comfort. 'You'll have to ask a local historian about that, I'm afraid. Personally, I have no interest in clocks. Even if we don't have a clock, we're *all on* the clock – from clocking in and out at work, to clocking in and out of this world.'

'That's true,' admits Jack but not at all surprised that Tony surprisingly knows zilch about the history of the clock.

At this point in the conversation, a smartly-dressed woman enters Reception, hovers around, and looks at the screen in front of Tony, muttering something in discreet German. She then disappears again without acknowledging Jack. But Jack *does* clock her name-tag: Adele, and she happens to be the hotel manager, if her name-tag is to be believed.

Tony cuts the conversation short by suddenly giving Jack the cold shoulder. 'Have a good night, sir.' Again, he flashes that celestial smile of his, prompting Jack to make a note of looking into whitening his teeth when he gets back to Old Castle – Jack drinks far too much tea.

Jack, taking this as his cue, moves away from the desk.

He's just about to climb the set of steps to the lift when he spots the manager briefly look over her shoulder and descending the same set of steps which boast an emergency exit.

Too excited and nosey to sleep now, Jack swivels on his heels and tails the hotel manager. He's just about to go down the steps when two burly workers appear from somewhere to the left of the lobby, and they, too, follow the manager. These two individuals are security; Jack has no doubt. It's the first time that he has seen security at the hotel.

Jack hangs back a minute before tip-toeing down the stairwell after them. He follows the voices ahead. The further down he goes, the cooler it gets, until he is once again in the same subterranean corridor he had been in a few hours previous.

He turns the last bend and stops.

The lighting is poor down here, but what he sees is not possible to mistake...or maybe just not possible. If his eyes aren't deceiving him, somebody has just come from the Dead End room and has entered through a door in the dead-end itself – the Disneyland dead-end.

Jack had been right.

Unable to focus in on what exactly he is witnessing, Jack is left with the first and last impression of somebody disappearing through a door in the Undead end held open by the hotel manager, Adele. His view is obscured by the burly guards and the feeble lighting.

Something else also disappears through the door...an *animal* of some kind, is all Jack sees. Something that moves along at hip-height of the individual who went through the door. A Saint Bernard dog is the only thing Jack can come up with, or another breed of similar giant size.

Jack cannot understand what he's looking at. How bizarre! Just above them is a building full of sleeping tourists, which begs Jack to have the opinion that they are *meant* to be sleeping. In other words, this little *Elvis-has-left-the-building* moment is *meant* to be done in the shadow of night. Not that it's possible down here to know whether it is night or day. And that doesn't really matter either because tourists don't come down here at any time of the day or night. Who goes down dark stairways marked Emergency Exit? So, Jack concludes this *is* indeed an emergency exit, but for who?

Chapter 17

Change of Heart

'Ruthy, it gives the term *Emergency Exit* a whole new meaning.' says Jack over a breakfast of frankfurters, hash browns, fried eggs, beans, tomatoes, and bacon. 'It's clever because the last place people go to are emergency exits...funnily enough. I felt like I was a character in a mystery novel...or a fairy-tale.'

Jack had just told Ruthy the sequence of events that happened overnight while she slept off her hangover. There has been no mention of Ruthy's drunken heart-to-heart with Jack.

Hotel Bladd's restaurant is alive with guests this Wednesday morning, the 2nd of March. The open fireplace is already ablaze, and everything is so cosy and happy and picture-perfect.

'But what about the dark underbelly of this prestigious hotel?' Jack contemplates, devouring a hash brown. 'Nobody knows or suspects that there's a mystery guest staying somewhere right below our feet.'

Ruthy isn't in much form to talk. She gazes at him blearily. 'Jack, I'm still suffering from my mini-fridge binge, but didn't you hear?'

'Hear what?'

'An important politician has been staying at the hotel right under our noses...literally.' She gazes tiredly at Jack from across the table and gobbles down a frankfurter. 'I can normally smell a politician a mile off because they tend to stink, but this slimy dog eluded me. He's the one you saw in the VIP room.'

'The Dead End room, you mean; strangest VIP room I've *ever* seen.' But Ruthy's news does disappoint Jack. 'Where did you hear that?'

As far as Jack's aware, Ruthy hasn't been out of her room since he had seen her nod off to sleep last night. Or has she? Jack hadn't heard any mention of this yesterday, and he had been with Ruthy all the time. 'When did you hear about this?'

'I heard the cleaners talking about it in the hallway this morning. If you want to know what's *really* going on in a hotel, and not the fake guest bullshit, then listen in on the cleaners.'

'Since when do you speak German?'

'I speak enough to understand.'

This is the first time Jack knows this. 'So why haven't you been practicing?'

'We haven't been spoken to in German...'

It's true, realizes Jack, *almost*. 'What about that waitress that got all shifty with me and spat something in German when I asked her the way to Olenberg Castle?'

'I didn't hear her. I was in the lobby when you were talking to her. We've been on the tourist trail since we got here, Jack, and everybody tends to fall into English to avoid wasting time. Look, let's just enjoy our time here and go home. How about that? Let's forget about Olenberg because *none* of it is true, Jack. Yes, he probably does exist, and he does make clocks and he is a reclusive Count, but *who* cares? Let's be honest with ourselves: there is *no* time-machine. Don't you think this trip has already been therapy enough? We haven't stopped talking about Jeanie. Learn to accept her parting gift and move on...'

Jack's taken aback by Ruthy's sudden sway of opinion. 'Why the change of heart? Pun unintended.'

'Jack, I don't think we were meant to find him *or* Jeanie. I think Olenberg was a diversion to bring us together and get Jeanie off our chests, so to speak. I think this,' she indicates at everything, '*this* is our getaway from Jeanieland. This is as good as it gets, Jack.'

Jack reflects on Ruthy's words. He knows, deep down, in his rented heart, that Ruthy is right in a way. He sighs.

'Jack, give up the ghost...'

Jack seriously mulls this over. 'I can't, Ruthy. If I travel to Mars, I cannot put distance between myself and Jeanie's heart. I'm adamant that this is something I have to do. I'm going to find the Count and ask him to his face if he has a time-machine and when he *laughs* in my face, I'll take that as a *no* and be on my merry way. The doubt will always be there if I don't confront him.'

'What if he has?'

'Hmm?'

'What if he has a time-machine? Then what?'

'Then I go back in time and start all over. Like the way I made that sound so simple? Ruthy, I bought return tickets, so let that clue you in on how much I believe in time-travel.'

'Are you sure it works like that?'

'What do you mean?'

'Look, let's say you do go back in time...'

'I'm only entertaining you because you're hungover and your Mohawk is crestfallen.' He points up at it; it really is crestfallen.

'Will you know that you've gone back in time if you go back in time? Or will it be like a déjà vu, like you get this feeling that all of this has happened before, but you're not conscious to the fact that you have travelled back in time? As a consequence, you will live Jeanie's death twice?'

'Deep,' is all Jack can say. 'I'd hate to see you without a hangover...' he jokes, but this notion frankly scares Jack. Ruthy's words turn his world upside-down. He hadn't thought it through, and Ruthy knows this by his reaction.

'If you don't realize that you've gone back in time, you're going to get on that rollercoaster without knowing the horrible truth.'

'Where are you going with this? Not to the past, that's for sure.' Jack seriously weighs up what he's about to say next. 'Ruthy, it's like this: I *won't* find out until I do it. Really, I cannot lose.'

'You can lose Jeanie...*again*.'

Jack looks at his delicious fry-up but has completely lost his appetite.

'All I'm saying is that just because you go back in time, Jack, doesn't mean that time can be altered. See what I'm saying? It's a period of time which you have to re-live and the consequences just might be the same whether you go back in time or not. All of this boils down to fate, Jack. Fate.'

'It's a gamble, but it's a gamble I'm willing to take. Going by what you're saying – fate – if I go back in time, I'll re-live what has already happened and be oblivious that I've ever lived it twice. So, don't you see, if I don't do this, I'll never know if I can change the past or not. Plus, if I have to go through it again, I'll be unaware because I won't be conscious of having previously lived the same events.'

Jack takes a deep breath. All of this heavy thinking has turned him right off his frankfurters.

'You're playing with hearts, Jack. Hearts Anonymous is what I'm going to call this chapter of my life because there's always one other heart we don't know about...'

'Sounds like a magazine column for the lonely.'

She chortles and chokes on some black pudding.

Jack catches her eye. 'There's so many things I never knew about you... I'm only finding out about you now.' Why he should say this now is beyond him; suffice to say that it feels right.

'See, Jack?'

'What?'

'*This* is how we get over Jeanie. Discover the things we never knew about each other.'

Jack's not sure he wants to continue this conversation. She's leading him somewhere with this, and it's not down the garden path. He suddenly finds himself uncomfortable with the topic of conversation and decides to gulp down the last of his tea dregs. 'Coming?'

'Where?'

'To follow the Yellow Brick Road. Where do you think? To find Olenberg...'

'You're wasting your time. They're not going to tell you.'

'We'll hit all the local shops and stalls. One of them will surely know something.'

'I guess I'll just tag along.'

Jack cannot fathom it. What's with the sudden change? 'C'mon, what happened to the Ruthy who rang me that night, telling me the fairy-tale about Olenberg's ancestors? You were as excited as I was.'

'Watching copulating dung-beetles is exciting if you drink enough Red Bull, Jack.'

Chapter 18

Urchin at the Cemetery

Jack and Ruthy visit a total of eighteen premises during the day in the fairy-tale town of Bladd, from year-round Christmas shops to frankfurter stalls.

Jack witnesses the same sequence of events each time: locals are very quick to offer their products in fluent English with Bladd's award-winning smile...but when Olenberg is mentioned, people suddenly forget how to speak English and shrivel back into their shells. Bladd lives on tourism, yet, locals become incredibly vague when hearing that name *Olenberg*, just as the staff at Hotel Bladd had done before them. It seems as if everybody has been sworn to secrecy in Bladd, not unlike citizens living in a dictatorship who are afraid to speak out. Bladd, Jack has decided, is a sinister place. Yes, it is a quaint, fairy-tale town with beautifully coloured facades, but inside the houses there is a secret, he's sure of that.

By four o'clock, the sun is beginning to set. Bladd falls into shadows once again and a mist descends over the hillside town.

Jack realizes that they have walked further than they had first thought. They have arrived to the outskirts of town, and Jack is surprised to find the old walls of an enormous, ancient cemetery. Inside the gates, lop-sided headstones fade into the darkness.

Ruthy asks, 'Do you mind if we go in?'

'Um, graveyards give me the creeps...especially on a foggy evening like this.'

As usual, Ruthy doesn't listen to Jack. She strides up to the large main gates and checks the time-table. 'It doesn't close until eight p.m. C'mon, there's no more we can do today. Maybe a *ghost* might give us the lead on Olenberg,' she jokes, showing no intention of ever finding Count Friedrich Olenberg.

At the rate they are going, Jack thinks this might be a possibility. For the first time since they have arrived, Jack feels himself waning as his hopes begin to go down with the sun. Ruthy has all but abandoned the idea of ever finding Olenberg, and she's just tagging along at this stage. Jack cannot understand her change in attitude.

'Miss, how about a nice wreath for your lost loved one?'

Ruthy whirls around to see a boy sitting on a small three-legged wooden stool with various plastic flower-wreaths displayed at his feet; the cheap papery-type found in Chinese bazaars and the kind of flowers that would be an insult to leave at the side of the deceased. Ruthy hadn't seen the boy in the shadows of the trees. She pauses for a moment and stares hard at the kid, so intense that even Jack notices.

'What's wrong?' he asks.

Ruthy hesitates. 'Nothing. He just scared me, that's all.'

Jack sees that he's more of an urchin; small, scrawny, weak, and perhaps a tad grubby or maybe it's just the dimness of dusk.

'Excuse me?' Ruthy had heard him the first time, but his striking presence seems to have caught her off-guard.

'Do you want to buy a wreath of flowers for somebody inside the wall? High quality, life-like flowers that will last forever.' He flicks a thumb over his shoulder at the tall sandstone wall of the cemetery. The way the kid says '...inside the wall' clearly marks the living from the non-living.

'No, thanks.,' Ruthy answers politely. 'We're just, um, visiting.'

'Everybody's *just* visiting,' the child answers back with a vague shrug. 'Half of that lot in there say that...' Again, he gestures over his shoulder at the cemetery.

What an odd sense of humour the kid has, thinks Jack. *He should be at home doing his homework or kicking a ball with other kids his age. There's something odd about the child.*

Ruthy digs in her pocket and hands him a ten-euro note.

His watery eyes widen, and he gleams at her with a mouthful of teeth not unlike the crooked nature of the old cemetery.

'Why are you here at this time of night?' she probes.

'I need to make some money for the family.'

'What's your name?'

'Johann...'

'Johann,' says Jack, 'do you go to school?'

'I sell wreaths.'

'Oh.' Jack throws Ruthy an *Ask a stupid question* look...

Ruthy looks at Jack and half mutters, 'I've a good mind to call Child Services.'

The more his eyes become accustomed to the low light, the more Jack sees that this pale child looks as if he hasn't had a bath for months, and his tousled hair has never seen a comb.

There is something odd about the whole situation, ponders Jack, not quite able to figure out the element of oddness.

Ruthy says, 'Where are your parents?'

The boy pauses. 'I don't have parents anymore.'

Jack and Ruthy both look through the graveyard gates and decide that it would be rude to ask what they think happened to Johann's parents.

'So who minds you?'

'I mind myself.'

So what family is he talking about? Jack asks himself.

Ruthy looks at Jack. 'Jack, this isn't right.' She asks Johann his age.

'Nine,' he answers back, 'eighteenth of August...'

Jack prompts, 'Two thousand and six...' doing the math.

'I always forget the year,' the boy giggles.

Jack is astounded by the boy's level of English.

Jack asks, 'Where did you learn English?' beginning to formulate a plan in his head.

The boy shrugs. 'Just listening. Sometimes, the hotel in the town square leaves out a hot cocoa for me. I sit down in the restaurant – where people can't see me – and I listen in on their conversations. It's free. I'm happy it's free because I spend most of the money I earn from the flowers on gummy bears and lemon drops.'

That explains the mouth of rotten teeth, Jack wants to add, out of pity rather than sarcasm.

By now, Ruthy's got tears in her eyes. 'But where do you live? Who minds you? You're just a little kid...'

'I live here.' Johann makes a general sweep of the place.

Jack and Ruthy look around. At first they don't see a house, but then Jack spots windows in the wall of the cemetery. As his eyes adjust, he realizes that the wall of the cemetery is, in fact, a row of decrepit, rickety-roved houses. Below these windows, on the first floor, is a row of tombs.

Jack gazes in amazement at the houses, which are really second-floor flats, with the first floor being sarcophaguses.

'The only advantage here is that there won't be much noise from downstairs,' says Jack, half joking, half in earnest. 'Talk about taking advantage of space... Don't know if I'd fancy living in a cemetery.'

'I bet it's cool.' Ruthy's eyes are back on Johann. 'So does your family think it's cool too, Johann?'

She's trying to get friendly with him to extract more information, thinks Jack.

'Yes. Cool.'

'Uh-huh.' Jack's not convinced; he's just told them that he has no family. There's something missing in the equation. The kid looks as if he's been here all his life selling flowers to grave-visitors. But, since they've gotten here, nobody has come to visit the cemetery.

Ruthy turns back to Jack and lip-synchs: 'This isn't right...'

Jack's not sure if she means it's not right because no nine year-old child should be out on a chilly night wearing next to nothing, selling wreaths to nobody, *or* that the whole situation is strange. He agrees with both, but the second option is a definite...

Suddenly, Jack has an idea. 'Um, Johann. Have you heard of Count Olenberg?'

The hardy-living boy, who appears a vagrant, pretends not to have heard Jack, but busies himself with his wreaths and tends to his little make-shift wreath stall.

Jack shares a knowing glance with Ruthy and nods a *here we go again*... They've seen this same reaction over a dozen times already today; they're used to it by now.

'I bet you know lots of places where people *never* go.' Jack has a plan... He doesn't know much about kids, but he knows reverse psychology.

Johann answers readily, 'I know this place *better* than anybody.'

Ruthy lip-synchs: *This kid's freaking me out, Jack.* She whispers, 'Let's go back to the hotel. C'mon, this is getting creepy.'

Jack tells Ruthy to wait up a minute and turns back to the boy. 'I bet I know this place better than you.' Jack tries taunting the boy. 'I *know* where the castle is. I asked you to see if *you* know.'

'Of course I know. Everybody knows where, um...' The boy stops speaking, realizing that he's already said too much. 'I don't know where the castle is...'

Ruthy steps in to stop his squirming. 'That's fine, Johann. We believe you.'

Jack gawks at the back of Ruthy's head. 'We *do*??' He stares at her with a searching look. *Surely* she knows what he's up to – they've just found their best lead to Olenberg!

Ruthy turns back to Jack and winks, telling Jack that she's got something else up her sleeve. But when she focuses back on the boy, he is already disappearing into the shadows.

'*Yoo-hoo!*' he shouts from the darkness. 'Come and get *meee!*'

'Ruthy! Why did you let him get away? I had him on the ropes. Jesus! He was on the brink of telling us where Olenberg is!'

'Jack, we were never meant to find Olenberg...'

'Yes, we *were!*' Jack's fuming. 'Let's follow him!' he suggests, all excited now. 'Look at him! He *wants* us to follow him!'

'*Now, Jack??* Call me crazy, but I'm not so keen on the idea of being led into the Black Forest at night by an undernourished, grubby kid with *no* light whatsoever. He's faking it, Jack. I'm *not* following him!' She waves him in the direction of the dark woods. 'Be my guest.' Ruthy makes a point of sitting down at the boy's makeshift stall. 'The whole thing is too creepy for me, Jack.' Grimly, she adds, 'This is the Black Forest; we don't need it any blacker than it already is.'

'Suit yourself...' Jack trots after the boy yelling out from the trees, giving clues to his whereabouts. 'You stay here and sell wreaths,' says Jack. 'Put one on Jeanie's *grave* while you're at it...'

From her vantage point, Ruthy watches Jack wander off into the woods where the orange sodium of the streetlights no longer reaches. She swears and curses to whoever and whatever will listen. She *knows* she has to follow Jack; he's only going to get himself into trouble. The mischievous Johann, might lead him astray and Jack is a good guy, but gullible at the same time, especially when he has been blinded by excitement. Ruthy *knows* what he's like. Plus, she doesn't like the idea of being around this unnerving place on her own.

She gets up from the improvised stall and skips after Jack. 'Wait up!'

When she catches up with him, Jack's happy to see her.

'There's something not right about that kid, Jack. He was just sitting there in the dark. Think about it. Who visits graveyards when it's dark? *Fucking* lunatics, Jack, with a capital F. I'm beginning to not enjoy this trip anymore. Why are we even following this little freak?' Ruthy spikes her Mohawk nervously with the tips of her fingers. 'We came here to put Jeanie to bed...to read her this – *our* – one last fairy-tale.'

This line melts Jack's heart right there; he knows she's right. He feels the anger ebb away.

'It's dark,' says Ruthy simply and finally.

Jack looks about him and sighs deeply. 'I had noticed.' He's well aware that they're definitely not prepared to hike into the Black Forest. What water they had in their backpacks has been drunk long ago, along with the mini-bar snacks which they had already eaten before they had come across the graveyard.

'I don't have any other bargaining chips,' Ruthy concedes, 'And speaking of chips – I'm *starving*.'

'Johann!' Jack suddenly calls out in desperation, scaring the wits out of Ruthy. 'Come back!'

They listen to the wind siphoning through the black firs.

'Johann?!'

'He's gone, Jack, he's gone. The kid will be here again tomorrow. We can come back when it's bright.' She listens to the night. 'All I can hear is my heart pumping in my ears, Jack.'

'Mine too – and Jeanie's.'

Jack walks off despondently, leaving Ruthy behind him.

She catches up with him. 'Hold my hand...'

Jack stops and turns. He can just about make out Ruthy's Mohawk in the blackness.

'Please, hold my hand. I can't see a *fucking* thing...Be a gentleman.'

'I can see your Mohawk. Do you have to swear so much?'

'I tend to swear when I'm at my wit's end, Jack. It's a nervous reflux, and there's nothing I can do about it.'

'Reflex...'

'No, reflux; I get indigestion, too. Now, please hold my hand and get me out of here.' She shivers involuntarily.

Jack didn't really care about Ruthy's profanities; he had asked her the question in some kind of attempt at offsetting her question. Holding Ruthy's hand now becomes one more awkward dilemma; a series of many that he's found on this trip. If asked why awkward, Jack might draw a blank, but maybe he's realizing that he has some kind of feelings for Ruthy, over and beyond the call of duty, as it were. On one hand, Jack wants to have the chance to help a pretty maiden in distress (what man wouldn't), but is he being loyal to the memory of Jeanie? He feels that if he takes Ruthy's hand now, then he would be turning his back on his fiancée. He has already felt guilty about taking her hand during the bumpy landing in Stuttgart.

I'm dead, Jack, dead. As dead as Clara the crow, stiff and stuffed on an imaginary pedestal...

Jack hears Jeanie's voice, but she's living inside him and giving him *life*. So what does that mean? Jack suddenly finds himself having an existential debate with himself on Wednesday night in the Black Forest on the 2nd of March, 2016.

Living is for the living, Jackie...

The more Jack mulls it over...

'Are you *going* to take my hand or do I have to break my perfect nose by walking into a *tree?!*'

...the more he feels that Jeanie would agree to him holding her best friend's hand rather than anybody else's.

He turns back and holds out his arm. In the darkness, he feels Ruthy's cold hand grasp his own and squeeze it.

They lead each other out of the border of the shady woods, back into the large parking area outside the cemetery. They find their bearings and retreat back through the winding, narrow streets of Bladd.

Jack, feeling that they are no longer lost, tries to let go of Ruthy's hand, but she's not inclined to let go. It feels comforting, yet not right. He plans how to take his hand from hers without wanting to make it seem too brusque; maybe check his pockets for something. But when he tries to ease his hand from hers, she locks down again.

They walk on, happily and silently getting lost among the snaking streets, but it is okay; it's *all* okay because they've got each other. The whole night becomes a surreal labyrinth. She eases her grip on Jack's hand, but Jack leaves his hand in hers because Ruthy is all that is left of a world he once knew. A wave of irrational fear ripples through him, prickling the hairs on his arms and nape of his neck. He shivers.

'What is it, Jack of Hearts?' asks Ruthy.

The way she asks Jack makes him think that Ruthy already knows. 'Somebody just walked over my grave...'

'Maybe it was Jeanie.'

Jeanie's heart goes *rat-a-tat-tat* in his chest, lending him the gentle reminder that she's always nearby.

They flash each other a rather shy smile, then break eye-contact.

Soon, they come out in a large opening, which they realize is the warm surroundings of the town square. Had they wanted to get lost in these timeless streets? Had they known all along how to get back to the hotel, but they had both wanted to be lost? At some point, Jack felt that Ruthy certainly knew the way home, but was prolonging the surreal, hand-in-hand, timeless walk. Maybe *he* had known too...

Only at the doors of the hotel do they realize that they're still holding hands.

'Why did you call me Jack of Hearts?'

'Because you like to gamble girls' hearts and play them close to your chest.'

What a bizarre thing to say. Jack's not sure if he likes his new nickname or the dark metaphor. He's not gambling anyone; the only gamble here is this trip.

Ruthy sets her hand free of Jack's. 'Don't look so shocked – it's a compliment.'

'Don't make light of what happened, Ruthy. Don't compare fancying somebody to a massive heart operation. A heart can be shared in many ways.'

Ruthy looks hurt. 'A life-time of love *isn't* fancying somebody, Jack.'

She dismisses Jack and climbs up the stone steps of the hotel, leaving him to his blurry thoughts as the first flurry of snow falls silently down around him.

He cannot shake the feeling that he's being watched. He had the same feeling as they meandered through Bladd's little tunnels and snaking, cobbled streets.

Giving one last glance over his shoulder, Jack ascends the steps, is greeted by the doorman's kick-ass smile-of-the-month which doesn't reach his eyes.

There's no sign of Ruthy by the time he gets up to his room. She has already closed her door in some kind of silent protest.

Better leave her to her thoughts, Jack decides, for the worst...

Chapter 19

Jack of Hearts

Your body isn't really yours, Jackie boy. Your body is mine, and I'm claiming squatter's rights. You're just the face, my friend. What counts is inside, and it's all me, Honey, 24-7. It's all me because you failed to save me, Jack. Now you're paying the price for your tardy response to that fast-approaching branch that just happened to snap my neck. You have my heart, but c'mon, let's face it; we both know that it is me who has got you. I'm growing inside you, Dear, like cancer, I'm spreading, spreading until there's nothing left of poor little Jackie. I am your hijacker. I will eat my way out and swallow you whole, my love...I am your praying mantis – you better pray, darlin'...

The following morning, Jack wakes abruptly from a disquieting dream with tears in his eyes.

Jack 'n Jeanie up a tree, k-i-s-s-i-n-g. First comes love, then comes carnage, here comes what's left of Jeanie wrapped in a bandage...

He still hears Jeanie's mocking voice in his head as he struggles to break free of nightmare gravity. Jeanie is the main actress on the nightmare stage, and she is busy telling Jack some home truths...or is it his conscience posing as a nightmare? Her heart; her *bloody* pumping organ has become a dark obsession, no doubt. That last line crawls under Jack's skin and stays there like a Demodex mite, leaving a plethora of haunting and horrid images of something obscene, pumping beneath a bloodied gauze.

Climbing out of bed, Jack douses his face in cold water to shake himself free of the bad dream. He looks at himself in the mirror and for a microscopic second, sees Jeanie staring back at him; pastel shades of deathly blanche, bordering on parchment-yellow.

He quickly switches off the en-suite light and traipses across to the window in a search for normality. He opens back the curtains and is flabbergasted to see the town square covered beneath a meter-thick blanket of powdery snow. The fountain in the centre of the town-square has turned to a semi-sculpted iced work-of-art.

Jack takes a few photos of the scenery outside his window with his phone, makes a cup of weak hotel tea, and then logs onto the hotel's Wi-Fi to do more research on the elusive Count Olenberg.

But as he flicks from webpage to webpage on his phone, he cannot get Ruthy's echoing words out of his mind: *you like to gamble girls' hearts...*

Then come 'Jeanie's' words again, tapping inside his temples: *I am your praying mantis – you better pray...*

Is there a hidden message in there? No, Jack. It's a flat-out threat. The more Jack thinks about Ruthy's new nickname for him, Jack of Hearts, the less he likes it. It leaves an acidic aftertaste on the palate. She even seems to be belittling the accident and, more so, the inextricable tie which links him to his living-dead fiancée. Because Jeanie *is* living-dead now, make no mistake. Jack had come to that realization without actually admitting it. She is literally living *in* him, and his hollow role is to be the host. If he's not careful, he fears that Jeanie may take him over – just like what she said in his dreadful dream. Between him and Ruthy, her memory is living on; they're keeping it alive and Jeanie is feeding off this...but Jack has to remind himself (though he prefers not) that she is cold and dead and will *never* leave the confines of Old Castle's cemetery. But not her heart; *there's* the problem, right there. 'This is what I call a messy finish,' admits Jack to himself.

Jack makes up his mind that today, Thursday, 3rd of March, will be the day that will decide *everything* once and for all, for better or worse.

He goes for a power-shower, pulls on a fresh set of warm clothes and boots. He stocks up his backpack with dry biscuits from the tray by his tea and coffee condiments. Then, purely for medicinal purposes,

Jack takes a few tiny bottles of whiskey from the mini-fridge. As a rule, Jack doesn't like spirits, but considering the weather...a hot toddy might be welcome.

He steps outside into the hallway and knocks on 2204.

After a few moments standing in the busy hallway, Jack knocks again but there's no answer. He puts his ear to the door and hears nothing. Is Ruthy still sour with him? Is it something he said? Surely it was Ruthy who had done most of the speaking. Maybe she's emptied the mini-fridge again...

Maybe she's downstairs having breakfast, ponders Jack.

Choosing the last option, he goes downstairs and scans the bustling restaurant, but no Ruthy. He sees the same smiling waiters and waitresses making inane small-talk with the tourists.

Jeanie's heart flutters and sends mild panic into Jack. He trots back upstairs and pounds on the door this time, so hard that a guest pops her head out the door a little further up the hallway and tells Jack, in German, to do something; *probably* keep the noise down.

He apologizes and sets off to look for the cleaning team that he had passed on his way down to the restaurant. He trot-walks a few hallways, one the same as the next, until he finds the cleaners.

He describes Ruthy, obviously choosing her Mohawk as a good starting point, but the cleaners look too vague for Jack's liking.

He remembers something.

He reaches into his pocket for his phone and flicks through the gallery on his phone's home-screen. He stops on a photograph of Ruthy and Jeanie he had taken on opening night of the amusement park. They are standing by the killer coaster, of all places, with wide smiles. Well, Jeanie's sporting a wide smile, but Ruthy looks troubled, for some reason.

He had forgotten that he has this photo; an overpowering surge of hopelessness and infinite sadness swells inside him and dissipates as quickly as it had erupted.

Jack explains to them that he needs to get the door open.

'If it's not, eh, your room,' the woman answers in broken English, 'then we cannot open it. Um, hotel policy.' She mentions hotel policy as if that closes matters and brings a neat, polished finish to this encounter.

'Listen,' Jack's getting a tad irritated now. 'I booked two single rooms; one for myself and one for a friend. We are here together. I think there's something wrong, so please, do me a favour and open the door. Leave me the room-card if you're not comfortable with the idea. I'll say I stole it from you.'

The woman sighs and reluctantly speaks to her workmates in hushed German. She grabs a stack of towels from her station.

Jack's just about to lose hope when she lets a room-card fall into the laundry trolley. She looks at him momentarily before ducking back inside another room.

Jack whispers a 'thank you,' grabs the room-card, and heads back the way he has just come.

He slips the card into the slot and it clicks green. Jack pushes in the door a little and knocks again, not wanting to make a surprise visit. The idea of catching Ruthy in her underwear (or less) would be awkward, yet strangely attractive to Jack. Better not let Jeanie hear his immoral thoughts or see the X-rated picture-show projected onto the wall of his mind. If Jack had to choose a single moment where his attitude toward Ruthy had changed on this trip, it would probably be when she had shown him her fuzzy-wuzzy tattoo. It had given Jack that fuzzy-wuzzy...scluggy feeling.

But Jack's becoming just an x-ray image of himself and Jeanie can see it all from inside, so clear your questionable thoughts, Jackie.

'Ruthy, are you here?'

The room is silent. Jack takes this as his cue to walk into the room.

The first thing he realizes is that Ruthy isn't in the room. The second thing he notices is that her bed hasn't been slept in. This is worrying. Now Jeanie's heart is really pounding in Jack's chest. Going by the layout of the room, Ruthy hasn't even been here.

But he had *seen* her go into her room...or had he?

Jack retraces his steps to last night when she'd left him at the doorway of the hotel. They had had a little difference of opinion regarding just how far one could steal a heart – Jack of Hearts, she'd called him before she walked up these steps...

...doorway...

...but he never saw her enter the building!

Ruthy, for some inexplicable reason, had gone off on another route when Jack had lost sight of her at the bottom of the hotel steps.

Jack leaves the room, locks the door, jogs back to the cleaners, and places the room-card neatly into the cleaner's laundry trolley. The woman is busy in one of the rooms, so he pops his face in the door and thanks her.

Going downstairs, Jack checks every nook and cranny of the old hotel. He even ducks down the Emergency Exit, but is swiftly stopped by a locked door. This door leads down to the dead-end room, but now there is only the double-doors of the genuine emergency exit, which Jack had overlooked the first time he had come down these steps. The passageway that leads to the 'special' room is now off-limits.

Jack climbs the stairs and is about to notify Reception of Ruthy's disappearance when something dawns on him...

He rushes outside. The air is biting cold; his breath fogs in front of him.

The doorman beams his Bladd smile at Jack and tells him to be watchful for patches of black ice on the steps.

Jack nods a *thank-you* and descends the black-iced steps with caution, then stands in the same spot where he had stood the night previous.

It's true; only the top part of the main doors can be seen from this vantage-point.

Climbing up the steps again, he looks for a possible route Ruthy would've taken if she hadn't gone inside.

The only possible way she could've taken, other than vanishing off the face of the planet, is an alley-way that leads down to the left of the hotel. His line of vision follows the path, and it takes his eyes up the hill that looms large behind the hotel...up the hill and into the woods. Squinting his eyes in the sun, Jack sees the peak of a distant mountain on the horizon above the woods.

On instinct, Jack feels he must follow it.

Chapter 20

Footprints in the Snow

Jack loiters around and makes chitchat with the doorman.

A taxi, full of tourists pulls up at the bottom of the steps, and the doorman goes to help with their luggage.

Jack takes this opportunity to duck down the alleyway, which seems to be off-limits (or feels off-limits, at least) to the general public. Careful not to break his neck on the ice, he walks briskly down the narrow alleyway. At the end of the lane, he is taken to the back of the hotel and is amazed to see that the woods begin straight ahead of the hotel. All that separates Bladd hotel from the tree branches is a couple of enormous blue rubbish skips. He hadn't noticed before how close the woods come to the back of the hotel because Bladd's sky-line is higher than the tops of the fir trees. Jack can see the mountain-peak engulfed in snow-cloud, just peeping over the tops of the trees. He is reminded, briefly, of the woods surrounding the amusement park (not so amusing) in Old Castle. He recalls his close-encounter with the branches hurtling past him in flashing images. He flinches as he sees that thick branch coming towards him; the same one which killed Jeanie. He seems to be coming full circle...

Before he knows it, Jack is following a vague path across open ground, which leads off into the darkness of the Black Forest. The sun bouncing off the frozen-over snow throws glaring white in Jack's eyes and gives him a spontaneous headache. He shields his vision, regretting not bringing his sunglasses, and quickly crosses the stretch of ground between the hotel and the fir trees, seeking the shade.

Then, Jack spots footprints in the snow.

He reaches down and touches the footprints, frozen into the snow some time during the night. For a second of vague hope, he thinks they might be Ruthy's, but these footprints are smaller than her feet, so he disregards them and walks on another few meters. Anyway, it's a tad presumptuous that these footprints belong to *anybody* he knows.

A second set of prints running alongside the footprints are now beginning to attract Jack's attention. But these are animal prints.

Jack follows the trail of prints a few more meters; the prints in the snow are perfect frozen moulds. The small set of footprints running alongside what Jack *took* to be paw-prints, now don't look so much like paws anymore, but *claws?*

Jack racks his brain to try and guess what kind of animal would be living in this forest that would have claws or talons of this size. Another thing is this: was this animal accompanying its owner (probably a child, judging by the boots) or are these the prints of a wild animal that happened to have passed by here some time during the night and the proximity between these animal prints and the human prints are merely coincidental?

More importantly than any of this: what was a kid doing walking around here during the night or early morning?

Jack quickly arrives at the conclusion that there's *nothing* odd about finding kids' footprints in the snow. He loved snow when he was a kid. Still...

Now a *third* set of prints materializes in the snow and these prints *could* indeed be Ruthy's. They do fit her size and he recognizes the familiar cross pattern set into the soles of Dr. Marten boots. He recognizes the vague cross because he used to have Dr. Marten's with the same Red Cross-type cross. Maybe he's jumping to conclusions? If he were reading this in a book, he would find it too much of a coincidence, but sometimes, coincidences do happen in real life.

The trail steepens as Jack moves further into the woods. He follows this hill-path through the firs for another half hour. Snow blankets overhead branches and blocks the sunlight. Everything is draped in an odd, filtered white, almost like a Disney studio.

Suddenly, a *fourth* set of footprints materializes out of nowhere in the snow...and these are fresh. *Now we've got a full-on party of footprints,* thinks Jack, growing excited by the minute and for no real reason. These new prints are so fresh that Jack actually looks around him for the first time. These footprints belong, he surmises, to an adult. Now, he's on the trail of four sets of prints in the snow. He's convinced that the prints were left at different times, the newest set being the freshest. The smaller child footprints and the Dr. Marten prints seem to be current with each other. But it's the animal prints that are confusing Jack. They seem to be old and new, appear and disappear...

Coming upon a clearing, Jack stops to take in the view and catch his breath.

Below, the size of a match-box, is Hotel Bladd.

Jack realizes just how far he has come up the hill and, at the same time, asks himself *why* has he come up here?

Because he'd been following footprints in the snow, that's why. In hindsight, Jack feels a little foolish now; these prints could belong to anybody.

But speaking of footprints: the snow is heavier up here and the last set of prints he had been following have disappeared somewhere along the way, which is confusing Jack because the path he's been on is a single line with no diversions. The footprints and the animal (if it is an animal) prints have vanished, and it isn't as if it has snowed since. The prints just stopped in the middle of the path.

Curious, he retraces his own steps back down the incline until he comes across the same prints again in the snow. There's no doubting that the prints do stop in the middle of nowhere. There's no logical explanation.

Jack gets a shiver down his spine, and it has nothing to do with the melting snow occasionally falling from overhead branches, and slipping icily down the back of his collar. A wave of insecurity causes Jack to look around him, scanning for movement in the trees. Several times he thinks he sees a face duck behind the trunks but when he looks again, it turns out to be a branch or something equally explainable; the woods are full of optical illusions and matrixes.

He climbs another hundred meters before he thinks he hears a giggle behind him. He twirls around and scans the woods, now feeling the adrenaline of fear. His mouth becomes dry.

A magpie squawks and makes a clatter in the branches above him, virtually sending Jack running back downhill. But he stands his ground, yet he senses he is being watched; he knows it. The trees are watching and whatever is hiding behind them is also watching.

He walks on, heart pulsating. As the snow crunches beneath his feet, he swears that he hears another mocking titter.

Jack just manages to convince himself that it's his own imagination when his rented heart skips a beat on hearing weepy, haunting sobs of a woman coming from somewhere up ahead. For a moment, he considers turning back and following the path back down, pretending that he'd heard nothing...but curiosity gets the best of Jack.

Warily, he carries on but stops when he sees what is in the middle of the path around the next bend.

Chapter 21

Count Friedrich Olenberg Junior

The snowman is sitting there, gazing back at Jack with stones for eyes and nose, and smiling with a twig mouth.

For a delusional moment, Jack associates the snowman with the crying and the irregular footprints. But snowmen tend not to have feet, and this snowman happens to be grinning at him. Besides, salty tears would melt his face off; it's counter-productive for a snowman to cry.

Jack surprises himself as a chuckle escapes him, but the crying wail freezes him to the spot.

He quickly locates where the crying is coming from, spotting a person sitting in the snow, head down, and sobbing.

There's only one Mohawk in the Black Forest...

'Ruthy?!'

The crying stops. 'Jack? J-Jack, is that you?' Ruthy breaks down in an uncontrollable fit of crying.

Jack runs to meet her, sinking in the snow as he makes long strides. 'What are you doing *here*??'

Ruthy's face is white, and her lips are a different shade of blue than the lipstick she normally wears. '*Jesus*, you're *freezing!*'

Ruthy shakes and jerks. She tries to speak through her chattering teeth, but she's unable to control her trembling jaw.

Jack takes off his jacket and puts it over Ruthy's shoulders. 'I've got to get you back to the hotel. You've been here all night, haven't you?'

Jack makes out Ruthy's nod in between jerks and twitches.

'Jesus Christ, Ruthy! *Why?!*'

'W-W-Where i-i-is he?'

'Who? Come on, we don't have time for this. You've got hypothermia.'

Jack uncorks a mini-bottle of whiskey. 'Drink this...'

Ruthy vaguely looks at the bottle before shakily putting the bottle to her lips. The glass clatters on her teeth before she swallows the amber contents. She squirms but manages the hint of a smile. 'I can feel the heat going down my gu-gullet.'

Jack gives her another bottle, and she downs it in one. She fights to control her speech. 'I'm muh-making a habit of these little buh-bottles...'

'It really is medicinal this time,' Jack smiles.

'H-He h-hides...' Ruthy struggles to coordinate her speech.

'*Who?*'

'I *saw* him, Juh-Jack.'

'Who, Ruthy?'

'Johann...the boy!' Ruthy's face twists in cold agony. 'He was h...hiding down a little lane that runs along the suh-side of the hotel...we just got talking.'

Jack's suspicions have been confirmed. 'And walking...'

'I'm s-s-sorry I hurt your feelings when I called you, y'know... Belittling this *thing* you sh-share with Jeanie helps me...it's my defence.'

Ruthy's teeth chatter crazily in her head, reminding Jack of those joke wind-up teeth, but it's no time for jokes.

'Maybe I'm a little juh-jealous. Puh-people get j...' Ruthy strains to control her quivering jaw, 'jealous b-because of a divided heart, but this is duh-different...' She attempts to laugh but it comes out as a horrible rictus grimace, and Jack has seen and heard just about enough.

'C'mon, I'm going to help you back to the hotel.' Jack's not entirely sure *how*, yet, but the first thing is to get her standing.

Ruthy goes into some kind of cold-induced stupor, rambling on about the good old days when they used to visit the scrapyard and how all that disappeared when the amusement park had replaced it. Then Ruthy goes into delirious mode and starts speaking about herself in the third person...

Then Jack hears that familiar impish giggle. He looks over Ruthy's shoulder to see Johann, the cemetery urchin, standing by the snowman, changing his happy face to a sad one by inverting his twig-mouth. He turns back to Jack with a similar mock sad face.

So the footprints were the kid's and Ruthy's, after all. Coincidence? *No,* thinks Jack, *more like fate.* Two sets down and two to go.

'You think this is funny?' snaps Jack. 'Hmm? You got her confused...you led her around in circles. You think that's *funny?*' Jack's fuming, ready to knock the kid's block off, simultaneously pondering that the kid is wearing the same clothes as he was last night, and it must be well below freezing.

'I'm bored; I just wanted to play.'

Jack suddenly feels pity for the lonely kid, and the fight leaves him. 'This the last time you play hide-and-go-seek,' is all the wisdom Jack can sum up in the moment.

'It's not his fault, Jack. I'm *not* lost...yes, I am; no, I'm not. I don't *know* anymore. It's not the boy's fault, that's all I know. It's all getting out of hand.' She looks at Jack. 'Why did you come, Jack? You shouldn't have come.'

'Huh?' Now Jack's lost with Ruthy's bizarre comments. 'Ruthy, if I hadn't come, the snowman would have a snowwoman for company.' Jack levers Ruthy up to her feet. 'C'mon, you're not thinking straight. Let's get out of...'

Somebody clears their throat a few meters away...

Jack turns on his heels to come face to face with, very possibly, the oldest man he has *ever* seen. The wizened and gaunt man's face is deeply furrowed and is a map of time itself and could be this mountain's brother. His cheeks and temples are so sunken that it is easy for Jack to imagine a skeleton standing in front of him. He is leaning heavily on a barley-twist walking-stick, bowed and crooked like an ancient olive tree. The old man is wearing an olive green robe. But it's his eyes though, his eyes, which throw Jack; either they are lying or his body is lying. One of them is lying because his intensely sharp blue eyes are not the eyes of the old man that surrounds them.

How long he has been standing here, Jack has no clue. What he does know, though, is this individual standing in front of them is the same man who he'd seen on that documentary.

Jack loses his breath momentarily, fathoming who is *actually* staring at him: Count Friedrich Olenberg Junior...

Ruthy falls limp in Jack's arms.

Jack has a dilemma now, thinking how far down the mountain he will have to go, wading through the snow with Ruthy over his shoulders. And why now? Just when he's found the Count. Talk about bad timing...Is bad timing also fate?

But his dilemma is soon solved as the old man leaves the path and pushes his way through the heavy snow towards Jack; his barley-twist walking-stick sinks halfway down into the snow and it looks, to Jack, as if the man is walking on his knees as the rest of him is below snow.

The aged man mutters lost words under his labouring breath as he slowly but surely approaches Jack.

Jack's becoming increasingly anxious... Ruthy will be frozen over by the time he gets to them – *if* he gets to them. Now Jack fears he will have two people to rescue...

The old man kneels down in the snow next to Jack and gazes at Ruthy's peaceful, pale blue face. Jack's not sure if the tears that have gathered in his eyes are related to the bitter cold or something on a deeper level. He strokes her hair and touches her sunken Mohawk.

His reedy voice commands, 'Come with me...*look lively*.' He speaks in English with a very strong German accent.

Jack looks questioningly at the old man.

'You had better bring her to the warmth of my house.'

Jack cannot quite believe what's happening. Yet another piece of the puzzle snaps into place, and quite by accident, as accidental as everything else that has led him here.

There are no accidents, darlin'...

'We are here,' says the man.

Jack follows his line of vision and sees a turreted tower reaching above the uppermost branches of the black firs. 'How did –'

'No time for talk, young man. Jack, is it?'

Jack nods. 'But how did you know my name?'

The stranger attempts to wave away Jack's question. 'Oh, the boy might've mentioned it...'

Jack's not convinced. He cannot recall ever mentioning his name to the boy. What boy anyway? *Johann??* But, it's true, the urchin might have easily overheard his name yesterday at the cemetery.

Olenberg orders in a strong voice (stronger than his feeble body): 'Bring the girl. My name is Count Friedrich Olenberg, by the way.'

Jack does as he is told and lifts Ruthy onto his shoulders with all his might...and almost drops her right over his shoulder when he hears that name coming from the owner of that name.

The Count walks off and Jack follows.

'Johann,' Olenberg prompts, 'give this boy some help.'

So he *knows* the kid, thinks Jack, starting to feel that they know more about him than he knows about them. For the first time on this trip, Jack is feeling vulnerable. Not without hope now, but it feels like Open Season on Jack.

Johann obeys the Count immediately, grabbing Ruthy's feet. Between them, they move further up the side of the mountain quickly.

'But I don't understand,' Jack observes.

'The boy led her around in circles...'

At this juncture, Ruthy vaguely murmurs disagreement with Jack, just as she had done when Jack had blamed the boy for getting her lost the first time 'round.

The old man pats the boy's head. 'The only way you can get to my house...'

Castle, thinks Jack...

'…is to come in circles. Yes,' he affirms, looking out at the spectacular view, 'it's probably the best way to my humble abode. Johann is a faithful companion. I don't want any tourists snooping around my house, and Johann likes to play hide-and-seek. Only he does all the hiding, and the tourists do all the seeking. Some determined tourists *do* manage to find my home. They come and take a photo or 'shelfie' as they call them nowadays.'

'Selfie…' Jack corrects the Count, but maybe he shouldn't've; maybe it's his Germanic accent. Maybe he isn't qualified to correct a Count.

'Selfish? Not at all. They…'

He is also hard of hearing…

'…don't bother me, and I don't bother them. Ninety-nine percent of the time, Johann confuses them in this labyrinthine wood.'

Jack wants to tell the Count that it's highly irresponsible, but doesn't feel authorised, *and* he's winded from the climb. Plus, he understands Olenberg's need for privacy.

They take a right, walk on a few meters through thick forest, then a left. Now it *does* feel that they are walking around in circles. Several times, Jack sees something moving in the tree-tops, rather, *above* the trees, as in *flying*. He catches the movement from the corner of his eye but by the time he looks, the flying object is gone, like looking for an army jet. It's substantial in size, whatever it is. The only thing that springs to Jack's mind are eagles which reach large proportions.

The Count, too, seems very interested in the UFO that occasionally passes over their heads.

The Count looks at Johann with a twinkle in his eye. 'Isn't that right, hmm? Johann? Hide-and-Seek?'

'I'm *only* playing.'

There goes the kid again, looking for pity with those big seal-eyes of his. That's his secret weapon, Jack realizes.

'I know,' says Olenberg with a slight smirk. 'But how many times have I told you about hide-and-seek in the woods? Hmm? You have to learn to know when the fun is over, Johann.' He turns to Jack. 'Johann is always hanging around the village below and the mountain up here, and he leads nosey-parkers astray...he leads them away from me and my house.'

Jack finds it amusing how the Count pronounces *'nosey-parkers'* and adds as an aside, 'It looks like Ruthy almost found it...' not expecting the old man to hear him.

Olenberg turns and looks him dead in the eyes. 'Oh, do you think she was lost?'

This question doesn't require an answer, in Jack's opinion. 'Of course.' Wanting to add: *What have we been talking about for the last five minutes?*

'Did she *tell* you that she was lost?'

'Well, no, yes...' Jack doesn't have an answer. He thinks back to those initial few moments when he had found Ruthy. She *had* said she was lost, but *not* lost at the same time. 'Not exactly, but...'

'The girl probably meant that she's lost here...' He knocks gently on his left temple with the handle of his walking-stick.

Jack whispers, 'Join the club...'

Chapter 22

The Kiss

Jack almost drops Ruthy for the second time when they come to a large set of ornate steel black gates with a pair of majestic stone-carved dragons standing high on their hind legs upon each of the two stone pillars on either side of the gates.

Jack then notices that the ancient steel gates are actually fashioned into clock faces.

Running along the high stone wall, various mythical beasts and gargoyles stare intimidatingly down on Jack.

Olenberg fumbles in his pockets and takes out a bunch of old keys. He inserts one in the gate and clicks it open. They walk through the gates into an impressive courtyard. Jack is greeted by the same imposing fortress he'd seen on the documentary that night in his bedroom.

The Count leads them to the great, old carved doors of the awe-inspiring Castle Olenberg, which looks more of a Gothic mansion with its time-stained sandstone. He chooses another key from the ring of keys jangling in his fist and slowly proceeds to open the front door.

The door creaks open, provoking a hundred-and-one Hollywood films in Jack's memory with that same creak.

They step inside to a large, dimly-lit, foreboding hallway. Arriving in Jack's nostrils are the suffused aromas of salad and incense.

Olenberg then guides them through another door to the right.

Jack finds himself in a large, high-ceilinged room. Across the way is an open fireplace, big enough to burn Jack's recently-purchased Mini. Thick fir logs crackle and spark on the hearth. Tapestries hang from the walls, depicting various scenes from what appears to be the Black Forest. The more Jack looks at the life-size illustrations and characters, the more they seem familiar in some way. He's *seen* those people on these walls somewhere else before…perhaps a long-forgotten fairy-tale his mother used to read to him to help him sleep. Each tapestry leads to the next, in consequence, reminding Jack of the fourteen 'Stations of the Cross' paintings in Old Castle's church. The last tapestry depicts a large grandfather clock and what appears to be boy and girl climbing into it…how bizarre.

He is carried away with the moment, and his attention is taken to the hall itself, full of dark carved antique furniture. Fawns, ogres, and strange creatures are carved from the wood, alongside fierce dragons in combat with helmet-clad knights while beautiful women with flowing dresses look on from a distance. Carved into the wood panelling is the head of a man who looks remarkably like the man standing in front of Jack now.

Jack then notices the stuffed crow standing on a perch in the corner of the room. It reminds him of Clara back at home, in his bedroom, that seems further away than the dark side of the moon right now.

'You can peruse my house at a later moment but for now, the girl needs attention. I'll run a hot bath. When I call, bring her, and you can undress her and lower her into the water. That'll bring her around.'

Undress her? This isn't on Jack's itinerary, but he nods nonetheless; the Count doesn't look like the kind of guy who is used to taking no for an answer.

Olenberg shuffles off, leaving Jack to lower Ruthy onto the thick rug in front of the fire. As he does, he hears something coming from a closed-off area by the fireplace; what looks to be a large hole in the wall. The hole in the wall looks as if it had once been a place for storage, firewood perhaps. Maybe it still is. A maroon curtain hanging on a simple pulley system is hanging across the entrance, but Jack's sure that he can hear heavy breathing from the other side of the curtain, like somebody is in a deep sleep. Then Jack hears a snort and shuffling. Something brushes against the fabric and appears at the bottom of the curtain... a foot, a paw, or is it a tail? The light is too dim for Jack to make out what he has just seen, exactly.

Before his eyes have time to adjust, whatever it was that had slipped out, creepily retracts behind the curtain again.

'Boy, bring the girl...'

Olenberg's voice breaks Jack from his trance. He takes a deep breath and lifts Ruthy over his shoulder and brings her out of the room.

The Count is standing further down the hallway, outside an open door, presumably the bathroom.

Jack walks down the draughty hallway, lit by low-burning oil-lamps from a bygone period and turns right into the bathroom as the old man indicates.

Once inside, Jack discovers a steaming bath of water; one of those old-style baths with claws-for-legs and brass taps. The rest of the bathroom is covered in colourful wall-tiles and a hole in the ground, which is in fact, the toilet.

'Undress the girl and allow her to soak for as long as it takes to get her ruby lips back. I have left towels for you. Bring me her clothes and I will put them by the fire to dry.'

Jack lays Ruthy on a thick sheep-wool rug, asking himself, not for the first time, how he has ended up in this situation; just a few days ago, he was watching a documentary about the famously reclusive Count Olenberg and here he is in his *bathroom*...

He begins to undress Ruthy, acutely aware of the old man standing by the door and watching him like a hawk.

Ruthy looks different in the candle-light with her crest-fallen Mohawk. With trepidation, he removes her top layers and is confronted by the straps and cups of her black bra, momentarily catching a glimpse of what's *inside* those bra-cups.

Dear God... Jack begins to sweat.

Turning squeamish, Jack opts for her jeans instead. He pulls off her Dr. Marten's and socks, then peels off her jeans. He strips her down to her matching black knickers.

Jack admits, though reluctantly, that Ruthy's got the curves of the Scalextric he had once gotten for Christmas. It's the first time he has seen Ruthy practically naked. Only now is he truly recognizing her beauty. She's been hiding away these curves under her baggy punk outfits since forever. Why?

He sees her fuzzy-wuzzy tattoo, and this sends Jack's on-loan heart beating faster. He stands there, ogling her, yet trying to be a grown man about it – but isn't this just the problem; any grown man can see that Ruthy is a beauty...

God help him if she should wake now – what would she think of him, up close and personal, perving down on her?

'C'mon, man.'

'Huh?'

'She needs to be put in the water. What are you waiting for?'

Jack grows nervous and is about to back-answer Olenberg when Ruthy begins to come around...

'Thank *fuck* for that,' Jack mutters under his breath, silently celebrating his lucky stars.

Ruthy focuses in on Jack above her then realizes that she is virtually stripped, lying on a sheep-wool rug in candle-light. 'We have to stop meeting like this...'

She strains a smile while Jack wipes sweat from his brow.

'Ruthy, um, I realize what this must look like, but I can explain. You passed out and we were brought here by, um...'Jack casts a glance at the doorway, 'Count Friedrich Olenberg.' Jack raises his eyebrows and throws big eye signals at Ruthy as he says this name. 'We've prepared a bath for you.'

Ruthy gestures for one of the towels. Jack hands it to her and she places it over herself, eyeing the man standing in the doorway. She smiles at him before grabbing onto the side of the bath and hauls herself to her feet. 'Close the door behind you.'

'No probs.' Jack is only too happy to leave the room (practically running), then easing the door-latch shut behind him.

'Little Johann told me about your case. Apparently, you two struck a chord with him. The girl,' gesturing at the bathroom door, 'poured out her heart to Johann, as your dead loved one poured out her heart to you.'

A shiver goes up Jack's spine, and he feels an intense pity and sadness in the grave voice of the Count.

'Johann normally doesn't entertain tourists when they come snooping around my house, but Ruthy is different. Johann has a soft spot for her since forever.'

'Sorry, I don't understand.'

The elderly man comes towards him.

Just when Jack thinks that Olenberg is going to hold him or slap him, the Count shuffles past him, leaving Jack scratching his head.

A few steps up the hallway, Olenberg says, 'You'll join me for supper...' without turning around.

He doesn't stop or wait for a reply so Jack takes it as a rhetorical question. Jack and Ruthy should be getting back down the mountain but with the events of the day, Jack hasn't realized how hungry he really is. 'That would be nice. I'm starving.'

'Then wait until you see the exquisite spread I've prepared for you both.'

Anybody would think that he's been waiting for Jack and Ruthy.

Jack's mouth waters, imagining the infinite exotic recipes the Count will have.

Jack waits outside the bathroom door for Ruthy, trying to block her beautiful body from his mind's eye with what's awaiting on the Count's dining table. What would Jeanie say? What *would* Jeanie say? If he listens hard enough, he might make out her answer in the Morse code of her heart-beats...

He's hearing that series of dots and dashes when the latch of the bathroom door rises. Ruthy appears in the hallway, draped in a long towel with another towel wrapped around her head. She's holding her clothes in a bunch close to her chest.

'You look younger with your Nohawk,' Jack jests. 'We've been invited to eat with the Count, Ruthy. We've made it!' Jack struggles to keep his voice in check.

'We're here, Jack,' she smiles. 'We're *finally* here. This is where fairy-tales are born and urban myths die in the wind.' While saying this, Ruthy leans over and catches Jack off guard with a soft kiss on his cheek.

The kiss makes Jack dizzy, like alcohol suddenly streaming through his veins. As her lips meet his stubble cheek, he hears the softness of *'fairy-tale'* in his ear. This brief moment in history is a drunken one for Jack, not that Ruthy will *ever* know.

But *Jeanie* knows; the unwanted guardian angel she has become....

Jack pulls back from Ruthy's lips faster than she had laid one on him.

'I don't think I've eaten garlic in the last twelve hours...'

'No, Ruthy, it's not you...'

'Oh, okay. It's just my breath, then? C'mon, Jack, it's just a harmless peck on the cheek. Your aunty Mary probably gives you the same type...'

'I don't have an aunty Mary.'

'*Everybody's* got an auntie Mary... Forget it. So what do you think we'll be eating?'

'Hmm, well, judging by what I've seen on the Big Screen, we'll be having a feast: turkey legs, entire roast pigs, and strong wine. And probably a few Irish wolfhounds by the open fire to throw the leftovers to.' Jack reminds himself of what he had and *hadn't* seen just a while ago, resting behind the curtain next to the fireplace. He doubts that it is an Irish wolfhound...but maybe it's a wolf.

'Do you think he has hold-fast hair gel?' Ruthy points upwards to her floppy Mohawk and looks at Jack with a grin.

'Of course ancient and reclusive Count Olenberg will have hair-gel, Ruthy.'

The two of them giggle in the hallway.

'I'll just tie it back.' She unwraps a rubber-band from her wrist and ties her Mohawk in a pony-tail. 'How do I look?'

'Good enough to dine with a Count.'

Chapter 23

A Supper Fit for a Count

They strut happily back along the hallway and enter the same room on the left.

The heat in the dining room is tremendous. Olenberg is sitting at the head of the long, carved table Jack had seen earlier. But now it is lit with red candles sitting in antique candelabras. There is silence save for the snap and crackle of burning firewood.

The whole thing strikes Jack as romantic, of all things. Yes, *romantic.*

'Welcome,' Olenberg gestures them to the table.

As they approach the expansive table, both Jack and Ruthy see that the menu tonight *isn't* like in the movies as Jack had understood when the Count had mentioned 'exquisite' – the immense table is laden with canned goods and air-tight jars holding various "Best Before 2050" foods and condiments. By each of their plates is a can-opener where a dainty soup spoon might go. What really cracks Jack up is that the cutlery and plates are the white plastic picnic type; the munch 'n run variety.

Almost in response to Jack's observation, the Count says wryly, 'I don't like washing up.'

'I can relate to that,' answers Jack, unsure whether to laugh or not.

His eyes skim across the table: pot noodles...sardines in brine... sardines in ketchup...mussles...artichokes... pickled onions...

'*Spam?!*' whispers Jack out the side of his mouth, and Ruthy almost bursts a blood vessel trying to keep a straight face. 'The last time I saw spam was in my emails...'

'Come,' invites their host, 'Ruthy, you can sit here next to me. Jack, there.'

Jack, already not liking the distinction, sits opposite the Count while Ruthy happily sits next to him. Jack notices that he's got the side next to whatever is sleeping in the hole in the wall by the fireplace. Great, now he's going to have a cramp in his neck, keeping an eye on that curtain.

'Wonderful spread,' comments Ruthy, scanning the various bottles, cans, and jars. 'All that is missing is a picnic basket.' She smiles and the Count's got a twinkle in his eye.

'There was a time when this house was full of servants. Every time I rang one of those bells,' pointing to the row of bells high on the wall above them, 'I'd have a servant waiting on me. But I travel light these days...' he turns to Jack. 'I am not partial to receiving guests. It's a genuine pleasure to finally meet you, Jack.'

Finally thinks Jack? *Really? Do you know me?* Jack is struggling with the tin of spam. He pulls on the ring, and it comes away on his forefinger. He reddens up... 'Trust me to pick the dodgy one.'

Olenberg gestures him to hand it over to him, so he does. The Count sighs wearily and gets up from the table muttering, 'That's the last time I'm buying cheap spam...'

He crosses over to Jack's side and passes his hand through the curtain.

For a moment, nothing happens, then Jack flinches as Olenberg's arm jerks and the Count is almost pulled in behind the curtain. 'Tina!' He struggles and scolds 'Tina' in German and pulls his hand back.

'Tina!?' Jack lip-synchs to Ruthy across the table. *'What the fuck...'* If he was confused before about the origins of the beast sleeping in the wall, then now he's really flummoxed. What kind of animal (that obviously has the strength to pull the Count's arm out of its socket) can be called *Tina?* It's the name that's throwing him...

Count Olenberg calmly returns to the table and seats himself. He sighs and hands the tin of spam back to Jack.

In amazement, Jack looks at the can that has been neatly punch-holed.

'Use the tin-opener to cut along the holes,' Olenberg drones, as if it isn't the first time he has done or said this.

'Oh, okay,' Jack responds with a vague shrug, eying the curtain which conceals whatever it is curled up inside that hole-in-the-wall. He flashes a wary glance at Ruthy, as if to say: *what have we gotten ourselves into?*

'Johann tells me you suffered a tragedy.' Olenberg speaks exclusively to Jack, 'You must've pulled the heartstrings on his dusty, cold heart. I'm sorry I ever interfered with the boy.'

Jack frowns, only hearing: *interfering with boys...*

Olenberg carries on. 'He doesn't know if he's coming or going lately.' The Count chuckles to himself, shivers a little, and asks Jack to pass the pickled onions.

Jack gulps some Dutch courage in the form of what he thinks is mead from a dusty bottle. 'We don't follow...At least, *I* don't follow what you're saying?' Jack glances across at Ruthy as if to ask if she understands.

She shrugs and vaguely shakes her head, telling Jack she's as lost as he is.

'But *he* followed *you.*' Olenberg is quick-witted. 'Little Johann doesn't miss a trick. You were lucky you found him. He doesn't normally speak to strangers, but he was attracted to Ruthy in a way only the Gods will ever understand. I've warned him never to bring strangers, and he promised me...until now. Then again,' he glimpses sideways at Ruthy, 'you're not strangers. But he doesn't know that...'

Ruthy diverts her gaze.

Now, Jack's definitely getting the distinct impression that he *is* missing something. He feels as if he might've just nodded off in mid-conversation and wakes up half an hour later in the middle of a different topic, trying to put the impossible pieces together.

Something grabs Jack's attention from the corner of his vision; he's sure that the stuffed crow has just moved...or had it been the dancing shadows from the spitting candles? He keeps his stare fixed on that corner when, to his surprise, the crow stretches its wings and falls back into its statuesque pose. The crow is *alive?*

'*So*,' Olenberg swiftly clears the air, 'here we are, fine-dining...'

Jack looks at the jars of jellied-eels. 'Yes, indeed...'

Ruthy smiles and feels compelled to fish a cold frankfurter out of a jar.

The more Jack looks at her, the more she seems relaxed. She doesn't have that unruly streak she has in the outside world.

'Where is Johann?' asks Ruthy. 'He disappeared in the forest.'

The Count chuckles to himself. 'I'm sure he's not too far away. There's no fear of him. He knows his whereabouts.'

'He seems to know his way around the forest quite well,' says Jack, chugging on his drink, which he thinks might be mead. 'He's not afraid of the woods at night...I've seen him in action.' The more Jack drinks, the more his tongue loosens.

'And why wouldn't he? Anybody would know this place if they had been walking its leafy tunnels for nigh on three hundred years.'

Bang on cue, Jack's mead goes down the wrong way. He tries to swallow the cough, but his head puffs out like a puffer-fish about to be puffed one inch too far. The result is that mead (if that's what it is) and phlegm are shot out from various orifices...

Jack apologizes and quickly wipes himself up with the roll of disposable napkins. He blows his nose and clears himself up after his spontaneous bout of internal combustion. 'Sorry, I'm not used to mead. If that's what it is?'

The Count nods.

'I like the occasional beer. I don't do wine. But this mead is a possibility...' Jack is nervous and doesn't know when or how to shut up. 'Um, what you were saying about Johann's age... As far as I can remember, he told us his birthday was in two thousand and six.' Jack thinks again. No, *he* had prompted the boy by telling him the year after Johann had told them that he was nine years old. Jack had done the math, but Johann had laughed at him and commented that he always forgets the year... 'But he told us he was nine years old.'

'Yes he is...'

Jack puts on a face. 'Then what's the confusion?'

'The only one confused is you, my dear boy. Johann is nine years old, he will always be nine years old. He has been nine years old for over two centuries.'

Jack's wondering if he's just heard right, while Ruthy looks composed. As matter of fact, she's giving Jack the impression that she *hasn't* just heard what he *has* heard. She sticks a plastic fork in an artichoke and nonchalantly swallows it. Going by Ruthy's facial gestures, this artichoke is her first and last. She gags and quickly reaches for the mead to wash it down. 'Now I understand why they call them arti*chokes*...'

'You used to love artichokes. Personally, I detest them. I got them in especially for you.' Olenberg smiles fondly.

Jack looks at Olenberg but no smirk comes. He decides to backtrack a little. 'What were you saying about Johann? Something about, um, being three hundred years old... And remind me to come back to why you have just said that Ruthy used to love artichokes...'

Panic begins to rise in Jack and the pleasant heady feeling from the alcohol isn't nice anymore...

Olenberg clarifies, 'Johann is a half-ghost from the past. I often wonder what he would've been like as a man, but we'll never know.'

More riddle talk...

Of course he is, thinks Jack; *not only is he a ghost, but he's a half ghost...*

Finally, Ruthy speaks, helping Jack to feel less alone. 'Sorry, I didn't catch that?'

Jack's beginning to regret drinking any alcohol. He suddenly feels exposed and wonders if the mead is playing with his perception. He sneaks a look into his plastic goblet to spot anything off-colour, like essence of Deadly Nightshade. He discreetly checks to see what Olenberg is drinking and is disappointed to see that his plastic glass also holds mead. Jack discreetly holds his mead up to the candle-light to see if he can make out the dregs of any powder that might've been slipped into his drink – the same powder the Count is obviously on.

There is too much information, vague subtleties, and hints at the table for Jack to absorb. Feeling that he's being kept in the dark, he finally plucks up the courage and speaks his mind. 'Surely, you're either a ghost or you're not?'

'Did you not see the lost expression on his face? Do you not see it on *my* time-beaten face?' Count Olenberg speaks in riddles.

Jack considers the old man's face: the deep creases around his forehead, the crow's feet at his eyes and lips, hollow temples and cheeks, but his eyes are on fire as the reflection of the flames dance in his pupils. Olenberg looks ancient, almost translucent. But just beneath his skin, Jack feels a younger man is ripening and soon Count Olenberg will slough his skin, as a snake would, and reveal his younger, fresher self once again.

Jack dismisses this wild folly in his head with another stiff glass of mead and makes up his mind to throw reality out the window because he's quickly coming to the conclusion that this event is turning into a fairy-tale in real-time, and Jack's one of the unwitting characters in his own tale...

The evening has taken on a dreamy, almost out-of-body sensation.

Jack sees Ruthy also gazing dreamily at Olenberg's countenance and his remarkable cerulean blue eyes, vivid and alive.

'Do you like the mead, my dear? Brewed it with my own honey from my own bees.'

Ruthy answers Olenberg in German, shocking everybody at the table, especially Jack.

'Very tasty,' Ruthy admits in English, flashing an apologetic glance at Jack. 'There is something very similar in Ireland. But it's for the tourists. I wish they would bring it back to the normal bars and pubs. It's such a sweet romantic drink. Lovers used to drink it before getting married – that's where the word *honeymoon* comes from.' She takes in Jack with wide sensual pupils. 'Don't you think so, Jack?'

Jack looks at his golden honeyed drink. He's *not* thinking romantic thoughts; he's just not thinking, full stop. But he is *wondering*, wondering if the bathroom he had been in earlier has a window? If so, is it large enough for him to climb out of?

The Count turns to Jack. 'You are from the Emerald Isle, Jack?'

'Um,' says Jack. 'Ireland, yes.' He can't ever recall divulging that information, maybe he had.

'Slowly but surely, the drink is loosening your tongue. May I dare ask, do you know *why* you have come to the Black Forest of Deutschland, Jack?'

The question should be: *Tell me why you've come to the Black Forest?* But it sounds more like: *I know why you're here, but do you?*

Jack answers, 'A wild goose-chase.'

'Do you not have wild geese on the Emerald Isle?'

Ruthy clarifies, 'Not this kind.' She smiles at Olenberg.

So Jack takes a deep breath, swallows another mouthful of mead, and relays his own remarkable story to Count Friedrich Olenberg: from the moment Jeanie and he get on the rollercoaster to Jack waking up in hospital with and without Jeanie. With a lump in his throat, Jack goes on to explain to the Count that it is Jeanie's heart pumping in his chest...

'The love story of the century,' adds Ruthy at this juncture, leaving Jack unsure whether she is being sarcastic or there's more than meets the eye.

Jack then goes on to explain how Jeanie's heart has become a dark obsession; which has led him to attempted suicide, saved at the eleventh hour by a crow named Clara, now stuffed in his bedroom (and Jack wishes he was there right now, feeling in over his head now).

Jack is also quick to add their life-time together; how they had been childhood friends until love blossomed between them. He doesn't want to give the impression that all of this is a spontaneous thing.

Jack finishes by repeating: 'Jeanie's heart *and* Jeanie have become a dark obsession for me.'

'A poisoned chalice,' Ruthy interjects.

Jack is quite drunk by the time he finishes his life-story. In the back of his mind, he's obsessing over the half-ghost child named Johann...but he needs to remain focused on his objective – to go back in time to save Jeanie. He needs to get his message across to the Count that this trip is no fly-by-night occasion.

Olenberg sits there, mulling over Jack's story before snapping in his face: *'You should be ashamed of yourself, boy!'*

Whatever is sleeping behind the curtain snorts, holds its breath, and falls back to sleep...

Jack's reaction is one of shock. *'Huh??'* This sudden outburst is the last thing he thought the Count would be capable of.

'You've been given an extraordinary gift – the gift of life. How dare you throw that back at the girl who *loved* you. Who do you think you are?' He stalls. 'If only *I* could turn back time...' The Count stares off into space before tears make him blink, bringing him back to himself.

Jack looks at Ruthy for some kind of answer. Why would Olenberg say that now? Of all times, why *now*?

Jack feels himself shrink inside. Has Olenberg just inadvertently admitted that he doesn't have the time-machine? It was an urban myth all along? Olenberg's reaction isn't the one Jack has been expecting. 'I don't think you understand...She didn't give up her life for me.'

'I understand *more* than you think, boy.'

'No, you see, she was already dead when I received her heart. She was brain-dead...on a life-support machine.' This is the first time Jack hears these words coming from anybody; *nobody* has ever spoken about this, not even at the hospital, but *alluded* to it. It's a bitter pill to swallow, and Jack washes it down with more honeymoon drink. Ironic.

'That's immaterial. You, *you*,' pointing across the table at him, 'are *alive* because of that girl. Dead or alive? Who *cares?!*' Olenberg turns away and snorts some angry words in German. 'That girl died to save your life. It was written that way. That's the way it was from the beginning.'

Olenberg gets up from the table, and gestures Jack to the window.

Jack leaves the table and stands next to Olenberg by one of the stain-glass windows. They both look out into the clear night. The Count points upwards to the sky with his long, gnarled fingers. 'It was written in the stars, Jack, and when it is written in the stars, it is there for everybody to see – you just have to know how to read it.' He marks individual twinkling stars.

As he does, Jack imagines them lighting up...

'Join the dots and read your fate. It is there to be read, but most prefer not to join the dots.'

The Count leads Jack back to the table. 'You see, boy, somewhere...' Olenberg gestures vaguely at the tapestried walls that surround them, 'there is a library of fairy-tales, and each one of these tales is our life story.'

'My best friend's death *isn't* a fairy-tale,' Jack back-answers.

Beyond the curtain, whatever is sleeping, suddenly stirs again.

Jack feels it holding its breath...

Olenberg informs him, 'You're wrong...'

The heavy breathing of Olenberg's pet returns to normal...

'What fairy-tale doesn't have a death?' he adds. 'Horrible, ghastly things happen in fairy-tales, but it is always for a reason and there will *always* be redemption in some form or another.' Olenberg repeats his message: 'That girl died for you. From the moment she was conceived, she would save a life to end hers.'

Tears well in Jack's eyes, listening to the Count's profound words. Who is Jack to say that it isn't true that life isn't already mapped from the beginning; that bad luck and good luck *don't* exist? But who is the Count to say that all of this is pre-written destiny? 'So, what you're saying is that everything happens for a reason?'

Olenberg nods and swallows a whole pickled onion, as if they were talking about a football match.

'Well, I don't agree with that!' Jack is growing angry at Olenberg's flippancy. He's not taking him seriously. 'How do you think I feel when you tell me that Jeanie died to save me? Now, I've got that extra guilt on my shoulders going home.'

Olenberg glances at Ruthy. 'Going home?'

Ruthy prudently shakes her head, as if saying: *Now's not the right moment...*

'I am only trying to tell you that life is meant to be this way. I am helping you, Jack; I'm telling you that there was never anything you could do to avoid the accident on that rolling...' The Count struggles to remember the word.

'Rollercoaster.'

'Even if we could turn back the clock, everything *will* play out exactly as it had the first time.'

Again, Jack glimpses Ruthy. Olenberg *knows* something. He wouldn't have just said that if he didn't know. Jack decides that it's about time to lay all his cards on the table. He takes a deep breath, closes his eyes momentarily, and opens them again. 'I could change things if I turned back time.'

If I Could Turn Back Time... Remember that old song, darling? Remember we danced to that one Christmas Eve?

Jack had forgotten about that, and Jeanie has just reminded him. Christ, she is growing...growing...*growing...* Jeanie is robbing him of his memories. That's where she's going to begin; the succubus will suck him dry until he no longer knows he is Jack...

Olenberg's features grow dark and sinister. '*Time* can be interfered with, boy, but never, ever attempt to change what happens in any particular second or moment, because that little tiny change will grow into a tsunami, and sooner or later it will drown you. You won't know your arse from your elbow...'

Either Jack's having an allergic reaction to the mead or Olenberg's thought process is far too clever for normal Jack from Old Castle, Limerick. Although if Jack's to be honest, that last line about comparing an arse to an elbow does mar the overall effect.

Count Olenberg gets up from the table and checks to see if Ruthy's clothes have dried. When he sees that they are as wet as when she had removed them, he takes them in his hand and leaves the room for a moment, calling, 'Tina, come...'

Before they can see anything for sure, something slinks out from under the curtain and shuffles beneath the table to get the quickest way out, stroking past Jack's legs.

Tina is gone out the door and down the hallway before Jack can figure out what breed of dog it is – if it is a dog, then it would have to be something like a Saint Bernard or a dog of equally giant proportions. But a Saint Bernard tends not to *slink*.

'*What the fuck is going on, Ruthy?*' screams Jack in a whisper across the table. 'And why are you so quiet? I'm trying to work on the time-machine thing, but your role is to get to the bottom of Johann, who or what is *he*? And how old is he really? The Count's made several odd remarks at the table, and I don't understand one of them. Jesus, I've got a million questions, but I'm not going to ask any until I find out if I can go back in time.' Now Jack turns on Ruthy. 'And *you??* You're acting real shifty, Ruthy. Is there something you want to tell me?'

She considers him. 'No, Jack.'

'Sure? You're giving me the impression that you've been here before, Ruthy...'

Just then, Jack suffers one of those moments of utter self-doubting clarity, wondering what or why he is here and *time-travel??*

Wake up and smell the coffee beans, darling.

He doesn't know where he stands with Jeanie any more. She's playing with his mind, and she's become more complex than when she was alive, if that's possible. When did all of this begin? It seems as if Jack's been strapped to a conveyor which has led him here, but it's all been of his own doing; he organized *everything*. Ruthy had even tried to talk him out of it.

Olenberg returns and hands Ruthy her clothes.

'They are red-hot,' she smiles, 'as if they've just come out of a tumble-dryer.'

'A what?' asks the Count.

'Nothing. Forget it.'

'You can change anywhere you want.'

Ruthy thanks the Count and takes herself to the fireplace. Jack watches from the corner of his eye as she pulls on her jeans beneath the towel, then gracefully contorts and twists herself into her bra beneath the towel, as elegantly and beautiful as Houdini dislocating a limb to slip out of a strait jacket...

'Now, let's deal with why you both are *really* here. I know you didn't come all this way to tell me this sad story.'

Again, Olenberg's tone of voice is a riddle; Jack's unsure if the Count is asking him for his real reason to be here or *telling* him that he already knows why he is here...which doesn't make any sense anyway because Jack has already told him everything there is to know...except the time-machine; he hasn't mentioned the magic clock, which is why he has really come.

The Count slobbers over a frankfurter, licks his fingers and comments to Jack, 'Come with me. I want to show you something.'

Chapter 24

Johann's Moon Walk

Olenberg gets up from the table and they follow him out of the room, Jack glimpsing the strangely familiar tapestries as he passes by them.

Slowly, the Count leads them down the hallway, leaning heavily on his barley-twist walking-stick which echoes *click-clack* on the cold flagstones. The Count carries a single candle in his right hand, lighting their way ahead.

Something brushes past Jack, making him squirm. Squeamishly, he skips aside as whatever it is trots ahead of them; its nails click along the dark hallway in front of them. The animal is too fast to make out for Jack, but big enough to know that it isn't a dog. Dogs tend to be covered in fur, but the slight glistening Jack has just seen under the candlelight makes him think that it *isn't* a big, cuddly Saint Bernard. Big? Yes, just maybe not as cuddly as he would like. The place is too dark to see anything; all he catches are glimpses of forms and shadows.

Jack asks the obvious, 'Why don't you get electricity?'

'For what?' responds the Count, as if electricity is the last thing he would consider installing in his 'house'.

Jack opines, 'Dishwashers are handy,' already realizing that Castle Olenberg isn't the type of residence where a dishwasher might be found.

'Have you seen my cutlery?' asks the Count with a smidgen of sarcasm.

Jack is about to name out a list of other useful electro-domestic appliances when he realizes that electricity is literally everywhere and everything nowadays. Anyway, if he has to tell Count Olenberg about the advantages of electricity, then it's probably better to keep quiet.

Moreover, electrical appliances are no match for half-ghosts, and Jack is still more-than-curious about that Johann issue. He had planned to ask about it again, but the Count seemed to divert the topic the first time. *Maybe the boy is closer to the Count than Jack thinks. He wouldn't like to hurt his feelings in any way or bring up a painful subject, which it seems to be. And he has seen how the Count dotes on the boy.*

'I do everything by hand; candlelight and lanterns are sufficient for all my needs. Why incur extra expense to line the pockets of the electricity-provider of this country? Mafia – their way or no way. Well, it's *my* way. I stock up on candles, wick, and oil a few times a year when I stock up on food and other provisions. Occasionally, after spending months of work on a particular clock, I like to treat myself and stay away from home for a few nights to be pampered and enjoy a sirloin steak, watch daytime television in five-star comfort. Tina also enjoys to be pampered, though the hotel staff don't like to get too close to her. Daytime television tends to send her to sleep, but she enjoys the sirloin steaks as much as I do – she likes her steaks *bloody*.'

Jack comes to a stop and stares at the back of Olenberg's olive-green robe as he recedes down the hallway, realizing that it was him, and not the *politician* Ruthy had convinced him of, staying in the 'Emergency Exit' Dead End room of Bladd Hotel.

No, Jack, don't jump to conclusions; it wouldn't be the first time.

He catches up with Olenberg. 'Um, when you say you enjoy to get away for a few days, do you, uh, travel far?'

The Count looks over his shoulder at Jack, and then at Ruthy walking along behind him. 'Yes and no...' before looking ahead again.

Jack glimpses over his shoulder at Ruthy, dramatically lip-synching his favourite expression: *What the fuck?* 'Uh-huh, but you mentioned you like to escape for a few days to be pampered. I've heard that the massages and spas in Thailand are second to none.' Jack already knows that the Count doesn't do massages, *especially* in Thailand.

'No, no. I go down the mountain and stay a few days at Bladd Hotel.'

A shiver creeps up the length of Jack's spine...

'It's a five-star residence, and the service is splendid. But more importantly, the staff are loyal to me and keep me a secret when I'm at the hotel.'

Jack already knows the answer, but asks anyway. 'How do you come and go to a hotel without being seen by guests?'

'I have a special VIP room underneath the hotel.'

Here we go...

'A direct tunnel from the mead cellar of my humble abode leads to the hotel far below...'

This just keeps getting better, thinks Jack.

'Hotel Bladd was originally an extended part of my house. It was where my ancestors held parties with aristocracy and presidents from around the world. Every room would be occupied in the Party House.'

Jack is unable to hide the stupid grin on his face. *'The Party House?'*

'Yes, *das Partyhaus.*'

Jack cannot believe that a subterranean tunnel exists between the castle and the hotel below. That explains the fake Disney dead-end that he had seen...it was concealing a door, so well concealed that Jack hadn't seen it. This has just been taken to the next level of crazy shit. Jack knows it and feels it. What next?

What next, darling? I'm going to wake you up. That's what's next...

Is all of this an elaborate dream? Jack, in a way, would like to wake up, but he also wants to know how this dream finishes. Maybe it's one of those bad dreams that will end when he jolts himself awake as he dies... if this is indeed a dream, and Jack believes it isn't.

The Count finishes by saying, 'I am also the owner of the hotel.'

Jack's flabbergasted. 'Just a minor detail...' realizing that he had paid top dollar for this hotel. Now that he thinks about it, it was Ruthy who had told him about the place. What gives?

He tells this to the Count, how he had opted for the all-in-one package.

'I'll reimburse you every penny.'

'No, I'm not complaining or looking for charity. I prefer to pay my way, whether you or Santa Claus is the owner.'

The Count grins. 'I wouldn't have Santa Claus as a business partner.'

'It was Ruthy who told me about the hotel...'

The Count lithely turns and stares at Ruthy. 'You let him pay? I know you're a shrewd businesswoman, Ruthy, but there are lines in business, and we don't cross them.'

Ruthy apologizes, all docile-like.

Jack's never seen her like this, and why would she let him pay? Jack's about to ask her what the deal is when Olenberg says, 'I have to move with the times, and this is how I maintain the cost of the building. Nice to see that it is a five-star hotel nowadays. I've been very fortunate.' Again, he studies Ruthy before tut-tutting her.

'I go to and from the hotel without fear of being seen. I stock up on provisions while I'm down in the village. Sometimes, more often lately because I am weak, I stay on a few days at the hotel to gain enough strength to take the walk back up the tunnel. I must set up a more efficient system, perhaps a little train or something.'

The idea of Count Olenberg sitting in a little steam-train blows Jack's mind.

'Other days,' the Count goes on, 'the days when I just can't walk anymore, Tina helps me.'

Finally, finally we're getting onto the subject of Tina, contemplates Jack. Now all that's left is the mystery boy, Johann...

'Does Tina carry a little barrel of brandy under her chin to warm the cockles on snowy mornings?' Jack's already re-convinced himself that it *is* a Saint Bernard.

'Dear God, man, are you crazy? She would be a ticking time-bomb...She gets a whiff of any kind of flammable substance, especially alcohol, and I can kiss my ass goodbye, um, as the saying goes.' Adding from the corner of his mouth, 'You'd be surprised what you can learn from watching daytime television in a hotel room. I find it an addictive invention, so I make a point of not getting one, for fear of it rotting the brain. I'd never build another clock. But, to answer your question: no, Tina doesn't carry a barrel of brandy. But she comes in useful in other ways.'

'Such as?'

'Well, she carries me up to my home when I'm too weak to walk myself.' The Count speaks as if Jack is already privy to what Tina is.

'From the hotel?'

'Yes.'

Jack's getting closer and closer to finding out Tina's true identity. 'Through the *tunnel?' Christ,* Jack ponders, *it's a donkey!*

'Up to last year she did, yes. She would carry me right up the tunnel, all the way up to my mead cellar. Oh, by the way, I have an excellent port wine I would like you to try. It's three hundred years old...'

The Count has an unsavoury habit of throwing big numbers out there; Jack's getting the whiff of a compulsive liar.

'Uh-huh, but getting back to Tina. Why, if you don't mind me asking, doesn't she take you up, like um, this year, for example? And more to the point, how does she take you up now?'

'You're very good at asking roundabout questions to answers you want straight.'

Jack's unsure how to respond so, like an idiot, he thanks him.

'She's gotten too big, is the answer to your first question, for the tunnel. She needs a lot of room to spread her wings and...'

Wait... *'Wings?!'*

The Count glances at Ruthy and back at Jack. 'Yes, Jack, wings.' Olenberg makes a vague flapping arc with his frail arms, spilling wax on the stone floor.

'Yes, I know what wings are, but when you say wings, what do you mean, exactly?'

'More roundabout questions. Good God, man, a pair of wings is a pair of wings...'

'No, sorry, it's just that when somebody tells me that their house-pet has wings, it's normally a budgie or a canary, but I can't see either flying you up the tunnel. When somebody is taken home by their pet that happens to have wings, then that sends off little alarm bells. I mean, unless you have a donkey, just like in the old days...a flying donkey.'

'All will become clear soon, Jack.'

Jack turns to Ruthy. 'Don't you have anything to say about the matter, Ruthy? You've hardly opened your mouth since you got here.'

'You're doing all the talking, Jack.'

Jack jibes, 'That's unusual for you.'

The Count stops and takes them into a room filled with the crescendo of *tick-tock...tick-tock* and *Cuckoo! Cuckoo!*

When Olenberg lights up the lanterns, Jack sees that the room is *full* of old clocks and curious automatons with little clockwork characters doing all sorts of quaint tricks. Jack scans the room, gazing at the clocks and the long workbench with neatly organized wood-carving tools and other fine instruments that have seen a lot of use.

Ruthy, in turn, is gazing longingly at Jack, relishing the childlike wonder in his face.

'This is my workshop. I make a few clocks a year and sell them. This is another way I finance myself – somebody has to pay for those fine frankfurters and pickled onions.'

Jack's about to snigger, but straightens up when he sees that the Count is serious.

'Many royal palaces have my clocks in their living-rooms. People pay thousands for these anatomical clocks; these are the Olenberg

Clocks. I have built a surplus which will keep me going for the rest of my life...and beyond, at the rate I'm going.' He throws a thoughtful glance at Ruthy.

Meanwhile, Jack's mind is doing over-time; does Olenberg mean that he doesn't have long to live, which is very plausible, or...*no*...don't be silly, Jack. 'But these clocks, are they original Olenberg clocks?'

The Count reacts as if he's just been insulted. 'Of course, they're original. I built them with my own hands.'

'Yes, but I mean, there are two clockmakers in your family; your ancestor Count Olenberg was also a clockmaker.'

'Come, come, Jack. We both know the clocks come from the same place...'

'Huh? What does...'

'Really, I don't need to build another clock, but I don't like the idea of retirement, so I will never retire – building clocks is a great way for me to manage my time. Get it?'

Jack's overcome with everything. 'Hmm?'

'My little joke.'

Ruthy giggles.

'Oh, yes, good one,' lies Jack. He hasn't heard a word the Count has said because he is looking for the *special* clock; the *special* reason he has come to this *special* place.

'Do you enjoy clocks, boy?'

'Um, I don't know if *enjoy* is the word I'd use. For example, I don't enjoy when my alarm clock goes off on Monday morning.' He regrets saying it already.

'Poppycock,' Olenberg answers and leaves it there.

'Are you sure you have no more clocks?'

Jack spins around on his heels and stares at Ruthy, amazed that she should, at last, open her mouth with such a bold question.

Olenberg turns and studies Ruthy's sincere candle-lit face. He pauses, as if waiting for something unseen or unheard to Jack. 'Yes...'

Jack's heart thumps hard in his chest, and now Jeanie's playing the bongos along his ribcage. So the goose *isn't* wild, after all, thinks Jack; the chase is coming to an end. He has all but forgotten about the true identity of Tina and Johann now.

'I do have one other,' he pauses to find the word, '*unique* clock. But it's not open to the public.'

Jack panics. 'But *nothing* is open to the public...and I'd hardly call us the public. We just ate spam together and drank your home-brew,' opines Jack, sweating now to get a glimpse of the so-called time-machine.

'Nevertheless, these are the clocks you need to see. All these clocks go forward.'

The electricity in the air is palpable, despite the Count not having any.

'As opposed to...'

'As opposed to clocks that don't always go forward. For the common man, these are the clocks that will interest you.'

'Common? We aren't here by chance, Count. Can I call you Count? It sounds cool.'

'Yes, boy, I am an official Count, so yes, you may.'

'I haven't told you how we found out about you. I've told you my story, but it was Ruthy,' gesturing to Ruthy, 'who first told me about you and your ancestor. She first discovered you, your *ancestor* rather, in an unfinished medieval fairy-tale that has sort of evolved into an urban myth.'

Jack recalls the night he left Ruthy sitting on her own at Joe Soap's in Limerick City and, after that how they had spoken about the fairy-tale over the phone. That was only recently, but it seems as if years have passed.

Ruthy chuckles, 'Count Olenberg Senior!'

Jack's blush is partly hidden behind the flush he sports from the mead. 'Um, yes. We gave your ancestor that name to avoid confusion...seeing as you both share the same name and title and both of you are clockmakers.'

Jack's looking into the eyes of the Count, but there's no reaction, not even a blink, and it makes him uneasy.

'Um, in a nutshell, it's a fairy-tale about a clockmaker,' he pauses, 'your ancestor living in the Black Forest who didn't let his daughter marry the man she loved because he was the son of a rival clockmaker. She tried to kill herself, and her clockmaker father promised he would, um, y'know, make a *special* clock to help his daughter.'

'I think, in a way,' Ruthy adds, 'the clockmaker actually died with his daughter's attempted suicide. That's the price he paid.'

Jack's more concerned with the time-machine part of the story. 'The clock, um,' beating around the bush, 'could be classed more of a, let's say...'

Ruthy elbows Jack to get to the point.

'I'm *getting* there,' Jack tells her. 'I can barely bring myself to say it aloud. I feel stupid. Why don't *you* say it?'

'C'mon,' Ruthy urges him again.

'Your ancestor, Count Olenberg Senior, for want of a better expression, was in possession of a special clock. This clock could alter time...a *time-machine*. A time-altering clock.'

There; it's out there. Jack holds his breath in nervous anticipation.

No reaction comes from Count Olenberg. The only sound in the room is the busy *tick-tock* of the clocks and the oblivious clockwork figurines going about their business.

'As opposed to time *altering* the clock,' Ruthy clarifies and shuts her mouth again.

Suddenly, they feel somebody else enter the room. They turn around to see little Johann standing there.

Olenberg turns to the boy. 'Scallywag, I've told you before not to sneak up on people like that. You know what I've told you about coming through the walls. You knock on the door like any normal living person would do. Try to fit in.'

'Sorry,' apologizes the boy. 'I forgot. It's just faster to use the walls...'

Not taking any of this seriously, Jack dismisses Johann and his apology with an anecdote. 'Don't be sorry for walking through walls, Johann. When I was your age, I was sure I had X-ray vision...I could *see* through walls. I had my classmates and myself convinced.' Turning to Olenberg, 'What do you mean, "coming through the walls"? Is that a local expression directly translated into English? Because it doesn't work if that's what you've done.'

The Count is watching the boy. 'I see your excitement, Johann. You want to show them, don't you? Hmm?'

The feeble child nods shyly and gazes up at them with his big lamp eyes.

Jack's really mystified now; thoughts are jumbled up into a mass of doubts. Several comments and happenings haven't made sense since he turned up at Castle Olenberg; namely Johann and Tina, but other little comments made by the Count don't tally.

Olenberg turns to Jack and Ruthy. 'Come with me.'

Johann rejoices and fists the air, then breaks into a high-mountain yodelling jig. Olenberg claps him on. Then Ruthy joins in... but not Jack, because Jack is too busy blinking and wiping at his eyes...

The dimness of the room, the castle in general, is playing with his senses.

Jack could've sworn just now that Johann was dancing in mid-air. Sometimes, his feet didn't seem to touch the stone floor, or they did but with a delayed reaction. His prancing feet seemed to stay airborne for longer than is possible, as if dancing on the moon. Johann's doing a *real* moonwalk, thinks Jack absurdly. What *is* this place?

They've slipped him a Mickey Finn in his mead...

Olenberg gets a great kick out of this spectacle. 'Come, Jack. Let's go to the tower.'

He leads Jack and Ruthy from the workshop. They leave the *tick-tock* behind them and follow the Count down another hallway. At the end of the corridor is a steep winding staircase running up through a round tower. The Count begins to climb the stone steps.

It reminds Jack of their day-trip to Bunratty Castle, not too far from Old Castle, just weeks before the accident; the accident is like an A.D. and B.C. in Jack's life.

They ascend the stone steps while the boy, Johann, bounds upwards ahead of them with unending energy.

Jack witnesses the boy glide upwards, clearing three or four steps at a time. Jack might *possibly* jump the distance of two steps, but it seems that Johann is on an escalator or on an invisible wire, so smooth is his movement. He's not jumping; he doesn't have gravity.

However, the old man, Olenberg, becomes slower and slower, until he comes to a complete stop and leans into an opening in the wall with a slit for a window. He looks at them, panting and pale.

Ruthy comes to his side and puts her arm around him. 'Are you okay? What can we do? We can do this some other day...'

'Some other day?!' asks Jack, disbelievingly. He loses control. 'Are you *crazy?!* But we've come so far.'

Chapter 25

Winding Staircase of Truths

Yes, Jack, Jeanie's voice whispers in his ears, *we have come so far, darling. I'm enjoying the ride. But there's one thing: if you go back in time, I'll still be in your chest – trapped inside your rib-cage prison. Have you thought about that? You think you can outrun a disease by going to Mars? You've been misled. Wake up and smell the coffee beans, Jackie. If you smell them long enough, you'll start to get the whiff of something else, something rotten, lingering behind the aroma of freshly ground coffee beans... I still love you, Jack, even after what you did to me... Yes, you could've saved me if you had really wanted to... But I still love you and am closer to you now than I've ever been. I want to tell you to listen to your heart, Jack, listen to your heart. There's something wrong...*

Jack snaps out of his momentary lapse. Jeanie's voice had been *so* real this time, and echoing, as if it was right here on this winding staircase. She really *is* taking over. Jack trembles, fearing insanity. She's getting stronger, he thinks deliriously. She's *feeding* off him as she had promised, but why is she asking him to smell the coffee beans? What rotten stench does Jeanie speak of? *Am I going insane?* Jack asks himself...

'No,' Olenberg responds, shaking Jack from his stupor. 'It has to be now. Tina, *lift...*'

Jack is wondering if he's starting to go around the bend, and speaking of bends; something comes up towards them from around the bend of the winding staircase...

Jack hears the same clicking claws on the steps just below them, galloping now...then the clicking becomes frantic as 'Tina' charges up the steps below...coming up towards them...

Coming around the bend, out of the darkness, swoops a creature, flapping wildly to stay airborne. The beast's leathery wings beat hard, buffeting wind in Jack's face and everybody else's.

For a hallucinatory moment, Jack cannot figure what he is looking at. It's not a bird – birds have feathers, nor is it a bat, though it does have wings similar to a bat. The more the creature swoops in and out of the oil lanterns, the more Jack remembers his childhood dinosaur books. The thing hovering in front of him could be a pterodactyl, but the only thing that Jack remembers is that pterodactyls have been extinct since forever and the 'P' is silent...

And then, something happens that gives the secret away; a little hint, and it is probably this moment which breaks Jack's post-Jeanie life (AJ instead of AD) into two: everything that happens is in the future...

A ball of fire lights up the entire stairwell, flashing everybody in strobing fiery red-orange.

'Stop complaining, Tina. I don't ask you to give me a lift every day.'

In the middle of this impromptu fire storm, Olenberg calmly tells Jack, 'She blows fire when she's not happy about something. I'm guessing that she doesn't have enough room to spread her wings here on the stairs. She's clipping her wing-tip claws. Can you see?' The Count points left and right; it's true, *Tina* is shearing her wings on the stone wall of the tower.

But Jack is more concerned with the actual beast. It's NOT a pterodactyl; it's, '...a dragon...' Jack doesn't hear his muffled words as another fiery flare discharges. This time, he feels the heat on his face, and he's immediately transported back a couple of decades to the fire-blower of the local circus in Old Castle. The creature's (*dragon's*) scorching fire-balls are exactly the same as those of the fire-blower, Jack recalls.

'A dragon?!'

For a crazy moment, Jack convinces himself that dragons have always existed, it's just that he's never seen one. They are everywhere in mythology, and half the population have the mystical creature tattooed forever to their bodies. Yes, maybe it's just that he has never actually seen a dragon. It's true that he has seen animals in zoos that he never thought existed...but a dragon is a stretch, admittedly.

'*A dragon?!*' he shouts again, nobody confirming or denying anything.

'Well, I did *mention* fairy-tale somewhere along the way,' quips Ruthy, now really fucking with Jack's mind. She's got a knowing smile on her face, and she doesn't seem all that bothered or confused by the sizzle coming from the dragon's blistering breaths.

Wake up and smell the coffee beans, Jack...There's a stench, darling, please...

He hears Jeanie again, trying to warn him from inside his head, but all he can smell is sulphur and something else like cheap incense coming from the dragon – *dragon?!*

But this is only the warm-up act, as Jack is about to discover.

The dragon lowers herself over Olenberg, opens her considerable talons, and gently grabs the Count around his shoulders and under his armpits, so careful not to slice his skin with her impressive spurs.

The dragon, possibly the same size as a calf with wings, then lifts Olenberg until he's airborne. The disgruntled dragon fights to stay in the air, puffing balls of fire as she flaps upwards...and around the bend.

Jack stands there on the step, frozen, despite the heat. He hears the flapping wings on the winding staircase above him, occasionally lit up as the dragon, lovingly named Tina, spits fire.

As Jack stands there, he recalls the prints in the snow – man and beast – and how they suddenly vanished in the middle of the path. Well, now, it all makes sense. Now that he knows what Tina is, Jack's not sure he wants to know what Johann is. But, going by what he's just witnessed, Johann is indeed a half-ghost, or fully-blown ghost, who cares, and he *does* take short-cuts through walls.

Jack and Ruthy are left standing in the hallway. They look at each other, and it is Jack who is the first to speak, 'So, what's the deal?'

'What do you mean?'

'Oh, c'mon, Ruthy, I've seen and heard enough to know that we're not exactly here by accident. We've been led here, most probably by you. Just answer this one question – it's a yes or no answer: you've been here before, haven't you?'

Ruthy looks him in the eyes. 'Yes.'

The bottom falls out of Jack's world on hearing this simple one-syllable word.

Racking his brain, he tries to think back to the first time on this trip when he had suspected something odd and now he realizes that *many* things just didn't add up in the moment, but he'd let them slide. But now, yes, he is starting to add them up into something that equals sinister. He is on the edge of a cliff, about to fall into a strange world of truths and half-fictions; a fairy-tale landscape of oddities awaits. He is on the verge of knowing *everything* and *nothing*. But where to start?

With Ruthy, of course...

'How about filling me in, Ruthy?'

Ruthy's visibly upset. 'I don't know where to begin.'

'At the start would be a good place.'

They begin climbing the stone steps of the tower.

'It may take a while...'

'To enlighten me,' he gently warns her, 'you've got to the top of the stairs.'

'But I don't know where to begin!'

'I tell you what: how about you tell me from that night when you told me about this fairy-tale or urban myth or whatever it is we are in...I'm *scared*, Ruthy. I feel vulnerable and alone. You haven't been honest with me, and you're all I have in the world.' *This world and the real world,* thinks Jack.

They ascend the twirling steps. 'It starts long before that, and we don't have that many steps...'

Jack doesn't follow. 'Before the accident?' Jack finds it difficult to think of anything before the accident.

'Before that...'

Jack and Ruthy slowly spiral upwards towards the top of the tower.

As they reach the top of the winding stair-case, Ruthy adds softly: 'Two hundred and thirty years before that...'

Chapter 26

Time will Tell

'Huh?'

By now, Jack's head is reeling in confusion; nothing, *nothing* makes sense anymore, and he's even starting to feel that he doesn't know himself any longer. The last hour has turned his world upside-down and inside-out. All this while Jeanie's consuming him from inside-out like a tsetse fly.

The Count is waiting for them on the top step of the winding staircase with an ominous smile on his face. He proceeds to light the oil lanterns along the walls.

The dragon, Tina, circles the floor, snorting and swiping at the shiny flagstones like a bull.

It's a dragon! Jack quietly rejoices. *A fucking fully-fledged dragon!* A small one, granted, but by Christ, it's a fire-breathing dragon! Jack cannot believe it. But dragons don't exist, yet there's no smoke without fire. Then again, they don't exist in his mundane world, but in this fairy-tale they do.

The Count lights the lanterns and turns to see Jack transfixed on Tina. 'Tina is a pygmy dragon, Jack. Dragons began to die out in the Black Forest in the late 1700's. Dragons still inhabited the Black Forest back in those days; in those days when the forest was actually black, not like now, teeming with happy campers – another daytime television expression. I came across a nest of dragon eggs one day while going for a walk in the forest, thinking over my next clock design. I took one of those eggs and kept the egg warm by the hearth in the dining room. She was born a few weeks later. I believe Tina is the last dragon to exist. She is the *only* one so when she goes, they're gone forever and no time-machine can bring her back.'

Jack's overwhelmed. He looks around the perfectly symmetrical room before gravitating towards one of the many stained-glass windows. Heavy mesh wire screwed into the stone walls prevents Jack from getting a good view, so he moves to the next window where Ruthy is standing.

He stares out into the dark horizon and vaguely makes out the lights of Bladd way off below. An immense sense of relief envelopes him on seeing those lights coming from a familiar place, proving that the outside world *still* exists...

Then he turns back to see something standing in the middle of the room. How had he missed it? Probably Tina's fault.

It's a grandfather clock, painted in black with gold-leaf running along its edges. But it's not any old grandfather clock; this is the grandfather of all grandfathers. The case is larger than usual and Jack, with wide eyes, realizes that the clock is just about big enough to hold two or three people in its belly.

He takes his gaze from the clock, just quick enough to see Ruthy who seems to be equally astonished – at least they've got this in common. But Ruthy is not Ruthy. Correction: Ruthy *is* Ruthy, but she's not the Ruthy Jack thought he knew. Yet, she is still his link to his previous life.

The clock is silent. In fact, the silence here is voluminous compared to the workshop down the stairs. The only sound up here is the howling wind whistling around the eaves of the tower.

Jack sidles up next to the large clock and stares into its golden face. The silvered chapter-ring has roman numerals which are cracked and broken in places. The large hands have been hand-cut and aren't symmetric. *Hearts*, of all things, have been ornately cut into the heavy hands, and the case lock is also the shape of a heart. Golden cherubs sing from the four corners of the clock face. There is an old key stuck in the heart-lock. Above the centre clock dial is a smaller second silvered plate, bearing the carved and black-painted initials: R.O. and J.S. Both initials are wrapped up in a wedding bow. Below the bow is the year 1782. This clock has five hands, descending in size, corresponding to the year, month date, hour, and minute. The fifth hand is directed at what seem to be coordinates.

In front of the clock is an empty audience in the form of a row of Jacobean carved wooden and green velvet chairs, facing the clock. Jack notices that the chairs, probably ten in all, are carved in the same pattern as the dark old furniture where they had dined on canned food. He sees the dragons, the fauns, folkloric beasts, and the carved face of a man coming out of the furniture. Jack is beginning to draw the conclusion that this face is the face of the original Count Olenberg Senior. He also sees the same engraved woman with the flowing dress he had seen downstairs on the other furniture. Her eyes follow him about the room, as does the carved head of Count Olenberg Senior.

Johann sits himself down on one of the Jacobean chairs.

It is cold up here in the tower, and Jack uses the excuse to find out, once and for all, about the cemetery urchin named Johann. 'It's freezing up here. He'll die of pneumonia.'

Johann giggles at this last observation.

A sparkle of a smile passes the Count's eyes. 'Now, now, Johann. He doesn't know...'

Jack gets defensive. 'Welcome to the *Let's Have a Laugh at Jack Hour.*'

Olenberg informs him, 'You were brought here by a memory.'

'Okay. I think I need to sit down.' Jack gestures to the chair next to Johann. 'May I?'

'Be my guest.'

Jack sits next to the boy, and the Count and Ruthy sit on either side of them. They become the clock's audience and the clock watches them.

Jack's not willing to sit around and be thrown half-truths any further. 'Will somebody puh-*lease* explain?' He turns to Ruthy. 'I'm sorry, Ruthy, but *nothing* makes sense anymore. I'm beginning to regret coming to the Black Forest.' For the first time, Jack appreciates the fact that he would merrily go home right now and happily accept that he's got Jeanie's heart forever and be damn glad of it.

Till death do us part, Jackie...

Count Olenberg takes Jack in with his cerulean-blue, hypnotic eyes. 'Johann was my little apprentice. He used to love coming to the workshop and help work on the clocks. Generally, I like to work on my own, but the child had an innate understanding of clockwork mechanisms, and I thought I'd found someone to carry on my business when I was no longer around. By then, I was alone in the house and happy for the company of an innocent child.'

The Count gulps and wills himself on...

At this juncture, Ruthy puts her arm around his shoulders in a show of support.

Something went down which Jack hasn't been privy to.

'Then I sort of brought him back to life and adopted him.'

Jack stretches his arm across to Ruthy. 'Pinch me.'

'Huh?'

'I think I'm dreaming.'

To prove that he isn't dreaming, Ruthy pinches Jack with gusto until he recoils. 'Okay, okay. So, I'm *not* dreaming!'

'Did you not already suspect that he was a little different?' asks Olenberg. 'The *floating* aspect might've been a good clue...'

Jack sees the smirk on Olenberg's lips, but he cannot bring himself to smile; not now.

'Floating tends to be a dead giveaway,' quips Ruthy, chuckling with the Count.

Meanwhile, Jack's abhorred. From far off, he hears himself repeat the Count's seven devastatingly simple words that could turn a lesser man than Jack-of-the-Killer-Coaster fame insane: "...sort of brought him back to life..." The more he studies Ruthy's little joke, the more he understands that Ruthy *knows* Johann. 'So, it's true. He didn't lead you around in circles in the forest?'

'Johann and I are old, *old* friends. Yes, it's true. Sorry.'

'But why did you let on that you'd never seen him in your life when we were at the graveyard? I don't understand.' Jack recalls how Ruthy had frozen when she had seen Johann that night at the cemetery. She was stuck for words, which is very un-Ruthy like. He even asked her what the problem was, so her reaction to the kid must've sparked something in Jack, but he hadn't copped anything at the time. This is starting to sound familiar.

'Jack, I didn't want to frighten you off. I wanted to get you here to explain things. I warned Johann to keep away, but he appeared anyway.'

Jack finds it incredible that the half-ghost kid had been acting all along. He's a good actor – he'll give him that much. 'You wanted to trap me so I'd have nowhere to run, more like.'

'I did what I thought was best. Can you imagine if Johann and I started talking like old friends? It would've kind of let the cat out of the bag.'

'I still don't comprehend, Ruthy. There's something missing. I'll tell you what's missing. What's missing is *why* you want to get me here.' Instead of running down the mountain screaming, Jack feels a crazy giggle-bubble erupt inside him before bursting out in unadulterated laughter. The whole thing is shit-fire crazy – crazier than carrying Jeanie's heart for the rest of his life. So, it's confirmed; Johann is a ghost...or half-ghost, either works. He never envisioned he would be sitting next to a ghost when he was booking his flight tickets to Stuttgart.

But enough is enough.

'Ruthy, start from the start...'

'I was going to tell you...'

'Tell me what?'

Count Olenberg interrupts: 'Johann fell out that window.' He points to the window in question. 'I don't know why, but people always gravitate to that window when they enter this room.'

Jack sees that it's the same window he had first tried to look through but couldn't because of the wire barrier. Now he understands why.

The Count speaks again. 'I never had the strength to tell his good parents that he fell. I am a coward, too guilty and ashamed. Their son disappeared one day, that's all they know. I thought that maybe, by him disappearing, they would never lose hope. I was right, but I was also wrong. The idea of their son returning home alive haunted them for the rest of their days. Knowing that their son died in a fall would ruin their lives, but they would know...they would *know*.' He pauses. 'I'm not sure if I've done a good thing, Ruthy.' Olenberg's chin begins to jitter. 'The shaman was right; remorse and guilt is man's worst curse, and it's all of his own making. What you see is his soul...a lost soul. His heart was still beating when I put him in the clock...but he died during his journey and returned a half-ghost. He's not a full ghost because he died during the time-travel...'

Jack hears the Count's words in the background, but time-travel is everywhere, echoing over and over again in his ears...

Time-travel... Time-travel...

'...he's a soulless child, part ghost, part playful youngster. I knew the boy when he was alive and the only difference now is that he no longer has nerve endings and is without gravity...but he's still the same mischievous, curious boy I knew when he was one of us.' He hesitates. 'A part of me is happy that Johann is a forever-child. He will never lose his innocence, and he is my best friend. Isn't that right, Johann?' Olenberg turns to see that the boy is no longer sitting next to them but is resting on his haunches next to Tina, playing with the tip of her tail.

Time-travel... Time-travel...Time-travel... Time-travel...

'He can't sit still for a minute, little scallywag. I also like to have him around because I feel it's my duty to look over him; the boy *did* fall from my window.'

Ruthy says, 'You cannot hold yourself responsible. It was an accident.'

'Yes, child, but it happened here. Do you see?' He nods at Johann. 'He haunts me... I shouldn't be allowed to forget that.'

Jack speaks, almost in an out-of-body experience. 'So it's true? You *do* have a time-machine?' Jack cannot believe this is happening.

'Oh yes,' the Count answers matter-of-factly. Olenberg notices Jack's expression of total mind-blown amazement and enlightens him, 'I set the clock back one day to just before the boy fell. The shaman had warned me not to interfere with time, but I'm stubborn and went ahead anyway.' He nods in Johann's direction. 'This is the result – dead or alive. I resurrected only half of him. He arrived in this century as a half-ghost. I won't be around forever but Johann will be, and he will forever haunt this house. He is wonderful company and a better watch-dog around the castle than Tina will ever be.'

Tina puffs a little cloud of smoke from each nostril on hearing her name while Johann climbs onto her back and wraps his arms around her neck in a tight hug.

Outside, the wind whips and whistles at the tower eaves while everybody gazes, in silence, at the clock before them.

Jack will savour this moment for the rest of his life. However, he's giving serious consideration to discreetly backing out of the room... *Now*, might be the best time before his head goes into overload mode.

'But the shaman is never wrong. He warned me not to mess with the natural process of time and I didn't listen. The shaman told me never, under *no* circumstances, alter the past; what happens, must happen. By changing the past, we create untold damage in the future.' Looking at Jack, 'You see, boy, when you alter your past, you *alter* your future. Terrible things happen. The shaman told me this, and the shaman is *never* wrong. He has lived a thousand years and has learned from time. He was once a child but was cursed to live a hundred life-times. He has seen the change of seasons over and over again, and he knows how time deals with its burden. Have you ever heard the expression: time will tell?'

Jack nods but finds himself in a sensory-overload stupor.

'Time will always have the answer in the end; whether you like that answer is immaterial to time because it tends not to keep friends.'

Jack waits for more, but no more comes. 'Which means?'

'Which means that, yes, you might save the love of your life, but you have disturbed time and everybody knows time stands still for no man, even if you have a time-machine. If you go back in time, you will knock something out of sequence...you will re-write your own history. Some morning you will get up from bed and something won't feel right. You might not know what that something is, but you will feel it in your bone-marrow – things aren't as they should be.'

It all makes perfect sense now; all those little gaps of doubt in Jack's mind begin to fill themselves in. A cold sweat beads on his forehead, and he feels his face redden up. The natural tilt and 24-hour revolution of the planet seems to slope a few degrees too far over to the left, and the turn of the world on its axis speeds up in a dizzying dervish spin. Jack's losing control...

He closes his eyes, takes a deep breath through his nostrils, and wills himself to float away... He is back at the scrapyard in Old Castle, sitting in the crocked Beetle with Jeanie, planning their non-existing future together. How simple, *simple* life was...

Turning to Ruthy, he admits: 'I asked you to tell me everything, but I think I know *too* much already.'

The unquestioning way she gazes back at him tells Jack that he probably does.

Chapter 27

Fairy-Tale in a Fairy-Tale in a Fairy-Tale

Ruthy is about to answer Jack when the Count interrupts, 'Johann fell out of the same window that...' shooting a fleeting look at Ruthy, '...Ruthy threw herself from, some eleven or twelve years before.'

'He doesn't know...' she utters before Olenberg has time to retract his words. '*Now*, he does...'

'*You haven't told him?!*' asks the Count, visibly gobsmacked. 'But when had you planned to tell him, girl? You cannot play with lives just because you play with your own.'

'I *tried* to tell him,' Ruthy explains in desperation, 'but I couldn't bring myself to do it...' She covers her face in her hands and begins to weep. 'I've tried to tell him four or five times since we got here to the Black Forest, but I always chickened out at the last minute.' She turns to Jack. 'I *almost* told you when you found me worse for wear after drinking the contents of the mini-fridge in my attempt to *forget*. I told you that I was trying to forget my past. Then later, when you found me in the snow, I was crying because I was feeling guilty about everything. It hadn't been anything to do with Johann. I *know* the way here. Why wouldn't I? It's my home. Johann just happened to come along, as Johann does. It wasn't his fault, and I wasn't lost. I nearly told you that day, sitting in the bumper car, remember Jack? We made that impromptu visit to the amusement park after I collected you from the hospital and...we almost kissed.'

How could Jack forget? He was kind of hoping that she hadn't noticed that.

'Jack, I tried to tell you so often, but I just couldn't. Everything just snowballed.'

He feels the blood drain from his head, and the world becomes a dizzy place to be in. Tina the pygmy dragon, and Johann the half-ghost, are only the side-show acts in this fairy-tale. The *real* freak is sitting right next to him. Finally, Jack fits the last (here's hoping) piece of the puzzle. His jaw hangs lower and lower as it dawns on him who Ruthy really is. Ruthy's words begin to twirl him in a swirl of lies, excuses, and unanswered suspicions...

Jack finds his voice, though feeble it is, 'You're the girl in the fairy-tale, aren't you?'

When Ruthy takes her hands from her face, Jack is there, staring at her in blank shock.

Even Jack's own words are hard to swallow. Now he remembers that she had told him in the restaurant at Bladd Hotel that the fairy-tale book she gifted him was a 'first and last edition.' It hadn't made sense then, but it does now. Ruthy had told him lots of things that didn't make sense in the moment, but do now.

He asks for a second time, 'Are you the girl?'

She doesn't confirm or deny this.

'I'll take the uncomfortable pause as a yes, Ruthy. This is *your* fairy-tale and...wait...'

Jack remembers something: the tapestries. The tapestries downstairs. Now he knows where he's seen those scenes. They're not the scenes from a bygone fairy-tale his mother had once told him as a goodnight story. *He* is in the scenes; he and Ruthy are in those tapestries, and not only them: Tina the pygmy dragon and Johann the half-ghost, are *also* there...and Count Olenberg, of course. Those tapestries represent *everything* that has happened this evening: finding Ruthy in the snow and meeting the Count for the first time. He recalls the snowman on one of those tapestries (which had struck him as odd when he had first glanced at it) and Johann in another tapestry. Then Tina carrying the Count up the winding staircase of this very tower. Jack racks his brain, trying to recall what the last tapestry was. He vaguely remembers a clock...this clock.

'And there is only one Count Olenberg – the same Count that lived in the past is here with us now.'

He looks at the Count, and the old man's gaze is just as undeniable as Ruthy's.

Jack knows, just by looking at how Olenberg observes Ruthy: just as a father lovingly adores his daughter. Under his breath, he mutters, 'You're Ruthy's father.'

Olenberg nods. 'I could be her great-grandfather...'

Jack doesn't disagree; it happens to be the truth.

'Look at me, old and haggard. I'm an addict to time-travel, Jack, and it has taken its toll on my body. I shouldn't go back, but I do, more often than I care to admit. You see, this is no man's land for me. I belong to the past...'

Yoo-Hoo, Jackie, coffee beans...

Ruthy cuts her father short, 'The past holds nothing for us, Father.'

Boom. *That's the confirmation right there.*

Ruthy finishes by telling Jack, 'We are time-fugitives.'

Jack can't quite believe what he has stumbled into and is really starting to regret it now. 'Time-fugitives?'

'Even Tina is a time-fugitive,' the Count points out. 'She has become too big to fit in the clock. Tina *really* is the last dragon on this planet.'

'And you really do have a time-machine...'

'Sometimes, I wish I didn't, Jack.'

Jack finally understands. Not everything, but just enough to get his head around this fairy-tale in a fairy-tale in a fairy-tale. 'What about *The Unending Fairy-Tale*?'

Jack recalls how Ruthy had cried when he had finished reading the tale in Bladd Hotel's restaurant. He had asked her why she was crying, and she mentioned something about reliving the story, telling Jack that she'd already read the story before giving it to him. This was a lie; she was crying because she was re-living her past.

'What about it?'

'When does it end?'

'Not sure...'

'Does it have an *end?*'

'Dunno...'

'What *do* you know?'

'I know that I'm in my house with Jack.'

'Oh, Ruthy, don't give too much away...'

Smelling that stench yet, Jack? Hmm, babe? Now that you've woken up and are smelling the proverbial coffee beans...

Jack flushes. 'I can't believe I'm sitting here with fairy-tale characters and a time-machine, a half-ghost, and a miniature dragon.'

The Count corrects him, 'Pygmy dragon.'

A spine-tingling chill skitters along his spine. On the one hand, this is nuts, plain and simple monkey nuts, yet there's something Jack finds appealing and magical about this whole surreal evening. And for just an infinitesimal twinkling of a moment, Jack believes himself to be still deep in his hospitalised, induced coma...

He casts himself back to his previous life and recalls all those little lost instances where things concerning Ruthy didn't add up – a list as long as his arm, the more he ponders on this. And now, thinking about it, seem completely outlandish, 'Your uncle doesn't have a rabbit farm, does he?'

Ruthy cannot help but smile and shake her head.

'*Rabbits?* Who would've guessed?' Then, Jack adds: 'You've been coming and going from the Black Forest all this time.'

Ruthy nods.

'And the degree in Children's Literature?'

Ruthy chuckles devilishly. 'I can't believe you never copped that one – neither did Jeanie. There is *no* degree in Children's Literature at the University. There is no *literature* degree. I liked the sound of it because I am a fairy-tale character.'

Coffee beans...

'So you see, Jack. We really *don't* know the ending of this fairy-tale because it is *still* happening. We have yet to write the ending.'

'*We?* I've written my ending: flying first class out of here, Stuttgart, Germany to Shannon, Ireland. Remember that place? Joe Soap's? Old Castle? Your apartment you shared with your B.F.F in Mount Kennett Place?'

'I do and I love the place, but it's not my home, Jack. *Circumstances* brought me there.'

Ruthy's got a strange gleam in her eye while Jack's struggling to hold onto reality, (if having your dead lover's heart thumping in your chest is indeed reality).

'Wait, why don't you just go back in time and undo the boy's death?' asks Jack. 'This is what *I* want to do,' pleading to the Count. 'This is why I am *here*. I want you to send me back to just before we get on that rollercoaster, so that I can save Jeanie – save *us!*' He squeezes the ruby and diamond ring in his pocket and for a tiny moment, he feels closer to Jeanie than he has *ever* felt. It's a comfort to know that he's got her heart; God-sent relief.

'I've already explained the dangers. The past holds nothing for you or for us now. I have dedicated my life to helping my daughter live her life again and undo what I have done in other ways. I also do the occasional favour for the people of Bladd; only those who want to travel to the past and watch from a distance but not *alter* the past. My most common requests are from people who want to see themselves as children again.'

Now Jack understands why locals were so slow to reveal any information regarding the Count.

The old man's eyes grow misty. 'In a way, I brought Johann back in some desperate attempt to reclaim the life of the boy who I had wrongfully poisoned.'

Jack sits up and gulps, suddenly overcome with sheer alarm. He feels the world closing in on him. After all, the Count is practically a murderer.

This revelation is too much to take on. Jack is cursing himself for not having read the signs, *so* many fucking signs that Ruthy has had a hidden agenda; a split personality.

He clearly recalls, on New Year's Day, at the abandoned amusement park, he had said to her that he was missing nine months of his life and how that time was lost forever. Hadn't Ruthy said something like: he *could* get that time back? *How* had Jack let that comment float by him? She had practically *told* him that time-travel was possible! Because he had thought that she had meant it in a metaphorical way, as in, he could *do* something to make up for that lost time. That's what he had understood.

The more he thinks back, the more Jack sees that he had taken many of her comments as metaphorical...

And now it hits him, like a stinging smack across the face; one final dig in the ribs.

Jack looks at Ruthy with tears in his eyes. 'You *knew*, didn't you? You knew that accident was going to happen, but you let it happen because your daddy told you not to mess about with what has already happened!'

Ruthy has already told Jack on a few occasions that she could've stopped the accident; she had told him that she had killed Jeanie and *almost* killed him.

Good ole' Jack had taken on this cry-for-help/confession as meta-fucking-phorical.

Ruthy begins to cry. 'I *didn't* know, Jack.'

'Of *course* you *knew!* You can travel to the future, Ruthy!'

'Yes, but this is the future for me.'

Can this get any more confusing? Jack's flummoxed. 'What *are* you talking about, Ruthy? If *that* is your name...'

'My life with you is my future; I haven't gone further into the future. I was happy with you and Jeanie; I'd found my place in the future, and I stayed there...'

'Except when you go to the fucking *rabbit farm*,' swears Jack acerbically. '*Funny* farm, more like.'

'I know the future no more than you do. But I did get a funny feeling about that rollercoaster. I told you that I'd seen it crash – but only in my imagination.'

'Premonition is a side-effect of time-travel,' adds Count Olenberg with the same sincerity as if he was reading off the back of a box of painkillers: *May Cause Drowsiness*.

For a moment, Jack thinks the Count is having a laugh, but evidently not. '*Why didn't you say anything, Ruthy?!*'

'Jack, what would you have done if I'd told you that I'd seen that coaster come off its rails? You would've laughed in my face and told me that I'd come off *my* rails.' She stalls. 'And I was already hurting that you and Jeanie were getting serious and leaving me. Imagine how I felt.'

'I didn't care how you felt then, and I don't now!' Jack's got one thing clear: 'I want to go back to the moment when Jeanie and I get on that rollercoaster. I've made my mind up. I'm going to the past, and I will alter it. I will save Jeanie – I will save Jeanie by not getting on that rollercoaster.'

The Count lays his hand on Jack's shoulder, and Jack shrugs it off. 'I cannot allow it. Jack, you must understand. Your survival and Jeanie's death have been written since the beginning of time. Say you disregard the wise words of the shaman and you save Jeanie, but Jeanie *will* lose her life in some other way and *you* will be saved. She was born to save your life.'

'If you're trying to make me feel better, then it's not working.'

'So you see, it is a lose-lose situation: to alter the past is a fruitless exercise, because everything will come to pass that is meant to be.' The Count glances at Johann (who is humming a tune to himself) and speaks low. 'Don't you see, Jack? The boy should've died in the fall, and…' he pauses, 'I should've left him. It breaks my heart to say it, but it's true. I've turned him into a lovable freak-of-nature. Jack, there is no way back. You must accept this, the same as I have accepted it and sealed my own fate. Don't you think I would like to go back and start again? It's a dangerous illusion…only a mirage, Jack; the gold at the end of the rainbow: you will *never* feel the gold in your hand.'

Jack ponders on this. 'Have you been to the future?' There's something nagging him, but he cannot decipher what it is exactly.

'Yes,' Olenberg responds, 'and no.'

Jack frowns.

'My – *our* – future is your present, Jack.'

'Okay, so I mean, *my* future?'

This question catches Ruthy's attention.

Olenberg responds, 'My old shell can only withstand so much time-travel-lag. I have no interest in going any further into the future; I have enough to worry about in the past.'

These wise words hit home for Jack. It turns out that he can relate to the Count on many levels if he looks at his own past. Come to think of it: he's got even more in common with Ruthy. In the past, they both have had lovers die on them.

'And remember this, boy; no matter how much distance you put between yourself and your past, the planets and all their moons, you,' poking his chest with his long, spindly forefinger, 'will-*never*-escape-your-heart.'

Jack's heart hammers angrily in his temples. This last sentence is the final nail in Jeanie's coffin, but Jack *can* face up to the idea that he's got Jeanie's heart, and he is okay with that. This has always been why he has come here: closure. Jack sees this now with great sadness and, it must be said, with immense relief. He nods to himself, slowly understanding. This irreversible situation helps Jack come to terms with Jeanie's death. He sees now that she *cannot* be saved; as matter of fact, it has always been the opposite: she *has* really saved him. Maybe this is the answer he's been seeking all this time; this is what Jack has come to hear. Let sleeping dogs lie, as they say...

Speaking of sleeping dogs, Jack is suddenly overcome by a swell of fatigue as the year-long tension and pent-up anger siphons from every pore of his body. He realizes that it is too late to walk back down the mountain and opting for a cable-car in the form of a temperamental taxi-dragon called Tina isn't an option. His legs wobble beneath him as the last of the anxiety he's been feeling washes from his system in something close to spiritual. 'I need to lie down.'

'Everything will be clearer in the morning.'

Jack seriously doubts Ruthy, but nods nevertheless, anything to lie down.

Count Olenberg says, 'I will show you where you will be sleeping. I'm afraid you will have to share the room for the night as the rest of the rooms are off-limits.'

Jack looks at Ruthy. 'You mean sleeping in the same room? Wouldn't you...Are you *okay* with that?'

Ruthy considers Jack with her wide pupils. 'We're just sharing a bed.'

'But maybe,' Jack intercepts, 'there will be two single beds?' Jack doesn't know if it's the drink or what, but Ruthy looks every bit the sultry fox in this medieval low-light setting, yet she's a spy: a spy-fox. He's all confused and rubs his face in an attempt to wipe away these jumbled feelings.

'But you lied to me,' Jack simply accuses her.

'I didn't lie,' Ruthy counteracts. 'Ask me no questions, and I'll tell you no lies. You never asked questions, so I didn't lie.'

'Because I had no reason to ask you if you were a two hundred and thirty-something year old spy. A Mohawk can take years off a person, Ruthy, but this is taking the piss.'

'...if you prefer?' finishes the Count.

Jack hasn't heard the first half of Olenberg's sentence. 'Hmm?'

'I said,' Olenberg repeats, 'I can ask Johann to take you back down the mountain, but I wouldn't advise it. Not on a freezing night like this, and Johann's sense of humour shines in the pitch darkness of the forest at four in the morning in sub-zero temperatures.'

Funny, but now Jack understands Johann, when he had told them at the cemetery that Bladd Hotel leaves out a hot cocoa for him and he sits where people can't see him. Ambiguous.

'Um...' Jack's even considering it. The last place he wants to be now is in a room...at night...in a bed with Ruthy. How can he trust her after tonight?

But more to the point, what would Jeanie's heart say? Would it murmur its disgust? Or would it go for the jugular by staging a heart-attack right there?

A drowsy cocktail of mead, heat, and body-shattering relief causes Jack to throw caution to the wind, so agrees to be put up for the night in Castle Olenberg.

The Count turns, and they follow him in mute silence: Jack, Ruthy, Johann the half-ghost, and Tina the pygmy dragon, following up the rear.

Over his shoulder, Jack sneaks a peek at the clock before they leave the room. He briefly wonders why he is going to sleep instead of running down the mountain like any sane person would.

Just listen to your heart, Jackie... whispers Jeanie.

Jack *does* listen to his heart and has made his decision by the time they reach the bedroom. He *cannot* give in to sleep.

Chapter 28

Heartstrings

The Count leads them to a bedroom in a different wing of the castle. He enters the bedroom and lights a lantern. Shadows dance on the stone walls.

Jack's worst fears are confirmed when he sees the double-bed and not two single beds. The bed isn't queen-size or king-size, but big-time COUNT-size. It is *immense*. The thoughts of climbing into bed with Ruthy are counter-intuitive right now. *This* wasn't in the itinerary either. Jack came here to find closure with Jeanie, which he feels he has done, *not* climb into bed with her best friend. This feels like extracurricular activity. Jack cannot believe how nonchalant Ruthy is about the whole thing...or maybe she hasn't realized the consequences of sharing a double-bed with her deceased best friend's husband-to-be? Then again, after tonight's revelations, nothing can sway Ruthy.

Or is the hand of something greater at work?

Jack and Ruthy have always been sworn enemies, but, yes, something has changed in Jeanie's absence.

Deceased, darling...I'm deceased...Does it really matter now?

Jack's not sure if that voice that he just heard is his conscience or Jeanie. Their voices are becoming one. Maybe Jeanie's voice has been his guilty conscience all along? Yes, Jack just might be over-reacting.

'I will bid you goodnight. You can rest assured that Johann will not be pestering you tonight. I have warned him not to visit you without knocking on the door first; that's if he doesn't float through the wall.' Olenberg goes to leave the room on this ominous note, before sticking his head back inside the door, 'It's a waterbed, by the way.'

Jack thought that he'd seen it all with the picnic cutlery.

The Count says to Jack: 'You can let me know your answer in the morning...'

'What answer?'

The Count gently eases the door closed behind him.

'What's he talking about?' Jack looks to Ruthy for answers, but she has drawn a blank.

He listens out. Once the Count's footsteps recede in the distance, he whispers to Ruthy. 'I've got to get to that clock tonight. I can't turn my back on her now.'

Jack's sudden change of mind shocks Ruthy. 'Jack, you heard him. Don't go messing around with shit you know nothing about. That stuff is black magic as far as I'm concerned. Look at my father; he's a wreck. He's like a drug-addict and *time* is his drug. I've used the clock once in my life and that was to come to the future, but my father is using it as we would use the local bus-line.'

'Have you forgotten why we came here?'

'*No,*' snaps Ruthy aloud. 'And how *dare* you for even suggesting it! Jack, we're both overtired. Everything will be clearer in the morning.'

'Will you stop *saying* that! I can't see what a few hours of sleep can solve in this particular situation...'

'Just go to sleep.' Ruthy climbs into bed, fully-clothed, shoving well over to her side of the Count-size waterbed.

Within seconds, her breathing slows down and deepens.

Jack shakes his head in disbelief. How can she sleep after tonight? He sits on the edge of the enormous bobbing bed, noticing how high up off the ground it is. It reminds him of the bed in the *Princess and the Pea*, not that he's going to mention that now; he's had enough fairy-tales for one night, thank you very much.

Jack be nimble, Jack be quick... echoes Jeanie's voice, only it isn't Jeanie's voice; its Jack's own conscience. It has always been Jack's own imagination, guiltily conjuring up what Jeanie might say. But, of course,

Jeanie would say nothing because she is dead, and Jack will love her forever and have her heart to prove it.

Slivers of moonlight shine silver through the narrow window, lighting up Ruthy's sleeping face. The more he stares at her, the more Jack finds it utterly incredible how she had pretended to be somebody else all this time. They've known each other for months...*years*. She just appeared one day. Jack and Jeanie had had conversations about that, how Ruthy slipped into their lives and they had practically grown up together.

Ask no questions, tell no lies, as Ruthy says.

Now Jack recalls how Ruthy dyed her hair blue the same day their old crock of a Beetle and the rest of the dead cars had been hauled away from their scrapyard headquarters. She had *known*, but she had told Jack that she had woken with a 'gut feeling...' She had dyed her hair blue to suit the sad day she had already seen.

He stares at her. She *is* beautiful, Jack thinks, and whether Jeanie were here (and she is) or standing atop a red-hot mountain on Mars, he would think the same. He has gotten to know Ruthy over the last few days and feels closer to her now than he ever felt to Jeanie; yes, it's true. There's a connection there that Jack cannot explain. If he were to study the topic in finer detail, he could make the assumption that their paths were *meant* to cross. Jack has always been a coincidence-man, but it's hard to dismiss fate tonight.

Seeing Ruthy lying in the bed next to him turns him punch-drunk on lust. Not love; just lust, which, depending on the man you're speaking to, is stronger and more dangerous than love because it's a spontaneous thing whereas love is a slow-burner. Then again, maybe all love starts with lust? Both start with 'L' and that's about as far as Jack's willing to question this for now.

With Jeanie's heart pumping in his chest, Jack climbs into bed with Ruthy, defenceless against her allure. He closes in and gazes at her face, up close and personal...when she suddenly opens her eyes.

'I wasn't asleep, duh.'

Pointless in pretending that he wasn't ogling at her, Jack stares into her eyes and she into his. There's nothing between them anymore, only the first move.

What has come over Jack? Why is he acting like this? Because he has harboured something for Ruthy for a long time, but Jeanie used to be the wedge.

But, wait, *Ruthy* used to be the wedge?

The bottom has fallen out of the real world and Jack's tumbling headlong into this dizzying fairy-tale where only Ruthy exists and the ghost of someone he used to know...

Jack, being led by the little Neanderthal monkey in his head nicknamed Instinct, guides him to what comes natural. He kisses Ruthy on the lips.

She doesn't stop him but grabs onto him as if her parachute had failed to open. Between kisses, Ruthy whispers in his ear: 'You won't believe how long I've been wanting to do this...'

Jeanie's heart is thumping in Jack's chest. He cannot stop, sinking deeper under Ruthy's magic spell. 'Ruthy, what's happening? Am I dreaming?'

'I was only Jeanie's friend because I wanted to be near you...It's always been about you, Jack.'

This last sentence comes at Jack like a bullet from a chamber. The world stops as the bullet comes towards Jack's heart at supersonic speed...

How could he have betrayed Jeanie like this? 'What am I *doing?!* What're *you* talking about?!'

He jumps out of the bed and jogs around in circles, tearing at the roots of his hair in bewilderment. 'I've betrayed her, and you were betraying her all that time?'

'I was in love with you, Jack. I *am* in love with you! I travelled through time to *find* you! Now, what girl is going to do that for you? Hmm?' Ruthy speaks as if none of this is a big deal.

This latest bulletin blows Jack's mind to kingdom come. 'Huh?'

'It wasn't betrayal; Jeanie *was* my best friend. But seeing you every day was an extra perk for me.'

Jack is flabbergasted. 'You never said anything.' He regrets saying this just after uttering the words. It almost comes out as: *you should've said something...*

'Some things are best kept a secret, especially when you are in love with your soon-to-be-dead-best-friend's-future-non-husband. Phew, that was a mouthful. I was happy in knowing that *you* didn't know.'

Ruthy's a *fucking* Pandora's box of secrets.

Jack approaches her and looks at her. 'What have you done?'

Ruthy begins to sob. 'I *knew* Jeanie was going to get killed on that rollercoaster. I told you that, and you wouldn't listen!'

Jack is livid and barely able to speak. *'Of course I didn't listen! Nobody can tell the future!'*

'I did it for us. I love you!'

'Did you love Jeanie?! Your best *friend!?*'

'Fate is fate. You and I are meant to be together, Jack.'

Jack remembers, quite clearly, what Ruthy had said to him and Jeanie after they broke the news that they were moving in together. With a strange look on her face, Ruthy had said: 'It's called fate, or shit happens, either works. You two are so predictable that I feel I'm living in a constant déjà vu...'

Just one more little hint that he hadn't picked up on...

'Did you know that I would end up with Jeanie's heart in my chest? Hmm? Kind of back-fired, didn't it?! You didn't know that I would have Jeanie's heart forever. Yes, you're right, our love was fate; our love was meant to be.' Jack pounds on his chest.

Ruthy waits for Jack to calm down before whispering, 'Jeanie's heart *brought* us here...brought us together.'

Jack almost falls back as he fits the final piece of this puzzle to get the big picture. 'All of this was planned, right from the beginning.'

'Jack, you were meant to fall in love with Jeanie, and she was meant to die. I was meant to fall in love with you, and I did and I let Jeanie die for that love. But I'm sorry,' she pauses. 'We both allowed Jeanie to die, Jack, not just you.'

Jack's legs grow limp beneath him.

Ruthy goes on. 'I allowed her to die when I let her up on that roller-coaster...You let her die when you didn't shield her from the tree-branch. We are both as guilty and innocent as each other.'

'No, Ruthy, you're wrong. You did it knowing that she would be killed. I never knew. Do you see the difference inside that tiny, twisted brain of yours?'

Ruthy begins to sob again. 'Jack, fate killed Jeanie, not me!! Do you think the camera-crew on the nature documentaries save the gazelle from the cheetah? *No*, Jack. It is the way of the world! *Shit*, in all its various hues and colours, *happens!!*'

'Cheetahs and Gazelles, *really...?* I don't think that will hold in a court of law.'

'And neither will a *fucking* time-machine, Jack!'

'But we can *change* fate with that clock just down the hallway! We can save a life. You had a chance in a billion to save Jeanie's life, but you didn't. Why didn't you tell me this the night I almost killed myself?'

'I didn't *know* you were going to kill yourself!'

'But you've seen all of this happen before...'

'No, how many times do I have to tell you? I saw that crash in my imagination! Hallucinations and predictions are a...'

'...side-effect of time-travel, yeah, I *know*. But forgive me for not having read the prospectus before I swallowed this bitter pill!'

'Huh?'

'Forget it!'

'Love knows no bounds, Jack. Love is timeless. *Our* love is timeless.'

'Our love!?'

'Oh, c'mon, Jack. Don't act as if you haven't thought about me in that way. I've seen how you've looked at me tonight. And not only tonight; you cannot deny those lingering glances. We look away, but our eyes always lock again...'

Jack's not going to lie. 'Okay, so we have become a little closer on this trip.'

'Because we're *meant* for each other, Jack. I know this might seem hard to believe, but Jeanie existed for us to be together.'

'That's crazy talk, Ruthy.' Jack cannot get his head around the events of this never-ending night. 'How do I know that you haven't been here before with me? Do you know what happens next, Ruthy? C'mon, level with me...'

'We are living for the moment right now. I don't know the future any more than you do. I stopped knowing the future when I first met you and Jeanie. I've told you this already.'

'You never told me why me...'

'Meeting you and Jeanie was just coincidence.'

'But you don't believe in coincidence.'

'I believe finding you that first time in the People's Park in Limerick was just coincidence, remember that? I offered you and Jeanie a bottle of cider. But I believe fate would've brought us together anyway, somewhere and some time. Sometimes, Jack, crossing paths with someone isn't just coincidence.'

'Your plan wouldn't be a success if that crow hadn't saved my life.' Jack hears himself and doesn't know whether to laugh or cry.

'That crow was mine, Jack, *is* mine. Didn't you recognize her when you saw her a while ago? The crow was your guardian angel.'

'Of course it was.'

'What makes a better spy than a silly old crow? She lived here in the castle with me. I found her one day in the woods with a broken wing. I put a splinter on it and nursed her back to health. She didn't want to leave after that. I taught her to steal coins from my father's pockets so I could buy sweets down in the village. I also taught her to follow my father and annoy him. I gave her the same instructions for you – to follow and annoy you. I'm not interested in stealing your money.'

'Very kind of you.'

'She understands me. I sent her to keep an eye on you, Jack, even when I wasn't there.'

'When you were with the rabbits...' Jack manages a tepid smile.

She nods. 'But you're right; Kray *did* save your life.'

'Kray?'

'That's her name...'

'I prefer Clara.'

So, Jack's got the wrong crow stuffed in his bedroom, after all. But who cares? Nothing, *nothing*, makes sense anymore.

Jack *actually* cracks a smile despite the crazy circumstances. Then he finds himself grinning. Ruthy is crazy, shit-fire loopy, but she loves him *more* than anybody ever has. Jack loved Jeanie and vice-versa, but there had always been that hairline fracture of doubt in his mind. He guesses now, that hairline fractures eventually become the crumbling point. Jeanie wouldn't move in with him, but Ruthy, in a way, let her best friend die to be with him. Is that to be admired or abhorred? Technically, Ruthy hasn't committed any crime...or has she? Can side-effect predictions stand up in a court of law? All Ruthy really did was stand back and let the cheetah mow down the gazelle.

'Come here.'

Ruthy beckons to him with her finger.

Jack has forgotten all about Jeanie, even though his heart is jack-hammering. He finds himself helpless against Ruthy's magnetism. 'You're one crazy bitch...'

'I've always been your *cuh-razy* bitch, Jack.' She removes her bra. 'Time to move on, Jack. You do know what the best antidote for Jeanieitis is, don't you?'

Jack had often imagined what she looked like naked. The only difference is that Ruthy looks better than she had ever looked in his mind's secret eye. She lives up to everything and beyond.

She slips under the blanket with feline finesse and undresses the rest beneath. 'There's no turning back the clock now.'

Well, that's it for Jack... The rest of the world has disappeared; he is under her spell. She is his vice, his bad habit, his addiction. 'I've never slept with a fairy-tale character. I always thought it would've been Snow-White or Rapunzel. But Ruthy? Never in a million years.'

'You do know that I wrote that book.'

Jack looks at her in the moonlight.

'There's only one book, Jack, first and last edition. I wrote it and printed it myself as my own sort of diary.'

'You're an indie author? Cool...'

'Now you know why the book isn't finished, because *we* aren't finished. To be continued...' Having said this, she kisses Jack on the lips.

Fully-clothed, Jack slides in next to Ruthy. The next few minutes become a lightheaded, dreamlike haze as Jack and Ruthy acquaint themselves a little further with each other; a self-exploratory mission to the netherworld. Surprisingly, the water-bed doesn't help proceedings, and Jack finds himself floundering and wallowing in the undulating mattress. He almost breaks down laughing at one point...but the smile is quickly wiped off his face when, quite unexpectedly, he catches a moonlit glimpse of the Fuzzy Wuzzy tattoo just above Ruthy's hip.

Then he feels it; his borrowed heart pounding, and his old friend – that old guilt – beginning to niggle in his bone-marrow. 'I can't do this. I've made a mistake, Ruthy.' He listens to his heart, as Jeanie had whispered to him, but all he hears is the mechanical *thump-thump...thump-thump...*of any old heart keeping him alive. He cannot hear Jeanie's voice any more. She has gone all quiet. Desperate, Jack wants Jeanie to yell at him for his infidelity; he wants her to get angry with him; he wants her to get something, *anything*, that will let him know where he stands – where they stand.

He's *listening* to his heart. By God, he is listening but hears nothing.

'This is no mistake, Jack. All of this has already happened. Everybody has to get on with their lives. This is you getting on with yours.'

She's right, but does it *have* to be like this?

'Was this also in your little scheme?' Jack's not sure if he wants to slap her or have her. 'It's like you're possessed...'

'I *am* possessed – by you. I've come a long way to be with you, Jack, and I've waited a long, *long* time...'

Jack's not sure of anything anymore. She has blinded him. He wants to stay with her forever in this Count-size waterbed, yet she is a traitor.

'I sat by your hospital bed when others had gone home to forget...'

Suddenly, Jack remembers his recurring dream while he had been in and out of consciousness at the hospital back in Limerick. 'You came to visit me...'

'I was always there when the others had gone home to their own little comfortable worlds.'

'So it wasn't a dream?'

She shakes her head.

'This doesn't feel right, Ruthy. What about Jeanie?'

'Who do you think she would prefer to see you with? A stranger or her best friend? Besides, don't you think it's a sign that Jeanie never actually got the wedding ring on her finger? She *never* made that promise, Jack.'

Profound...

Jack shakes his head in disbelief. 'Somebody, please wake me up.'

Ruthy, from nowhere, jumps up and screams in his face, *'Wake up 'n smell the coffee beans, Jackie!'*

Jack starts. 'What the f...?'

'See?' she giggles wildly, 'you're already awake.'

Chapter 29

The Time-Machine

Jack storms out of the room and sprints down the shadowy hallway. At the end of the hallway, he begins to climb the steps of the winding staircase to the tower, jumping two steps at a time, spiralling upwards...

Quickly, Jack reaches the top of the tower and enters the room where the special clock is housed. He briefly studies the various clock-hands and their corresponding times, dates, and coordinates.

He turns the hands back to 1st March, 2015...

Jack swears to himself in desperation. *'What fucking time?'*

It's only a matter of seconds before Ruthy catches up.

The world of Old Castle seems so far away now, the town itself shrouded in a forgetting mist. However, he distinctly remembers that Mayor Arthur Lawless and Bonnie, his chimpanzee monkey-advisor, took to the amusement-park inauguration stage at about five pm, so Jack moves the smallest hand back to that time exactly.

In the back of his mind, Jack *knows* that he could go back to any date before 1st March, but this way, he's hoping that the consequent damage is minimal and that post-tsunami won't be as destructive as the Count makes him believe.

He twists the key in the heart-shaped lock. Just as he's about to climb into the clock, he hears a snort behind him.

Jack turns to see Olenberg's pet, Tina, staring at him from the shadows; her mouth open and hissing like the reptile that she is, tendrils of smoke wafting outwards with her breath.

The dragon rises up and flaps her wings in anger at Jack.

If this is a pygmy dragon, then I wouldn't like to see a normal dragon, thinks Jack in the heat of the moment.

The smell of sulphur in the room almost gags him. The dragon sizzles and fizzles and opens her jaws wide. Where the epiglottis is on a human, Jack sees a glowing amber ball and is mesmerised by the sight, until a flame comes at him, peaking out centimetres from the tip of his nose.

'Do you like her?'

Standing at the door is Olenberg's silhouette. 'She is the clock-guardian. I was thinking about getting a German Shepherd, but they don't blow fire. So, unless you want first degree burns, I would suggest you step away from the clock in a gingerly fashion, Jack. It's not me; it's her. She's got a connection to the clock – maybe she knows she's the last living dragon and would like to go back and meet her old friends. But, as you know, she has gotten too big and is destined to live her life out in this century.'

'I have to save Jeanie...'

'The clock is NOT for altering history – it's an escape vehicle. Do you *want* to escape, Jack? I can make you disappear. I can help you as I helped my daughter find you.'

The world halts temporarily as Jack understands that he *does* want to escape. It's the answer he's been looking for.

He decides to speak the truth. 'Yes, I do.'

'Sorry, I didn't catch that?'

Jack raises his voice. 'Yes, I do! I want to escape from anything that reminds me of Jeanie!!' His heart pumps in his chest. 'I can't go back to Old Castle – I see her around every turn, and I can't live with the idea that she's not around because I didn't save her...I want to get far away from here, where everything is new...where I can forget my past.'

'Take me with you!'

Ruthy comes running into the room. 'The only way we can outrun this nightmare is to go to the future, Jack. Don't you see? I came to the future to find a new life after my husband-to-be was poisoned. Now, you're doing the same. Jack, my father built this clock to help me find a new man in my life after he took my first away from me. He made a promise to me all those years ago that he would find my soul-mate.'

'So, he's a matchmaker *and* a clockmaker? It did seem a little odd that we were put into *one* bedroom with *one* bed when there are more rooms here at the castle than a hospital.'

Jack's using his old humour line-of-defence to handle the situation, but Olenberg's haunted face is furrowed with shame and guilt. He doesn't need to verify his daughter's version of events to Jack; Jack can see the truth in his face. The Count is haunted by his past. Will Jack suffer the same fate?

Jack doesn't have time to reflect on this as Ruthy adds, 'I chose you amongst millions of light-year men. This is meant to be.'

Jack's panicking. He's never been a science-fiction fan. All of this has come out of nowhere... To go or not to go?

And then he catches sight of the initials in the silver plate in the clock's face, above the roman-numerals chapter-ring; *JS* in fancy Gothic script, and below it, *RO*. Around these initials is an engraved wedding bow. Of course, why hadn't he seen it the first time? JS: Jack Stack and RO: Ruthy Olenberg. He half points to the initials in amazement, and Ruthy smiles at him and Olenberg tries too.

'I've known about this for over two centuries, Jack,' the Count informs him.

'So, you'll forgive me if I seem a little impatient,' grins Ruthy. 'Just let yourself go, Jack...'

Now, Jack remembers the last scene of the last tapestry in the dining-room downstairs. It's an image of a boy and a girl getting into a giant grandfather clock. It looks as if Jack's past, present, and future have already been written for him. 'What about Jeanie?'

'We came here to forget Jeanie. Am I right or wrong?'

It sounds very final, but yes, it's true. They came here to put Jeanie to rest.

'We will always have a piece of Jeanie with us.'

'That's an understatement,' answers Jack. 'But it's true, and I've learned to accept it.'

Maybe Jack could go back to Old Castle, after all. And get on with his old life as best he can. But he doesn't want to; he's got too many questions now. He has seen too much in the last twenty-four hours to ever be content with mundane Old Castle. And, he must admit, he will *never* find another girl like Ruthy Olenberg – his light-year girl-spy. 'I want the future, and I want to share it with you, Ruthy.' *Am I crazy?*

Ruthy grins back at Jack and they embrace.

'It's now or never...' says the Count.

Hesitantly, Jack nods. 'I guess I wasted money on return flights,' he says, managing a shit-scared smiling grimace.

Olenberg opens the clock-case...

Jack stalls, like a parachutist chickening out of his first jump, before climbing into the belly of the clock. Ruthy squeezes in next to him.

Olenberg closes the door shut, leaving them in complete darkness.

'Wait,' shouts Jack, 'which year are we going to?'

Count Olenberg answers back cryptically: 'To a place and time so far away, yet so close to your heart,' before closing them in and locking the case.

Above their heads, Jack hears the clock-hands turning, before wheels and chains are set in motion.

'Where are we going?' Jack whispers.

Ruthy speaks softly, 'To the future...'

'Could you be more specific? The future tends to be infinite...'

'I *don't* know, Jack...that's the fun part. I didn't know where I would end up either the first time I went to the future. I don't think my father even knows...'

'Oh, great. I love surprises...' Jack's heart thumps hard in his chest. 'Ruthy?'

'Yeah?'

'I'm scared...'

'Don't be, Jack. Our future awaits. Wait...'

'What? *What?!*'

'What'll we do for money??' asks Ruthy.

'How am I s'posed to know what we'll do for... Wait...Your father said he'd return me the price of the hotel – full package deals don't come cheap.'

Ruthy giggles a little. 'Yeah, but, like you say, the future is infinite. Maybe we'll need more than that to set ourselves up.'

Goosebumps erupt on Jack as he remembers the blood-money in the shallow grave under the crab-apple tree in his backyard. He clearly recollects his father telling him, on New Year's Eve, that the insurance money will come in handy 'in the future'. Just how far into the future, Jack would've never guessed. 'We have enough money – as long as it's valid currency in the future.' And if all else fails, Jack still has the engagement ring...

Jack grows dizzy; his insides flutter as the clock begins to make him feel as if he is spinning, then he experiences a surge in his stomach.

Ironically, the last time he felt this was on the doomed rollercoaster...

In the darkness, Jack hears Ruthy begin to cry. 'What?'

'I have lots of great memories, Jack. Our lives in Old Castle. It was such a beautiful and precious time we spent together. The three of us.'

'Ruthy...'

'Yeah?'

'I'm not going to forget Jeanie. She'll always have a special place in my heart.'

'Nobody's asking you to forget her, Jack. We're moving forward, that's all.'

Something trembles inside Jack, and he cannot stop the tears that pierce his eyes. 'Me, too.' For a moment, he feels impending claustrophobia coming in on top of him, and he wants to smash his way out of here.

Has he made a terrible mistake?

Jack just about finds time to get his arm around Ruthy before they both become weightless and float through a black-hole into the future, happily ever after.

The End

Toledo, Spain.

Oporto, Portugal.

October, 2015 – April 9th, 2016.

Jonathan's other novels:

Balloon Animals 2012
Living Dead Lovers 2013
The Nobody Show 2014
Hide the Elephant 2015

Jonathan can be found here:

Goodreads @ https://www.goodreads.com/author/show/
6546212.Jonathan_Dunne
Blog @ http://jonathanwdunne.wordpress.com/
Twitter @ WriterJDunne

Don't miss out!

Visit the website below and you can sign up to receive emails whenever Jonathan Dunne publishes a new book. There's no charge and no obligation.

https://books2read.com/r/B-A-CNCJ-MFODB

BOOKS2READ

Connecting independent readers to independent writers.

Also by Jonathan Dunne

Hearts Anonymous
Lighthouse Jive
The Squatter
Billy's Experiment
Crazy Daisy

Watch for more at https://www.goodreads.com/author/show/
6546212.Jonathan_Dunne.

About the Author

Admittedly, Jonathan has done things arseways most of his life, from completing a BA in Literature in his thirties to fitting teeth brackets (30's, porcelain). During this general confusion, Jonathan has had various short stories published. Jonathan suffers from photophobia though has a tendency towards fireworks. Originally from Limerick, Ireland, he now lives the reclusive life in Toledo, Spain, as a bearded hermit, with his wife and three daughters. He is known to be found in the local cemetery at the weekend during daylight hours, though for goodness sake, don't sneak up on him.

Read more at https://www.goodreads.com/author/show/6546212.Jonathan_Dunne.

www.ingramcontent.com/pod-product-compliance
Lightning Source LLC
Chambersburg PA
CBHW020909160726
47993CB00005B/1895

9798215427156